ALI'S PORTAL

SAYLOR STORM

A Novel

ISBN 978-0578-69100-8

Dedication

For Judith Ann. You are missed.

Saylor Storm
Ali's Portal

CHAPTER 1

I push the pungent mystery meat in congealed sauce around the oblong plate. As uninviting as the lifeless meal is, I still can't help but feel the familiar urge to eat and count every bite. For as long as I can remember, counting has been my constant companion, a silent voice in my head dictating every morsel that enters my body. But for me, the act of counting was not just a harmless habit, it was an obsessive disorder that threatened to consume me entirely.

Deciding to save my bites for something more appealing, I cover the plate with a napkin and decide, instead, to stretch my legs. The familiar whirring of the engines helps to drown out the sounds of chatter from my fellow passengers as I make my way to the tiny bathroom. As I pull down my favorite black travel pants, I see the all too familiar gush of fresh crimson blood in my underwear. I feel the color drain from my face, and I suddenly feel dizzy and disoriented. Every month, the same disappointment was unbearable with the crushing weight of the reality that, once again, my body has failed me.

I grab a tampon from my purse and try to compose myself as I splash cold water on my face before heading back to my seat for the long ride home. I dig around and find a Xanax in my purse and conclude taking it is a better option than being fixated for the next eight hours on my lack of fertility. I open my new copy of *Getting the Love You Want*, hoping to learn something that will bring me the connection I long for with Rick. Halfway through chapter three, the pill begins to take effect.

I'm startled out of sleep by the overhead announcement that we are landing in Detroit. I suddenly have an urge for a Cobb salad and wonder if that little bar still has them on the menu. I have an hour-and-a-half to kill before checking in for my flight back to O'Hare.

I locate the restaurant, step inside and am promptly relaxed by the dim lighting of the room after having spent a week in meetings under severe fluorescent lights. The room's central attraction is a dark wood mahogany bar and it reminds me of an upscale old time gentleman's pub, like one you might find in Boston or San Francisco. I find the ideal spot for myself at the bar, a seat near, but not next to the server's station and I park my roller and trench coat on the bar stool next me.

"Good day!" the tall, slender bartender greets me with a warm, friendly smile. He is attractive in an earthy and almost exotic way. His curly, light brown hair is tucked neatly into a ponytail and his deep-set green eyes sparkle slightly as he speaks to me, "May I tempt you with some of this delicious iced tea? I just made it myself, it's a recipe from home."

"And where would that be?" I ask, detecting a Caribbean accent.

"Jamaica. I'm James, nice to meet you," he extends a lanky hand to me. He is a refreshing change from the business travelers that I've been encountering all week. I suddenly realize that he is much taller than I first thought, perhaps 6'5" as he leans over the bar to shake my hand.

"Nice to meet you, James. It's a pleasure. My name is Alison."

"Alison, hmmm. Have you ever wondered what you might be like if your name wasn't Alison. How different might you be if your name was perhaps Beatrice?"

"Beatrice? Where'd you come up with that? I can't imagine myself as a Beatrice!" I giggle.

"Why not?"

"Because I've always been Alison."

"So you do think that a person's name effects who they become."

"I guess so, I've never thought about how my name has effected me." I shake my head slightly at the ridiculousness of his line of thought.

"Where are you off to today, Miss Alison?"

"Home to Chicago. I'm just stopping through here on my way back from Beijing where I've been working all week. I make this same trip every six weeks or so."

I can't quite tell if he's trying to flirt with me, so I subtly twist my wedding band several times, hoping that James will notice.

"That's a lot of travel, Miss. Here, this will pick you up!"

He passes me a tall glass of tea with several sprigs of fresh mint in it.

I take a small sip from the paper straw and can feel a slight tingling sensation on the tip of my tongue. "You are right about this tea, this is delicious! It's just what I need. Do you still have that wonderful Cobb salad?"

"We do; it's the best in town if you ask me."

"Great! I'll have one of those too."

While I wait, I check my phone; there are six messages from work and two from my mother, Carol. What does she want this time? I find that not having to deal with Carol's phone calls is one of my favorite parts about traveling to China. I listen to the messages, shit! Carol's birthday is coming up. I send a text to my brother, William.

Are you going to Mom's BD dinner?

Can't. I'll be out of town.

You can't do this to me.

Sorry, Sis.

I won't forget this.

What a welcome home, dinner at my mother's without my brother there to buffer the situation. Carol will just have to wait a little longer to hear my answer about dinner and tell me how I don't measure up to her expectations.

James approaches me with a new topic. "They say that everyone has a book in them. If you wrote one what would it be about?"

"It wouldn't be my life story."

"Why not?"

"It would be boring."

"I'm sure you underestimate yourself. I want to hear your story." He leans in, placing his left elbow on the bar.

"Okay, but only because you asked. I was born and raised in the Chicago area, Evanston actually. I went to Northwestern, where I met my husband, Rick. I work for a large firm that manufactures products in China and sells them to companies here in the US; automotive parts mostly, like those tiny electronic components that allow the most modern cars to do everything from warning you if your falling asleep at the wheel to parallel parking for you. It involves a lot of paperwork and a fair amount of sales skills. See, I told you my life is dull."

"That might be your perception, but to me your life

sounds interesting. I have another question for you to ponder: Where do you suppose a person's self-worth comes from?"

I giggle at the oddity of his questions. This guy must be interested in me, why else would he be interrogating me? I twist my ring again nervously. "Lots of questions," I say.

"I want to know about you and how you think. What better way than to ask?"

"I guess you're right."

Is part of his job to make conversation like this? I'm not used to a stranger probing into my thoughts.

"So, what do you think about where self-worth comes from?"

"Certainly not from my mother."

"What's that about your mother?"

"Oh, nothing really, she just didn't do anything to help my self-esteem. It was very clear from day one that my brother was her favorite child."

I sit up straight, bracing myself for more questions.

"And why was that?"

"I have no idea. I've been trying to figure that out my whole life. I try and try to please my mother and no matter what I do, she is always dissatisfied with me. Maybe it's because William is a boy and I let her down by not being a boy. I don't know. Maybe it's because she viewed me as being defective."

"Defective? I can't imagine why."

"I had a speech impediment as a child and even though I worked hard to overcome it, I think it embarrassed her and reflected badly on her as a parent."

I've just revealed more to this total stranger than I do to most people who I've known my whole life. I've never even told my own husband about my childhood speech issues.

"So we've ruled out self-worth coming from your mother. Do you think anyone can give it to you or is it something that has to be earned by you and you alone?"

"Yes, I think you have to earn it for yourself. What do you think?"

"I agree with you."

"Now tell me about you." I want him in the hot seat for a moment.

"What do you want to know?"

"Any family?"

"Just my mum and two little sisters. There's a big age difference. I'm more like a dad to them than a brother. My dad ran off and I've been the man of the house for most of their lives."

This is not what I expected. He looks like the kind of guy who would be free and easy, not taking care of his entire family.

"That sounds like a big responsibility. Are they still in Jamaica?"

"It is a big responsibly, but I love them, so I don't mind. They live with my aunt in New Jersey, but I hope to bring them here one day. Now, back to you. You said you are married?"

Does he want me to be married? He can't possible find me attractive; I must be at least five or six years older than he, and for another he looks so hip. He must see me as a complete square in my unimaginative business clothes. There's nothing edgy about me. I can picture him with a stunning, young artist, with a small, yet tasteful nose ring and lots of tattoos.

"Yes, Rick and I have been married for three years. He's an attorney, which makes my mother happy since she thinks they walk on water. My brother is a lawyer as well.

She wanted me to be one too…another reason she's disappointed in me."

"It sounds like there's no pleasing your mother."

"You can say that again." I observe the unique amber shade of the tea.

James places a crisp white napkin on the bar in front of me and another on top of it, rolled with silverware inside. "Excuse me, I'm going to check on your salad. I'll be right back."

I twirl my straw in a circular motion as I look around the restaurant and notice that all of the tables are set with freshly pressed white linens. I can hear through the loudspeaker a flight being called to Mexico and I feel a tightening in the pit of my stomach. Suddenly, in my mind, I'm walking down the sandy beach in Playa la Ropa, listening to the rhythmic crashing of waves, the birds chirping and children playing at the shore. James returns with the salad in hand and startles me as he places the large, white ceramic bowl in front of me.

"It's beautiful! Just as I remember it." The artistic presentation of the salad is appealing with rows of blue cheese, egg, turkey, bacon, avocado and tomato lined up uniformly.

"Would you like me to leave you alone while you eat?"

"No, please stay and keep me company. It doesn't look as if I'm keeping you from anything." I look around at the empty bar and realize that I am James' only customer and I'm grateful to have a distraction from my thoughts of infertility.

"Do you mind my asking, Miss?"

I find it kind of cute and quirky that he keeps calling me "Miss".

"Asking what?" I place my hands in my lap and give James my full attention.

"Are you down about something? There is a sadness about you. You seem a little heavy-hearted, if you don't mind my saying so. What is it in life that might lift you up and bring you joy?"

How can he see that about me? Does it show that I'm as devastated as I am every month when my period arrives?

"I don't mind you asking, but I don't think of myself as miserable. That's a really good question, James. Funny, but I don't think I can answer it. I used to know what made me content, or at least I thought I knew. I'll have to give that some serious thought. Everyone should at least know what makes them happy, right?"

"Yes, Miss, it's essential to know in life," James replies as he refills my glass of tea.

"Yes it is, and somehow not only have I forgotten about it, I don't even know what it is anymore."

"It's never too late, Alison, to change your life and do whatever makes your heart sing. We all need to have a life that makes our heart sing, no matter what it is."

"You're absolutely right."

This revealing myself is so unlike me, but somehow I feel that it's safe to tell my feelings to James. I count out my maximum 15 bites of my enormous salad as I try to wrap my head around what I want and what might be making me discontent; other than my inability to conceive. I check my watch.

"What do you suppose is the best way for a person to attain happiness anyway? Have you ever thought about it?"

"I haven't. Do you ever get exhausted from thinking so much?" I grin. "I've got to run, but it has been an absolute pleasure and you've certainly given me a lot to think about today. I hope to run into you again, next time." I give him two 20's for a $32 tab. "Keep the change." I stand and stretch, feeling stiff from too much sitting.

"I'll be here, Miss Alison. You have a good trip and I look forward to our next visit and hearing more about your life's story. More than anything," he pauses and smiles, - "don't forget to be happy."

I smile back and study his face one last time. He has the most beautiful olive skin. How odd that we connected in a conversation about happiness and self-worth today. I was feeling miserable when I walked into this place and he certainly lifted my spirits and helped me forget to feel sorry for myself for the time being.

I make it to the gate just as my plane is beginning to board. No time to return any calls. Everyone will just have to wait, especially Carol.

I get comfortable in my seat and think about what James said. My mind wanders to my home life and my marriage. Truth is, there is no joy between Rick and me, and the sad part is, I'm not sure there ever was. When we met in college, I thought that marrying him would please my mother, but did I ever truly feel that he made me happy?

We've become adept at going through the motions and looking like the model up and coming urban couple. Rick, dark and fit, like the hockey player he was in high school and college and me, looking like the wholesome, freshly scrubbed Midwestern girl. We could pass for the couple on top of a wedding cake. We look good in person and on paper. But in reality, there's not much of a marriage there at all. I wonder if Rick realizes this as well, and this is just a dirty little secret that we keep quiet amongst ourselves; a knowing that is best left unspoken. Do I really believe that things will get better, and that having a baby will somehow make us stronger as a couple?

I continue to read, *Getting the Love You Want,* until exhausted, I fall asleep and dream of a trip to Mexico. I am blissful there and annoyed that my dream ends just as the wheels touch the ground in Chicago.

Time to go home and back to my life.

~

CHAPTER 2

J ust once, I wish I could return home and not have to fight the traffic in the rain. I'm so sleepy now I can't even see straight! It'll be wonderful to crawl into my own bed.

An hour-and-a-half later I pull into my driveway on Holland Court in Lake Forest. I am immediately sustained and restored by the beauty of my adorable little two story yellow house with black shutters and my pristinely manicured lawn. It's really too bad I don't get to spend more time here.

I can see the lights on upstairs at the Miller's house as I look across the street. Cass must be up with the baby; poor thing probably never gets a full night of sleep these days.

My beautiful, old Springer Spaniel, Gracie, greets me warmly as I carry my bags through the garage door into the kitchen. The house smells of pizza and I immediately notice the dirty dishes piled up in the sink and on the shiny, new, gray granite counter tops. Why? I ask myself.

"Rick? Where are you?"

The TV is blaring from the study, so I follow the noise.

"I'm home," I say, trying to get Rick to notice me as he

keeps his eyes glued to his laptop. He's wearing the same navy Northwestern t-shirt and gray sweats as when I left for my trip. His plentiful dark brown hair is disheveled as if he has been continuously running his fingers through and pulling at it out of stress. I can see the reflection of his reading glasses on his laptop screen.

I just came halfway around the world, and he doesn't even make the effort to look at me. Exhaustion takes over and I suddenly feel as if I can barely stand.

"How was your trip, Babe?" he says to the screen.

"Tiring; same as always. How was your week?"

"Great! I've got to study for this case, Babe, sorry." Rick casually brushes his lips past the general direction of my cheek, and again, I'm not sure if he even bothered to look at me and I am too tired to bring it up.

Gracie follows me upstairs and she wants my attention. I haphazardly wash my face and brush my teeth before slipping on my favorite pink pajamas and crawling into my fresh, white sheets with Gracie at my side. I don't wake for 14 hours.

Feeling disoriented, I look around and realize that Rick never came to bed last night – a frequent occurrence lately. The blinds are open and the light is giving me a headache. I suppose I should be upset that he didn't come to bed again. Maybe I've been traveling too much and getting too used to having a bed of my own with no one to bother me.

"Come on, Gracie, let's go outside!"

I notice a note from Rick on the counter.

I didn't want to disturb you, so I slept in the guest room. Have an early morning court case. See you tonight. XOX

I make a pot of coffee and wonder if sleeping in separate rooms is normal for married couples. Certainly, it's not what I want from my marriage, but honestly, I get more sleep this way. I flip open my laptop and go to work answering dozens of follow-up emails from my trip.

At two in the afternoon I am interrupted by a call from my best friend, Cassie. "Are you up for a walk?"

I met Cassie three short years ago, when I first moved to Lake Forest and we clicked the instant we met, thanks to her honest and comical outlook on life.

"I could certainly use one. Swing by and get me in ten?"

I throw on a pair of black leggings and a plain, white t-shirt and grab Snuffle's leash as Cassie heads up the driveway pushing a brand new designer stroller with the latest addition to her family sleeping inside.

"You look beautiful, as always!" I say, looking at Cassie's exquisitely styled shoulder-length black hair and nicely done, but not over done make-up. Her top-of-the-line black yoga outfit and brightly colored running shoes complete the look.

"Well, you don't, you look like hell."

"You mean you don't like the giant bags under my eyes?" I quickly pull my sunglasses from the top of my head and slide them over my eyes.

"At least I'm truthful, you can always count on that."

"True, but you wouldn't look so hot either if you had just flown to China and back." I try to keep up with Cass' brisk gait.

"You would think you'd be used to it by now."

"You never get used to it. Tell me what I missed while I was away, and slow down, I'm not up for our usual power walk today."

I temper my pace and enjoy the beauty of my unspoiled neighborhood as we walk around the Deer Path golf course that both of our homes back up to. There is nothing like these quaint sidewalks, freshly cut lawns lined with majestic Maples and Oaks in China. I appreciate my idyllic surroundings even more each time I return from Asia. The sun and fresh, crisp air feel almost foreign as they bathe my face.

"Okay, miss cranky, whatever you say. Let's see, you missed a bunko party at Heather's. It was a high drama evening. The only thing anyone could talk about was the Hendrix's divorce and who is sleeping with whom. I get bored with all of the gossip in this town! You didn't miss a thing, oh, and George surprised me with a new Audi."

I love the fact that Cassie dislikes the town gossip and drama as much as I do.

"Another new car?"

"Yes, every time I pop out a kid, he buys me a new car; one of the perks of owning a car dealership. Speaking of kids, how's that going?"

"Don't ask; it's not."

"You guys are still trying aren't you?"

"Sure we are, but with all this travel it throws off my cycle and then I'm not home at the right time…" I can feel tears welling up in my eyes.

"Whoa! What's going on? Why the tears?"

"I'm just exhausted I guess and I started my period. It's not fair, you can get pregnant without even trying and we've been trying for three years now."

There are many things I envy about Cass, but her ability to get pregnant is at the top of the list.

"I know it's not fair, but you can't give up. Are you still taking your temperature and checking your, what's that stuff called?"

"Mittelsmertz mucus."

"Yuck, that stuff. Why do you suppose you are so desperate to have a baby?"

"Probably because I never felt the mother-daughter

bond with Carol even though I tried and tried. In fact, the more I tried the more she pulled away from me. I would have done anything to gain her approval, but I was always disappointed. Why do you think you wanted to have kids so much?"

"Kind of the same thing. I wanted the type of family that I never had growing up. What sort of things did you to do to gain your mother's attention?"

"You name it, anything I could think of, but the worst disappointment was a school play. I worked so hard at my part, rehearsing tirelessly to overcome my shyness and self-consciousness about speaking on stage. I imagined how proud she would be of me."

"What happened?"

"Carol didn't even bother to show up to see it. I was crushed. When I asked her why she didn't come she said it interfered with her regular bridge game. Can we please change the subject?"

"Sure, why don't you and Rick come over for dinner Saturday night? Seeing my kids will make you feel lots better about not having any." Cassie grabs me around the shoulders and squeezes hard. She does know how to make me feel better.

"Sounds great. Can we walk back now? I'm too tired for this."

"I think maybe you should go back to bed."

"I wish I could, but I have a pile of work to catch up on. What are you doing with the rest of your day?"

"The usual, pick up the kids at preschool, then spend the afternoon keeping them occupied while I prepare George's favorite meal. It's our anniversary, but who has time to go out with four kids at home? We can always go out to dinner later."

"I'm sorry, I forgot all about your anniversary!"

"Don't be silly. I wouldn't expect you to remember that. Go home and don't push yourself too hard. I expect to see you and Rick at our house on Saturday at seven. Don't bring anything, just come and relax."

Cassie hugs me again before stepping up her pace towards home. I realize I am so lucky to have her.

Gracie and I walk back to the house, and she curls up on the floor next to me in the kitchen, somebody who loves me. I pour another cup of coffee and reluctantly open my emails, one by one.

Rick arrives home at five, looking professional in a gray suit and red tie. I, however, am still in my leggings and t-shirt and I haven't moved since my walk with Cassie, not even to take a shower.

Rick presents me with a dozen red, long-stemmed roses. "How was your day?" he puts his arm around my shoulder and presses his lips firmly against my cheek.

"You're looking at it," I say, as I try to rub the headache away from my forehead. "They're beautiful, thank you!" I take the flowers from his hand.

"You look like hell!"

"Thanks a lot! Cassie said the same thing."

"Then we're both right. Did you bother to eat anything today?"

I run water into a tall, crystal vase.

"Of course not, you know me, when I get working I lose track of time and forget everything." I hate it when he calls me on my lack of eating. I don't like it when anyone brings attention to my intentional food deprivation.

"You are going to put that laptop away now and take a shower, and I'm going to order your favorite Italian take-out and we are going to sit and watch one of those classic movies you love."

I place the flowers on the polished counter top.

"You would do that for me? I know how much you hate old movies."

"Yes, but you love them."

I put my arms around Rick's neck and get a whiff of his familiar cologne; a combination of spicy and sweet. He slaps me playfully on my right butt cheek.

"Ouch!" I protest.

"Don't take this wrong, Babe, but you stink! Go take a shower. I'll take Gracie for a run, and then swing by and pick up the food."

"Thanks, Rick, I love you."

"Love you too; now go!"

I let the bathroom fill with steam as I examine my face in the mirror. Cassie and Rick are right; I do look like hell! My normally petite frame looks emaciated. I restrict my eating as it is and I've yet to acquire a taste for some of the Asian cuisine. I will never get the image out of my mind from when I was invited to a business dinner and was served an entire turtle! It is supposedly a delicacy because that type of turtle is known for urinating out of its mouth, gross! As a result, I always come home from China thinner than when I left. Added to that, I'm terrified of eating something that will put me in a Chinese hospital.

I need to take better care of myself if I'm ever going to get pregnant. Maybe it's time to add more bites to my daily count. I meticulously examine my skin; it's so light it's almost translucent and the circles under my eyes are so dark, it looks as though I've been in a fight and lost. I undo the baby-fine, ash-blonde knot on top of my head. My hair is stringy and needs color as well.

Feeling defeated by my appearance, I let the hot water pulsate against every pore, hoping to cleanse the stench of travel off of me. I take a stiff brush; cover it with lavender soap and scrub hard against every inch of skin that I can reach.

Feeling clean and fresh, I wrap myself in my favorite fuzzy pink bathrobe and head to the living room sofa in search of a beloved old movie to watch. I'm delighted to find my all-time favorite classic; *The Wizard of OZ*.

My cell rings; it's Carol, ugh; it's time to face the inevitable and get it over with. I grab my favorite pigeon blue pillow from the sofa and clutch it to my belly before speaking to her.

"Hi, Mom." I focus on my articulation as I speak.

"When did you get back? Can't you call your mother, just to let her know that you're okay? I left you two messages you know."

"I know, Mom. I'm sorry, it's just that I'm so tired." I squeeze the pillow tighter.

"It's that job of yours, it's going to kill you."

"Please don't start. We've been through this a million times," I sigh.

"I'm sorry, but if you had become an attorney like your brother you wouldn't have to travel like this."

"I know, Mom, but I didn't get into law school."

"It's never too late."

I can feel my blood pressure rising and I don't respond to her comment. I take a deep breath.

Carol changes the subject, "Are you coming to my birthday dinner?"

I wish I had an emergency trip to Beijing right now, but I'm out of excuses.

"Rick and I will be there. Can I bring anything?

"No, dear, we'll have a quiet little barbeque, just the four of us."

This sounds like my worst nightmare.

"Okay, Mom, we'll see you then."

"Before you go, did you hear about your brother's good news?"

"No, what good news?"

"He and Beth are expecting twins!"

I feel a sharp pain in the pit of my stomach; it is so unfair! Everyone is having babies, except me! What is wrong with me? Why can't Rick and I have a baby like everyone else? And now my faultless brother is having not just one, but two babies! I restrain the tears before responding to my mother.

"That's wonderful news. I'm very glad for them."

"What about you? Any news to share in that department?"

"No, Mom, I really need to go now. I'll call you tomorrow." I toss the pillow to the floor.

Feeling utterly inadequate, I silently wipe my tears as Rick comes in with the food.

"I found a movie. I hope you don't mind watching this again." Poor Rick has probably sat through this eight times before.

"Whatever makes you happy, Babe."

"Before I forget, we're going to Carol's birthday dinner at her house on the 18th."

"That bothers you a lot more than it bothers me."

"It will be torture for me."

"It'll be fine." Rick puts his arm around me.

We curl up on the sofa and I take seven bites of Italian chopped salad before falling asleep on Rick's shoulder. I awaken at dawn with my neck feeling sore and find a note on the dark stained coffee table from Rick.

Headed to the office early. See you tonight. XOX

CHAPTER 3

I feel rested and almost back to normal by Saturday. Some of the color has returned to my face and I have even managed to consume my maximum allotted bites during the week.

This evening, I decide to put a little more thought into my look following Cassie's lead. I add some extra conditioner to my fine, lifeless hair and apply some colorful blush and lipstick to my pale face. Rick is pleased by my efforts, and compliments me on my new look.

I prepare a fruit salad of melon and berries to take to Cassie's, even though she instructed me not to bring anything. Rick picks up a six-pack of IPA to take along. He rings the Miller's doorbell as he leans in to kiss me.

"You look beautiful tonight."

"Thank you." I beam as I look down at my crisp, white jeans and off-the-shoulder black blouse. I'm glad he notices the extra effort I've put into my appearance. "You look very nice too," I remember reading how important compliments are in a marriage.

George answers the door, beer in hand. His white golf shirt is a bit on the small side and accentuates the slight paunch in the middle of his belly. He looks relaxed even though the household is in a complete uproar, as usual, with four kids under the age of six. Cassie somehow manages to keep the house clean and well organized, even with the constant chaos. No one would ever guess that Cass had given birth to her fourth child just a short six weeks ago.

"Here, you get to see what it's like," Cassie says as she hands me the newest addition to her family.

I can't recall ever holding something this small and fragile. I stare at little Sophie with awe as she yawns and stretches slowly inside her swaddle.

"I wasn't kidding when I said that being around my kids tonight will make you feel better about not having any. They are all yours for the evening. You get to discipline, change diapers and put them to bed. Do you think you're up for that?"

"I would love that!" I say as I marvel at the small bundle in my arms.

I look across the room and catch Rick watching me intently as I hold the baby. I smile at him, but he doesn't return the smile, then swiftly resumes his focus on the conversation he's having with George about golf.

"Here, you're going to need this then," Cassie hands me a beer in a frosty glass.

I watch Cass as she skillfully chops fresh basil and adds it to her aromatic marinara sauce. I'm impressed by her ability to innately know what ingredients to use and how much. She is quite a natural cook, preparing an elaborate meal for her family each and every night, a skill I envy as my cooking abilities are limited to spaghetti and omelets.

The children play noisily in front of the massive television as the men chat about the golf tournament that they're half paying attention to. I watch the men briefly and think that George looks like he could be Rick's slightly chubby uncle. Rick is many years younger than George and still in great shape, thanks to his dedication to running several times a week.

"You're not doing your job, Mom." Cassie nods towards the children in an argument about a doll across the room.

"Oh, yeah, I forgot. Children, keep it down over there, the men are trying to watch the tournament," I say in the sternest voice I can muster.

Cassie smiles; amused by my timid attempts to temper her children.

"How are things going?" Cassie asks, while raising her right eyebrow.

"You mean the baby stuff? Do we have to talk about that every time I see you? Oh, I didn't tell you the latest. William and Beth are expecting twins! As if I weren't feeling inadequate enough."

"Ouch, that must hurt. I'm sorry, Ali, really."

"It's okay, I really am pleased for them. I would be even happier if Rick and I were expecting too."

"Maybe you should lay off trying for a while, stop with all of the testing and timing and just let nature take its course."

"I'm too far gone for that, I've been at this too long. It has become an obsession. I think about it all the time, every time I see a baby or little children playing. It's constant."

"I wish I could understand what you're going through, but I've always had the opposite problem, getting pregnant at the drop of a hat."

"How many more are you planning on having?"

Cassie shrugs her shoulders nonchalantly, "I don't know, we'll see."

"Do you feel like you've created the family that you didn't have growing up?"

"Absolutely, my life with George and the girls just fell into place and it's more than I ever imagined."

I wish I could say that my life with Rick is more than I ever imagined.

It's time for you take the girls up for their baths."

I gather the little girls and herd them to the bottom of the stairs all the while holding sleeping Sophie in the cradle of my left arm.

"Follow me," I order, "I'm the mama duck and you are my ducklings. Now quack!"

I giggle as I hear the various quacks behind me while marching up the stairs. I return to the kitchen forty minutes later with three clean dark-headed children in pajamas.

"How did it go?"

"They were little angels."

"Ha! I know better than that! Why don't you put Sophie in her cradle and come eat some dinner."

I carefully count out three bites of pasta and five bites of fruit salad. I allow myself ten sips of beer to give the illusion of consuming it, but am mindful never to go beyond my allotted amount. I allow myself a maximum of 15 bites for an exceptional meal, but normally keep the count under 15 for most meals; a habit of calorie restriction I've had in practice for my entire adult life.

After dinner, I put the kids to bed. I know that Cassie is trying to teach me a lesson, but she has no idea how delighted I am to take care of the children for an evening. Instead of turning me off the idea of having kids, being around them makes me want a child even more.

After dinner, we adults adjourn to the expansive sectional sofa.

Cass suggests we play a game.

"Do we have to?" I ask. "I'm terrible at games."

"This will be easy. Certainly you've played Pictionary before."

"Sure, I guess it's not so bad."

The men refill the drinks while Cass sets up the easel.

"Couple against couple," Cass says.

I'm anxious to get my turn over with right away, so Rick and I get the first clue. I start to draw a stick figure and Rick guesses correctly that I'm drawing a farmer within three seconds.

"You're cheating!" Cass exclaims.

"How do you cheat at Pictionary? He guessed correctly because of the rake." I say defensively.

"It's a terrible drawing," George chimes in.

"Everyone's a critic."

Now it's their turn and they run out of time before George can guess that Cass was trying to draw an igloo.

It's Rick's turn to draw and I guess high-heel correctly within five seconds.

"You two are definitely cheating!"

"Explain to me how that's even possible. Rick and I are just better at this than you two."

The Millers keep trying to beat us, but Rick and I leave them in our dust. For once, we are better at something as a couple than they are and it feels good!

Not taking well to losing, Cass quickly ends the game.

"Let's just talk," she suggests.

"Do you remember how I first met George?" I start.

George looks a bit stunned.

"I caught him sunning himself in the backyard in nothing but a speedo." I cringe waiting for George's response.

George replies red-faced, "I had no idea you were there, Ali."

"I rang the doorbell a dozen times and then I just followed the sound of your music. I'm sorry, George, but it was funny."

"Maybe to you, but not to me."

George is a very private guy and I'm sure he was not happy about his new neighbor seeing him nearly naked.

"Okay, your turn now. You can tell an embarrassing story about me."

"Here's one that I never told you about."

Uh oh, what have I started?

"Early one morning I stopped by your house to drop off a putter that I had borrowed from Rick. Your window was open and I could hear you two going at it."

My face suddenly feels hot. "Why didn't you ever tell me?"

"Because I don't like to embarrass my friends like you do!"

The humiliating stories continue and I laugh until I almost cry. This is the most relaxed I have felt since I can remember.

Rick and I hold hands as we walk across the street home; this is the closest I have felt to him in months. Once home, I lead Rick directly to the bedroom and remove my clothes, dropping them to the floor.

"Are you sure about this?" he asks. "Is this the right time?"

"I don't care about that right now, let's just make love."

I didn't have to ask him twice.

~

CHAPTER 4

I purchase sod, hydrangeas and new patio furniture that includes a chat set with a fire pit for our unfinished back yard. I've never planted or grown anything before in my life, but I want to create an inviting area in our back yard, one that would make our friends and future children want to spend time there. I'm confused by the directions for the hydrangeas; I thought I purchased shades of blue but can apparently change them to pink by changing the ph level of the soil. I am not a chemist! I work tirelessly digging, planting and carefully watering every evening. Rick helps me on the weekends as much as he can. I even purchase a small swing set for the Miller girls to play on and hopefully our baby too one day will use it as well.

"Why don't we hire someone to do this like the Miller's do?" Rick asks.

"Because we don't have the kind of money that they do, we just spent a fortune on redoing the kitchen and living area, remember? And we just got finished paying for redecorating the dining room last year."

"Oh, yeah."

"Don't you want to work on the yard together? I think it's kind of fun. It's very satisfying work."

"No offense, but honestly I would rather be playing golf with George."

"I think you can give up a few of your weekends to make our back yard look presentable. You and George are golf obsessed, you would think that you would welcome a break from it for a change."

"Never!" he grins at me. He can always win me over with that smile. "Between work and coaching I put in long hours and I need to relax on the weekends.

"I know you work hard, but come on, Rick, we even bought a house on the golf course, isn't that enough?"

"There's no such thing as enough golf."

"What should our next project be? The bathrooms? We still have a lot of work to do to get this house to where we want it, and I want to save enough to buy another Irena Kononova painting for the living room."

"I don't know, Babe, but whatever we decide to do next, can we please hire someone to do the work? We can afford it as long as we don't do it all at once. I really need my golf. That and hockey are the only things that keeps me sane."

Somehow I had imagined my life with Rick as the two of us fixing this house up as a team and that he would be eager to do so on the weekends. I guess marriages are never the way you expect them to be. When we got married, I thought that Rick would end up being my best friend, my confidant and that we would share our inner most feelings, but these days we rarely share anything.

I watch Rick carefully as he digs a hole large enough for the Japanese maple we purchased. Sweat is pouring from his brow as he concentrates on the task at hand. He is hard working and capable and still looks like the young, preppy looking man that I fell in love with; the good looking all-American guy of medium height and build with thick, brown hair and hazel eyes. He's vain enough to stay in good shape. He was quite the ladies man when I met him and could have married anyone he wanted; I'm fortunate that he wanted me.

I don't miss a day of watering and after a month of focused work we are pleased with the results. The back yard is fit for entertaining.

The eighteenth arrives and it's time for the dreaded dinner at Carol's. I spend too much time lamenting over Carol's gift. I want it to be perfect since gift giving is such a focus in her life. Out of ideas, I visit her favorite Tiffany's in Skokie and look for a gold bracelet to add to her collection, but I soon learn they start at $1,500, way out of my budget. I settle on a gold heart charm for her bracelet at a mere $450! I hope she likes it; she should as she only likes the best!

I'm tempted to take a Xanax as I get ready to head out the door for dinner, but I fear it will make me too sleepy.

"Do I look okay?" I ask, tucking in my silk blouse.

"You look great."

"Carol will find something to comment about my appearance."

"Relax, Al. You're just sensitive to her criticism. I'll be there tonight and I won't let her devour you with negativity."

"Promise?"

"Promise. I've got your back."

Ricks words are reassuring, but in reality nothing can protect me from Carol's attacks.

My anxiety mounts as we make the drive and I'm just about in a full blown panic attack as I imagine the worst possible scenarios for the evening.

We pull into the drive and the massive two-story brick house resembles a fortress more than a home with imposing black shutters and perfectly sculpted boxwoods all around. The house is brightly lit and the lawn has been freshly cut.

Mom greets us at the front door wearing a Chanel jacket, of course, what else would one where to a simple family barbeque?

I hand Carol a plain bouquet of white lilies and a bottle of her favorite Chardonnay. She doesn't thank me, but simply says, "You look comfortable." An apparent reference of disapproval to black jeans!

"Happy birthday, Mom," I say as I take a deep breath and focus on my annunciation as we walk into the foyer.

"Happy birthday, Carol." Rick kisses her politely on the cheek.

"I'm always happy to see you, Rick, dear."

I don't think she's ever said that to me.

"Come on out to the patio. Your father is warming up the barbeque. What would you like to drink?"

Daddy looks at home with tongs in hand.

"Have a seat," Daddy instructs us to sit at the wrought iron patio table.

I can feel my body relax with Carol out of my field of vision. Daddy asks us what's going on in our lives and we tell him about working in our back yard.

Carol returns with a tray of drinks in hand. "Charles, why are you wearing that shirt? I told you to wear the striped button down, now go change."

Poor daddy looks stricken, but does as he's told quickly before Carol has a chance to bark another order at him.

"Mom, can I help you with anything?"

"Thank you, but no, Dear, I've been cooking for days."

What happened to the simple barbeque?

As we adjourn inside, I marvel at the formal décor of the dining room. The room is impeccably newly redecorated with mahogany walls, a granite fireplace, a navy tapestry rug under the massive, oval table, upholstered chairs and an ornate crystal chandelier to complete the effect.

"Charles, the chicken is burned! Can't you do anything right?"

Daddy sits in his chair at the end of the table without uttering a word.

"Honestly, I only asked you to do one thing."

I want to tell Carol to shut up and leave daddy alone, but I know that would only makes things worse. We are all terrified of Carol's rages. I learned as a child that Carol wears herself out trying to make everything perfect and by the time dinner arrives she's usually so exhausted that she lashes out at one of us, mostly Daddy.

We survive the meal with the normal superficial chitchat. Carol doesn't ask questions about our lives, but instead drones on about various relatives and neighbors. We pretend to listen intently as this seems to please her and we are motivated to keep her from erupting at any cost.

At the end of the meal, Carol presents us with her own homemade seven-layer vanilla cake. She makes the same cake every year claiming that no one can make her favorite cake as well as she does. We pretend to like it as much as she does, though I've only two bites left for the day and don't want to insult her.

I hand Carol her gift and she opens it without a response. I can't tell if she liked it or not. A simple "thank you" from her would have been nice.

After dinner, Rick and I offer to do the dishes, but Carol interjects, "That's your father's job, he'll do the dishes, just leave them."

Daddy earns the paycheck, does the yard work and the barbequing, why does Carol make him do the dishes as well? Can't she let the man relax for a change?

We survive the evening and head out with the excuse that Rick has a five-a.m. business call.

"Well, that was hell!" I say once safely inside the car.

"That must be humiliating for your father to be emasculated like that."

"She just doesn't let up. Either he adores her or is terrified of her to allow himself to be spoken to that way."

"You think he still adores her after years of being treated like a dog?"

"I do. She's a very attractive woman, has great taste, and is a fabulous cook. She has a lot to offer. I think Daddy feels lucky to be with her and looks the other way when she's so negative."

"I could never put up with that. It's like watching a castration over and over again."

"I keep thinking she'll mellow out with age, but she just gets worse."

"If you ever speak to me that way…"

"Don't worry, I'm nothing like her."

Time is passing much too quickly and before I know it I'm packing to go back to Beijing. As I add my toiletries, and as I look for my tampons, I realize I'm past the expected date of my period. I check my fertility chart and I'm three days past my normal period. Too soon to tell anything. I've had so many disappointments, so I pack the tampons just in case.

The next morning I leave at the crack of dawn and still have no signs of my period. I feel a little excited about the possibility as I drive to O'Hare.

I make a beeline to my cherished restaurant at DTW, hoping to see my favorite bartender, James. Looking healthy and relaxed, he greets me warmly with a huge smile.

"Miss Alison, so lovely to see you again! Are you on your way to or from China this time?"

"You have quite a memory, James!" I make myself comfortable on the tall bar stool.

"I would never forget you, Alison. Would you like the usual?"

"I have a usual? I guess I do. Yes, please, iced tea and a Cobb salad."

I am impressed that he not only remembers me, but also what I ordered. Most people don't remember me at all; with my fair skin, pale blue eyes, faint eyebrows, light ash-blond hair and petite frame, I've always felt as though I disappear into the background, something that I'm sure has added to my insecurities over the years.

"So, Miss, did you give any more thought to my questions?"

I had completely forgotten about the conversation I had with James about what makes me content. That was quite a conversation, and not one that I would have expected to forget about. I take a sip of my tea through the straw and notice, again that it makes my tongue tingle slightly.

"You should bottle and sell this tea!"

"I plan to in my own place. I'm working on opening my own bar."

"That's exciting!" I take another sip and focus on James' story.

"It is, but it's going to take a while. You do seem a bit more cheerful than the last time I saw you. Have you done anything different?"

"Can I tell you a secret?" I ask as I lean in close so no one else would hear me.

"Of course you can. Your secrets are safe with me." James gently places his right hand over his heart.

"It's a little early and you're the first person I'm telling, but I think I'm going to have a baby."

"Congratulations, you must be transported."

"Is that an airport pun? You have no idea; I've been wanting to have a baby for years and now it finally may happen. I'm keeping my fingers crossed."

"I will cross mine for you as well then." James holds up both his hands and crosses his middle fingers over his index fingers.

"May I have some more tea?"

"You may have all the tea you like, after all you might be drinking for two now." James gives me a wink.

He certainly knows how to make me smile.

"I'll be right back with your salad, don't go away."

"I wouldn't dream of it."

I feel like bursting. My dream of the ideal family is finally coming to fruition.

He places the ample salad in front of me and continues the conversation. "What is it about having a baby that is important to you?"

What does he mean, what is it that's important to me? What kind of question is that?

"Well, it's the whole thing about having a baby." I suddenly feel confused and defensive.

"Is that what will bring you fulfillment?"

I feel a wave of panic come over me. I'm somehow unable to answer James' simple question. Why do his questions have this effect on me? And why is he so personal? I like it and don't like it.

"I don't know."

"Didn't you give this some thought after our last conversation?"

"I did, but then I forgot all about it. I guess I need to think about it again. I will, I promise. And I'll give you my answer when I see you the next time."

"I will be anxious to hear it." His eyes twinkle as he speaks.

What is with this guy? Why in the world would he care about what makes me feel complete? No one has ever asked me that before. James tends to some customers as I count my maximum 15 bites of salad and ponder his questions and why I'm unable to answer them. I check my phone and realize that I'm going to be late for my flight. I stand and lay my credit card on the bar.

"James, I've got to catch my flight, but you've given me more to think about, and I'll be back, I promise. Thank you for the food and the company. You are a delight, even though you overwhelm me with questions."

He laughs quietly, "Thank you, Miss Alison. Safe travels and I look forward to our next visit. Take care of yourself, and don't forget to be joyful!"

I look at him with disbelief. Really, is he going to say that to me every time he sees me?

I settle into my seat with one thought in mind. I pull out a paper and pen to make a list and suddenly I'm not so excited about the baby. What was I thinking? That somehow having a baby with Rick is going to fix our empty lives? Why does James want to know why I want a baby, doesn't everyone? In my deepest heart, I sense the marriage is not what it should be and has been for a long time.

Rick and I rarely sleep together these days and I've tried to tell myself that this is just normal with some couples. Maybe I have been justifying this to myself, to make it somehow seem acceptable in our marriage when I know that it's not. Naturally, I want a close relationship with the person I'm married to: I want to be held at night and told that I'm loved and appreciated.

Rick never asks me anything about my thoughts, dreams or desires. Does he even know who I am? Maybe James knows me better than my own husband!

Why do I try and justify the inadequacies in our marriage? I know I should confront them head on or just move on if things aren't working between us. It's not acceptable for me to continue to look the other way and allow our marriage to collapse one fragment at a time.

Obviously, I forget all about the list.

I sleep heavily for the majority of the 13-hour flight and dream over and over again of Mexico. I was elated when my mind placed me there. I wonder what happened to Marcos? Did he ever marry? Have children? Has he ever forgiven me for leaving abruptly with no explanation?

Arriving in Beijing is always a jolt. The crowds, pollution and poverty disarm me every time. Watching the hordes of locals walk around with face masks makes me depressed and homesick. My week is filled with meetings with manufacturers and I sleep as much as I can in between. I make an appointment with my OBGYN for the day after my return. I don't want to get Rick's hopes up about a baby until I know for sure. As the week progresses, my excitement about the baby mounts, and I can't wait to get home and share the good news with everyone. The doctor confirms my suspicion. I am six weeks along.

"You need to take it easy. The first three months are delicate. I want you to rest as much as possible; eat as healthy as you can. I'd like to see you gain at least ten pounds over the next two months, and absolutely no overseas travel for a while."

I eagerly comply with anything the doctor suggests, though ten pounds sounds like a daunting task.

This moment has played out in my mind a thousand times. I spend the afternoon preparing the only meal that I know how to make well; spaghetti. The evening has to be special and memorable.

Rick is suspicious the moment he arrives home.

"It smells wonderful in here. What's going on? Why are you cooking? Flowers? Did somebody die?" His slightly hooded eyes crinkle as he speaks.

"Of course not," I giggle. "I just want us to have a special evening."

"And why is that?" he asks while tasting a spoonful of my sauce.

"I have some news, some big news."

"Really, and what would that be?" he looks at me with skepticism.

"We're going to have a baby!"

"Are you sure this time? You've had false alarms before."

This is not the reaction I was hoping for. I expect him to be a little more excited about our news. We've wanted this for a long time.

"Yes, I'm sure. I've been to the doctor and everything. She says I need complete rest and I need to start eating more."

"I would agree with that. Congratulations, Babe! You're finally going to have your baby." He wraps his arms around me.

This baby isn't just something I want; it's an extension of us, and something that I wish he desired as deeply as I do.

I correct him, "We are going to have our baby."

After dinner I feed the outdoor shrubs with plant food following the directions precisely. As I water them I feel satisfied knowing that I'm bringing life and vitality to plants. After, I go to bed alone and retrieve my relationship book from my suitcase. I read about resolving childhood wounds though I'm finding it difficult to concentrate on anything but the baby. If Rick and I are going to have a baby, we need to build a better foundation between us.

CHAPTER 5

The following morning I'm bursting with excitement and can't wait to tell everyone the good news. My first call is naturally to Cass.

"Do you think you could stop by this morning for a cup of coffee? I have something exciting to tell you!"

"I guess so, but I'll have to bring the babies with me, and it'll take me a while to get everyone together. Can't you just tell me over the phone?"

"No, I can't. See you when you get here." I hang up before Cassie has a chance to pump me for any more information.

Nervously, I dial Carol, knowing she'll find some way to disapprove of my news. I take a deep breath, grab my favorite pillow and prepare myself for that possibility.

"Mom?" I clutch the pillow tightly as I speak deliberately.

"Yes, Dear. What is it? Is anything wrong? You never call me in the morning."

"Quite the opposite, Mom, Rick and I are going to have a baby!"

"Are you sure this time? You've thought this before."

Can't she just congratulate me? Why can't she be supportive like normal mothers? I squeeze the pillow harder.

"Yes, Mom, I'm sure. I've been to the doctor and everything."

"Well, that's wonderful news. Maybe you'll have twins just like William."

There it was, the zinger! Can't she just be delighted for me without comparing me to my perfect brother?

"I'll be content to have one healthy baby, Mom. I thought you would be too."

I fight back the tears.

"Of, course, Dear. I'm very pleased for you and Rick."

"Got to go, Mom. Someone's at the door," I lie. I toss the pillow down on the new sofa; it's always excruciating having a conversation with her.

I prepare a plate of fruit and cookies for the kids and warm the water for the coffee. At least Cassie will support me. I can count on that.

Cassie arrives looking totally put together, hot pink and black yoga clothes with three babies in tow. "Help me with the carriage?" she asks as we pull it into the marble foyer. "This had better be good!" she adds. "It wasn't easy getting all these little people over here."

"It will be worth your while, I promise! Come in, I've got treats for the girls."

"Let's get them busy with their coloring books."

I watch Cassie as she takes command of her children with complete confidence. I can only hope that I will be as good with my child as she is with hers. By summer I will actually be a mother; I can hardly believe it!

"Have a seat, Cassie," I say handing her a cup of coffee with her favorite vanilla flavored creamer.

"Well, you are in a hurry this morning. What's going on?"

"Rick and I are finally pregnant!"

Cassie's eyes fill with tears as she grabs me tightly. "Oh, honey, I'm so thrilled for you! Tell me everything!"

Cassie pushes her hair off her face and listens to every last word as I babble on about the details of my pregnancy, so far.

"You had better have a girl! Think of all the hand-me-downs your child could inherit from my brood!"

"But, you and George might have more kids, right?"

"Who knows? Maybe. After four, what's one more?"

"You're amazing. I can't imagine."

"You'll see," she says, patting me on the knee. "I'm taking the girls to the pool at the Winter Club this afternoon if you'd like to go."

"I'd love to."

Cassie stays all morning. I am on cloud nine. At least I have one person in my life whom I can share my elation with.

The next day, my elation dissipates as I see through the door, when the bell rings, Carol.

I have no choice but to answer. I remind myself to keep my tongue behind my front teeth as I open the door. "Mom, what brings you here?" My heart is pounding, waiting for the worst possible response, whatever that might be.

Every time I see her I am struck by the contrast in our appearance and wonder if we're even related. She's at least six inches taller than I, with auburn hair and freckles, and her frame is much more solid, though no one would ever accuse her of being overweight, a chronic dieter, her figure is to be envied by women of any age. I look much more like Daddy; paler, more fragile, more Nordic. Maybe that's another reason for Carol's disappointment in me, I look nothing like her and everything like the man she abhors.

"I just came by to bring you a baby gift. Is that okay, or did I need to make an appointment with you first?"

Carol always brings gifts. Is that because she knows on some level that no one likes her? I am surprised though that she's brought a baby gift. Maybe she actually does care.

"I'm sorry, Mom, please come in. I'll make some tea."

"Thank you, Dear. Here, open it now," she hands me a white box with a large blue ribbon.

"Thanks, Mom, this is so thoughtful."

Maybe my pregnancy will bring us closer together.

"Come, let's have a seat in the living room. I'll start the water for tea."

"Are you sure you like having your living room open to the kitchen like this? Your guests can see all of your dishes.

"Yes, this is the way Rick and I like it; it's conducive to conversation."

"I don't understand your taste."

I return with the tea and open the package, it's an adorable blue Onesie with a big bear embroidered on the front.

"It's darling, Mom, this is so thoughtful of you."

"It was really no trouble, since I was shopping for William's twins anyway. Did I tell you they found out he's having boys?"

Stupid me! Naturally she was shopping for William and of course he's having boys.

"It was nice of you to think of us anyway, Mom."

"Oh, it was no bother, really."

I believe her.

"What if I have a girl, though, can I exchange it?"

"Oh no, Dear, just keep it for the next pregnancy."

So what she's telling me is if this baby isn't a boy, I had better keep trying until I have one. Suddenly, I can't wait to get away from her.

"It was nice of you to stop by, but I just remembered that I have to be somewhere."

"Okay, I'll be on my way." She stands and straightens her hot pink Pucci blouse and grabs her matching Hermes handbag.

I think she's as relieved as I am to get out of here.

"I'll walk you to the door."

It's going to be a nightmare for my poor child to have this woman as a grandmother, especially if it's a girl, poor thing.

Mid-afternoon I meet Cass and the girls at the Winter Club. It's early in the season and the pool is packed with moms and their young children.

Cass has saved me a lounge chair close to the shallow end of the pool. Her oldest, Giorgia, is taking a swimming lesson while three-year-old, Nicole, plays in the shallow water.

Cass is sporting a navy bikini and her dark skin looks as though she's just returned from a tropical vacation.

"Cass, your figure is amazing. You don't look like you've had any kids."

"Thanks. You haven't exactly let yourself go either."

I'm hesitant to expose my tan resistant skin to the ultra violet rays, so I keep my cover up on for the time being.

"Do you mind if I ask you a question?"

"Shoot."

"Did you have your breasts done?"

"Oh yeah, years ago. I was flat as a board which made my butt look huge, I needed some balance."

"Was it painful?"

"Not really, are you thinking of having it done?"

"I'd look ridiculous, like a stick pin with two balloons attached to it."

We both giggle.

"See that woman over there in the black one piece?"

"Yeah."

"She and her husband have an open marriage."

"How do you know that?"

"You'll know everything too once you have kids in school."

"Why would anyone do that?"

"I see it happen in couples in their 40's, the marriage starts to get boring, and the men threaten to leave. The women go along with the swinging in order to hold on to him, but it never works. Someone is always jealous and they end up divorced anyway."

"I would never do that. I want no one but Rick for the rest of my life."

"You're pretty happy now, aren't you?"

"Yes, and I can't wait until I can bring my own kids here and watch them swim."

"That's going to happen before you know it."

Cass and I relax as we watch Nicole learn how to hold her breath under water for the first time. She's so excited that she does it over and over until we are finally the last ones at the pool and have to drag her home.

When I get home, I continue to share my thrilling news with friends and family by phone, email and text messages. I call my boss, Katherine, and inform her that I won't be able to travel overseas for a while. Exhausted, I nap until Rick wakes me up.

"What time is it? It's dark out. I didn't water the plants."

"It's okay, I did it. It's seven; I had some work to finish at the office. I brought take out."

"Did you tell anyone about the baby?"

"Sure, a couple of people." Rick looks disinterested.

"And?"

"Everyone is excited for us, of course." Rick leans over me and kisses me on the cheek. "I'll make you a plate. You need to eat you know."

"I know," I smile.

I feel exhausted most of the time and sleep, as I never have before in my life. I buy an arsenal of books on pregnancy and spend as much time reading them as I can. My mind is consumed with thoughts of the coming baby; a dream that is finally about to come true.

At eight weeks, I make a drive alone into Chicago, to the Water Tower. This is a trip that I've dreamed about for a long time. I head straight to the maternity store and try on nearly everything in the store as I try to imagine what I will look like at nine months along. I end up with an abundance of maternity clothes and am ecstatic to finally be in a position to need them.

Pregnancy has brought minimal changes to my body, so far. My normally flat chest has already increased by one bra size, but the rest of me feels pretty much the same. It will probably be some time before I will actually show. With the addition of morning sickness, gaining weight is nearly impossible.

My shopping spree wears me out and I return home loaded with six bags of clothes. Rick is watching a hockey tournament in the den when I return.

"Geez, what did you do? Buy out the store?"

"Don't worry, you're not paying for it. I'm going to put these away and come back downstairs and join you."

"K, Babe. Do me a favor and hand me a beer before you go?"

"Sure." I think of the relationship book and how I should be doing simple things to please my husband.

Maybe Rick will be more interested about the baby when I actually start showing.

I fetch Rick his beer and then haul my loot up the stairs. I spread all my new outfits carefully over the bed, so that I can get a look at each and every one. Me in maternity clothes, I can hardly believe it! I can't wait for Cassie to come over and see it all.

I step into the bathroom for a quick freshen-up before heading downstairs. I brush on a little blush to brighten my cheeks and add some pink lip stain. I know how much Rick likes it when I make the effort to look good for him. I stop to pee for the twentieth time today and my heart stops as I see a spattering of blood on my underwear. No! It can't possibly be! I feel a sense of panic, not knowing what to do. I quickly layer a few tissues in my underwear and hope that the bleeding will stop as quickly as it started. This happens sometimes in pregnancy, I tell myself.

Slowly, I walk downstairs and find Rick on the phone with his sister. "Oh, here she is. I'll let her tell you the rest of it. Thanks, Sis, we're over the moon."

I sternly shake my head back and forth, feeling like I'm going to faint.

"C'mon, Al. You know you're dying to tell her."

Rick shoves the phone towards me as I feel the room spinning around me. The last thing I want to do is talk about my pregnancy now; the pregnancy that might already be over. I reluctantly take the phone and answer my sister-in-law's questions as best I can while fighting back tears.

I get off the phone as fast as I can and make myself a cup of tea before joining Rick on the sofa. He's engrossed in his golf as my head reels with fear. Maybe it's normal to bleed like this, I tell myself. I'll just try not to think about it, but of course, that doesn't work.

The tea takes effect and I find myself needing to pee, yet again. I don't dare go to the bathroom and find out if there's more blood. I can just sit here and pretend that it's all going to be fine. I finally give in and quietly step into the powder room. The tissues are soaked through with fresh blood and I know my worst fears are realized.

After cleaning myself up, I go upstairs to the bedroom sobbing silently so Rick doesn't hear me. My heart sinks as I see the maternity clothes strewn all over the bed. Methodically, I pick them up and place them over the upholstered bench at the foot of the bed in one massive pile. I turn off the lights and stare into the vast darkness in front of me. All of my fantasies about the perfect family are gone now and I can't imagine my future without a baby in it. My hopes and dreams have vanished in an instant. I have never felt this empty or alone in my life.

CHAPTER 6

Rick abruptly enters the bedroom and flips on the lights.

"You didn't even say goodnight and you skipped dinner again. You know you have to eat. Do you want me to bring you a tray?" He sounds annoyed until he notices the tears streaming down my face.

"What's wrong, Al? Are you in pain?" He looks alarmed as he sits cautiously on the bed next to me.

"I'm bleeding," I say in a feeble voice.

"Well, that could be anything, couldn't it?" He pushed his hands into his pockets.

"It can't be good, I'm sure of that."

"Let's look it up in one of your books or on the Internet."

That's just like a man, to be pragmatic about something at a time when I am so emotionally compromised.

"I did that." I sit up and push the pillows behind my back to support me.

"And?"

"It's inconclusive." I pull up the blankets and straighten them around me.

"Let's call Dr. Stevens."

"If it's bad news, I don't want to know."

"You have to know, Babe. Either way, you have to know."

"Will you call for me? I'm just not up to it right now." I pull the covers up around my neck.

"Sure."

Rick speaks with Dr. Stevens out of my hearing range for several minutes only to return, phone in hand with lots of questions. My heart is in my throat.

"She wants to know when it started. Why don't you just talk to her yourself?"

"No, I can't." I shake my head back and forth.

Looking irritated, he continues the phone conversation. "Uh huh. I'll ask. Hold on."

"She wants to know if the bleeding is getting better, worse or the same? Is there any cramping?"

Rick repeats my answer to Dr. Stevens, then listens intently and keeps repeating, "Uh huh," into the phone.

My stomach is in knots as I wait to hear the inevitable diagnosis.

"She says you are probably miscarrying and that it could take a while. If you want, she will meet you at the office and do a D and C, whatever that is."

"I know what it is." My heart sinks. It is all over as quickly as it had begin. This is so unfair. Why me?

"Do you want me to call her back? Take you in?" Rick nervously plays with the change in the pocket of his khaki shorts.

I shake my head.

"I'm sorry, Babe. Maybe we're just not meant to have kids. I'll leave you alone. Call me if you need me. I'll sleep in the guest room." Rick kisses me delicately on the forehead.

"Won't you stay with me?"

"You need your rest."

"Turn out the light please."

Why didn't he stay with me and put his arms around me? I'm not going to beg him! The last thing I want now is to be alone! I stare at the slate gray wall for hours, hoping to get through the worst day of my life. At three in the morning I finally get up, change my blood soaked pad and take a sleeping pill. It is going to be a long, desolate day knowing I'm losing my baby.

It is ten when I finally awaken in a fog, slowly recalling the events from the day before. The pit in my stomach returns immediately. I only wish it were a bad dream.

I notice a tray on the bedside table with a glass of orange juice and a bagel. The note from Rick reads:

Hope you are feeling better. Have an early meeting. See you tonight. – Rick XOX

Feeling better? Is he kidding? I am lying in wait for my dead baby to expel from by body. How could I possibly be feeling better?

There is only one person who could cheer me up, so I give Cass a call.

"I need you. Can you come over?"

She doesn't ask any questions, just like a true friend.

"The door is open, just come on up to the bedroom."

I'm sure she has a good idea of what is going on. The pile of used tissues on the floor by the bed is a dead giveaway.

"Uh oh. What happened?" She's wearing a royal purple warm up jacket and matching running shoes.

"The doctor thinks I will miscarry sometime today. I'm

just waiting." The tears are flowing uncontrollably down my face.

"What can I do?" She pushes her straight hair out of her eyes.

"Just be here. Talk to me. Distract me."

"Is there anyone that you want me to call? Does Rick know what's going on? Doesn't he want to be here with you now?"

What a sight I must be; swollen eyes and a puffy face.

I shake my head. "I can't face anyone right now. Rick knows, I told him last night what was going on and trust me, he doesn't want to be here right now." I grab a fresh tissue.

"If it's distractions that you want, then it's distractions you shall have. Let me just make one quick call."

"George? It's me. Can you handle the kids for a while? I don't know exactly. I'm at Ali's. She needs me. Thanks."

"Kids are under control. I'm all yours. I'm going to make us some tea first. A shower will make you feel better. Why don't you take a quick one while I make the tea?" Cass grabs the waste basket and expeditiously picks up the crumbled tissues from the floor, tossing them inside.

"I'm afraid standing will make me lose the baby faster."

"Really? Go take a shower, Ali. And put on some fresh clothes. How long have you had those pajamas on?"

Cassie returns with the tea and a deck of cards. I've showered and changed into a fresh pair of leggings and a pink sweatshirt.

"I know how competitive you are. A game of gin rummy should take your mind off things."

Cassie deals as I talk. "I feel like such a failure, Cass."

"Why? It's not like you have any control over your body's ability to carry a child."

"Having a child is something that people take for granted, it's just not fair. I feel incompetent at everything; I always have."

"Where did that come from? You're one of the most capable people I know." Cass shuffles again.

"Seriously? That's not how I see myself. Carol wanted me to be a tennis player, but I wasn't good enough to compete. She wanted me to be a lawyer, but I fell short of that as well. Then there was the speech problem too, that didn't help things."

"Speech problem?"

"Yes, as a kid I couldn't say my s's. Can you imagine? When I said my name growing up, it came out as Alishun Andershun. Carol was horrified."

"You'd never know you had a problem now."

"Thanks to years of speech classes. Every year they'd test me and every year I'd fail. I was pulled from class twice a week to go to a special class and was given exercises to practice at home. I can't count the number of times I've rehearsed, 'She sells sea shells by the sea shore'. Carol couldn't handle having a child that needed to be in a special class. It felt like each year when I failed the speech test, she pulled a little further away from me."

"Having trouble saying your s's sounds like a pretty minor thing."

"To you maybe, but not to Carol. Today my name would be Alishun Davish." I giggle. "There's one more thing and I've never told anyone this before, Cass, but I've been starving myself since I was 12 trying to get Carol's attention. It never worked, of course. If anything I think it made me even more invisible to her. I have to wonder if I caused the miscarriage, because of my eating disorder. Maybe I starved the poor thing to death."

"Ali, stop. You know that's not true. Your mother is an

idiot and doesn't deserve you. She can't see what a wonderful, smart and giving person you are. You always try and please everyone around you. Maybe it's time for you to start doing what you want, not what everyone else wants. You should get some help for your eating disorder. What do you do, just not eat?"

"I'd say Carol didn't like being a mother except that she seemed to enjoy mothering William. When I was 12 I overheard a couple of older girls at school talking about something called the five-bite diet and it suddenly clicked in my head. I started limiting myself to five bites for each meal and I lost 20 pounds in a month. I felt empowered and in control for the first time even though it didn't work to get Carol's attention."

"You only eat five bites per meal?"

"Now I'm up to 15. I've played with it over the years. A bite is 11 calories, so I calculate from there."

"That's less than 500 calories a day and you've counted every bite for years; it sounds exhausting."

"Sometimes I'll add a snack or a beverage."

"Still, that's not enough food."

"I'm working on it. I feel like I have things under control." I had added two extra bites to each meal since I found out about the pregnancy. "How am I ever going to face everyone? Now I'll be an even bigger failure in my mother's eyes."

"I'm glad your eating is better; I've often worried about how thin you are. You've done nothing wrong and you will hold your head high and go on with your life. What they think doesn't matter. My mother thinks I'm nuts to have so many kids. Do you see that stopping me? I could care less what anyone thinks. It's my life and I'm doing what I want with it."

"I do love that about you, Cass. You're wonderful that

way, not caring about what others think. I wish I could be more like that."

"You can, starting now."

"It's working, Cass."

"What's working?"

"You made me forget about the miscarriage for a minute. Amazing!" I place my cards on the small table. "Gin!"

"Mission accomplished then. How are you feeling?"

Cass counts the points and hands me the deck.

"There's some cramping. At this point I just want it to be over as quickly as possible."

"I'm really sorry, Ali. I know how badly you wanted this baby."

"More than anything in the world."

CHAPTER 7

Two days have passed since I lost the baby and Dr. Stevens is insisting that I come see her, a visit I am dreading.

"How are you doing, Alison?"

I'm always taken off guard by Dr. Stevens' appearance. Being a doctor, I would think she would care about her health and looks, but at 50 pounds overweight and an inch of gray roots showing, that doesn't seem to be the case. She came highly recommended, but she must be near retirement, I conclude.

She gives me a thorough exam, poking my insides and tells me to sit up.

"Everything looks fine. The good news is you are able to get pregnant." She gives me the statistics on first trimester miscarriages, hoping to cheer me up.

"I'm writing you a prescription for progesterone. It will help prevent a future miscarriage, so I want you to take it the minute you think there's any chance you're pregnant and I want you to wait a full three months before trying to conceive again. I also want to test you for a genetic mutation called MTHFR, it can be the root cause of miscarriages."

"What if I have it? Does that mean I'm doomed?" I hold the front of my gown closed by crossing my arms.

"Not at all. It means that we can give you supplements to fix the problem. The results will take a while."

I feel numb as I make my way through the following days. Rick is thoughtful enough to call family and friends saving me the embarrassment. I beg him to call Carol and I know I did the right thing when Rick relays the conversation to me later.

"What did she say?" I ask.

"She suggests that perhaps you should wait past the first trimester before telling anyone next time."

"So much for motherly comfort in my time of need."

Rick also calls my boss, Katherine, and lets her know that I am available for overseas travel. China sounds good to me for the first time in a very long time. I want to get as far away from the reminders of the miscarriage as possible. I make plans to leave the following week. I arrange for someone to water the garden in my absence in case Rick forgets.

I expectantly look forward to conversing with my new friend, James, at the airport. As I walk in the restaurant, I immediately spot that enormous smile.

"Good day, Miss Alison, lovely to see you again. How are you? Still excited about the baby?"

I'm sure that the color drains from my face as he asks me this question.

"Oh," he says immediately, "I'm sorry, Miss, if I have misspoken." He wipes down the bar in front of me with a damp rag.

"You didn't know. How could you? I lost the baby, but everything is going to be okay," I lie.

Changing the awkward subject, he asks, "May I offer you a Cobb salad and some tea?"

"I've been dreaming about your salad and tea for weeks! Thank you, I would love that."

I make myself comfortable at my favorite spot at the bar while James pours me a tall glass of tea and I can feel it tingling all the way through my extremities; it almost feels healing.

James asks, "Did you ever come up with any answers to my questions? Did you ever decide what renews you?"

"Funny how I keep forgetting that. I started to make a list last time I left here. Let me see if I can find it here in the side pocket of my bag." I rummage around and find a half finished list on a crumbled piece of paper.

"Here it is! Funny, I don't even remember what's on it." Looking at the faint writing, it all starts coming back to me.

"Will you share it with me?" He continues to dry a rack of beer mugs.

I take another long sip of my tea and feel it tickling my tongue.

"I wrote that I want to live on the beach, ride horses and draw. How odd!"

"What's odd about it? It sounds beautiful to me."

"It's odd because I don't remember writing this at all, but it is in my handwriting." I stir my tea.

I observe James' slender fingers with subtle tattoos and wonder how the two of us became friends; by looking at us one would imagine that we wouldn't have a thing in common.

"Why don't you write some more when you get on your flight and maybe it will come back to you."

"That's a good idea, I'll do that."

Feeling confused, I look around the bar. "Business seems to be picking up."

"You're not the only one who likes the food here," James laughs.

"I can see that. Good for you. How are the plans going for your own place?" I'm impressed that James' button down shirts always look freshly pressed.

"Coming right along, thanks for asking. My mum is helping me put some recipes together. It should be quite something when it's all done."

"I have no doubt that it will be, James."

"Do you ever give any thought to parallel universes?"

"To what?"

"To other universes where other selves just like us are living entirely different lives than what we are living."

"Where do you come up with this stuff? Do you watch a lot of science fiction?"

He chuckles. "No, this is real, look it up sometime. There's science behind it. Imagine that there are dozens of other Alisons out there just like you, but maybe one of them is a famous dancer and another is a mathematical engineer. Think about all of the versions of you that could be running around out there."

"That's a little mind boggling."

"Maybe there's even an Alison who has a loving, supportive mother."

"Now that would be something! You are intriguing, James, with these ideas of yours."

"Don't you ever talk about stuff like this with your friends?"

"Never. I have to run, but may I have one more splash of tea before I go?"

"You may have all the tea you want, Miss Alison. I'll give you some in a take out cup. Please take care of yourself out there. You look a little pale if you don't mind my saying so."

"James, you are one of the few people who are welcome to say anything you want to me." I conclude that I have absolutely nothing to lose with being completely open and honest with this man.

"Then, don't forget to work on that list as soon as you board the plane, promise?"

"I promise."

I don't know what it is about James, but I just can't help smiling when I talk to him. He has a way of making me feel better about everything.

I get acclimated in my seat and I can't stop thinking about the possibility of parallel universes. I try to imagine what it would be like to have a house full of kids and a mother who adored me. I suddenly remember the list. I take out pen and paper and memories about the beach, horses and drawing start to appear. I was thinking about Mexico and how joyful I was there. I start adding to my list and my mind wanders to my marriage and my life in general.

I can't believe that I feel a sudden sense of relief floating through me as I think about losing the baby. Rick was distant through the miscarriage. Is that what I would consider acceptable behavior of a partner? Of course not. I notice that I feel a wave of exhilaration as I picture myself being free from Rick and Carol. Why did I always work so hard to please them?

Soon, I'm asleep and back in Mexico. The dreams of Mexico continue for the following two nights. Why do I always dream of Mexico after my visits with James?

My week in Beijing flies by. This time I'm really dreading coming home and facing the empty feelings that have consumed me.

As soon as I get home I check on the shrubs and am pleased to see a visible increase in size. Life resumes and the miscarriage is never mentioned by Rick or anyone else for that matter, except for Cass, of course. She has a way of keeping after me and not letting me avoid things that I find uncomfortable. Now that I've told the truth about my eating disorder, she's all over me about that too. Cassie is never subtle, that's for sure.

Cass arranges a babysitter for the afternoon, and to cheer me up, surprises me with a Saturday lunch at our favorite spot, just the adults. It's a gorgeous, sunny, yet breezy, afternoon and the four of us, bundled in our down jackets, make the short walk to the Deerpath Inn and head downstairs to the dark, wood paneled pub.

"They only agreed to come if they could watch golf," Cass leans in and whispers to me.

"That figures! At least we are out of the house and having a change of scenery."

We pass the afternoon placing silly bets on the golf tournament and Cass and I take side bets on how many times our husbands will use their favorite golf terms during the course of the afternoon; for George it's "handicap" and for Rick, it's "in the zone". Cass and I are wildly entertained by our silly game and she wins by a whopping 24 points.

After passing such a relaxing afternoon, my mood changes and I feel de-stressed and grateful to have good friends and such an incredible environment to live in.

The weeks pass and Rick and I go about our business as if nothing has ever happened and I try to push the thoughts of the baby out of my mind as quickly as they enter.

∾

CHAPTER 8

I'm feeling isolated in my grief. Rick doesn't understand, Carol is unable to give me emotional support and I don't know James well enough to discuss the intimate details of my miscarriage. Cass would listen, but she just can't understand either. I do a search on the Internet to find others who have been through the same loss. I find a list of support groups and decide to give one a try.

I make an afternoon trip to the city to try a group meeting. I'm quite nervous as I enter the building, having no idea what to expect. I find a group of 10 or so women chatting quietly when I arrive. I'm welcomed warmly and instructed to take a seat. There's nowhere to hide in this room and no way to sneak out should I decide to leave early. I'm not sure if this was a good idea.

I grab a bottle of water and listen to the heart breaking stories of these women who have suffered far more than I, losing multiple babies or losing them much later in the pregnancy. One young woman tells of how she was repeatedly blamed by her family members for the loss of her babies.

Should I tell my story? Mine is not dramatic, but I feel a need to talk about what happened, after all that's why I'm here. I despise public speaking and I can feel my heart race as I think of everyone watching me. I finally get up the nerve to speak and am mindful to hold my tongue carefully behind my teeth as I say any words containing the letter s.

"My name is Ali. I'm 28 and I started trying to get pregnant the day I got married three years ago. Every month was a huge disappointment to me, but I kept trying, kept being hopeful. I had just booked all of the fertility tests for us when I found out I was pregnant. Calling to cancel those tests made me deliriously happy. I was not looking forward to going down the road of infertility treatments. For three years I had watched everyone around me have babies without effort. I'd be so angry when I'd hear moms talk about their unwanted kids and how they wish they weren't burdened with them. I couldn't understand why life was so unfair that way, giving babies to those who didn't want them and denying them to those of us who did. After three long years of trying I was finally going to have what I had always wanted, always dreamed about. But then, in an instant, it was gone, the moment I saw that stain of red blood; that damned blood. If that part isn't bad enough, then there's the embarrassment of having to tell everyone and worse yet, when people congratulate you and you have to correct them. I came here today because I felt a need to talk about what happened and I feel a little embarrassed about it since my story isn't tragic or unique. Thank you for listening."

One of the women asks, "Do you have anyone in your life to talk to about it?"

"I've got people in my life who love me, but they don't know what losing a baby is like."

"I know what you mean. People just don't understand; it's the loneliest feeling in the world." One of the women agreed with me.

I feel like a weight has been lifted and I'm glad I spoke. A couple of the women give me their numbers should I feel like talking. Very nice of them, but I don't think I'm going to need to keep talking about it.

I'm ready to look forward, not back, so I decide to tackle the renovation of our spare bedroom. I had planned on making the room a nursery, but it's time to move on. The room is currently outdated with tired looking yellow walls and floral linens that I've had since college.

I spend time choosing the right color for the room and decide on a sophisticated gray-blue shade called boathouse. I spend a couple of hours each day painting the room and finish it off with a bright white paint on the crown molding.

Rick is forced to sleep with me each night as I work on the room, something that I am enjoying. I miss the sound of his breathing next to me at night when he's sleeping in the guest room.

I'm pretty exhausted by the end of each day and Rick is being helpful by bringing in takeout each night. He surprises me one evening with a small wrapped box.

"What is this?"

"Just open it."

It's not my birthday or our anniversary, but I'm curious so I tear off the expensive looking paper. Inside is a delicate silver bracelet with tiny opals and diamonds set inside.

"It's beautiful, but why?"

"I know you've been through quite a bit lately and you're working hard on the house. It's just a little I appreciate you gift."

"That's so sweet, thanks Rick. Will you help me put it on?"

It feels good to be appreciated.

I continue with the spare room, making several trips to Target to purchase a gray and white rug, navy and white sheets and comforter plus white blinds for the window. The finished product is picture perfect, just as I imagined it.

When the room is complete I invite Cass over to show off my talents.

"You did a great job, it looks like a magazine layout."

"It's more like Pinterest." I giggle.

"There's nothing wrong with that, everybody does it these days. I've been getting new recipe ideas from Pinterest recently."

"You know decorating this room wasn't exactly easy for me."

"What do you mean?"

"It was supposed to have been the baby's room."

"Oh, I didn't think about that. It will be a baby's room at some point, but for now you get to enjoy this beautiful décor."

"Hockey is starting up. Do you guys want to come to some of the games again?"

The Millers have been very supportive of Rick and his Winter Club hockey teams.

"Yes, we love that. Watching the games and dinner with you guys is one of our favorite activities. Even the girls like the games."

"Go figure."

Even though the guest bedroom is completed, Rick continues to sleep with me most, but not all of the time.

∾

CHAPTER 9

As the weeks progress, I successfully manage to avoid Carol and the topic of pregnancy altogether. I request an extra trip to Beijing, just so I can escape the constant reminders of what I've just lost.

My trips there allow me a temporary escape from my problems and I manage to pay a visit to my favorite bartender on the way home.

"This time I remembered!" I say as I slap the crumbled list on the dark mahogany bar. "You and I are going to have a conversation about this!"

James laughs. "I'm looking forward to that, Miss. Let me just take care of a few customers and I'll be right back. The usual, right?"

I'm convinced that James has no interest in me romantically, that he just likes connecting with people and learning what makes them tick.

I nod and straighten out my list to get a better view.

"It's so odd, James," I start, once he makes his way back.

"What's that?"

"I only think about Mexico after I talk to you."

"How did you feel in Mexico? Were you excited about life?"

"Very." I think of Marcos and the enthusiasm I felt for life when I was with him.

"That's why then, we've been talking about contentment. It's a logical jump. Let's see your list then." I'm surprised he can make out my childish scrawl.

"See, it's all about the things I did in Mexico."

"Why don't you do more of those things?"

"Those things don't fit into my life in Chicago."

"Then maybe you shouldn't be in Chicago."

What did he just say? Not be in Chicago? What an absurd thought. I've never considered anything else.

"Now you're just being silly, James."

"Am I?" He looks at me quizzically.

I had to sit a moment and think about what James was saying. The thought of me living in Mexico, or anywhere else, was ridiculous. Chicago is my home. Besides, Rick would never want to leave. I try to imagine an alternate me living in Mexico romping on the beach in a bikini.

"I didn't know you're a provocateur."

"More people need a provocateur. We need to prod ourselves, from time-to-time, out of the mental haze of being complacent and think radical new thoughts while provoking those around us to do the same. I learn a lot listening to folks here at the bar. I just pay attention, that's all."

"Most people don't listen at all. We could all stand to do more of that. What about you? What exhilarates you?"

"That's pretty simple. I want my own bar and I just want my family to be taken care of."

"What about a family of your own? Don't you want a family of your own one day?"

He shakes his head, "All of my friends who are married are miserable. No marriage for me."

He is full of surprises.

"At least you know what you want, it's more than I can say for myself."

"You're getting there."

"When you imagine yourself in other universes what do you see yourself doing?"

"I'm inventing new forms of space travel, visiting other planets and communicating without words."

"You really are a science fiction guy, aren't you?"

"I guess I am. I have a new assignment for you."

"And what would that be?" I ask, smiling.

"I want you to make a new list of how you can incorporate the things that make you joyous into your life. You'd be amazed how quickly life's anxieties can dissipate when we focus on what we love in our life rather than on what we don't have or what's not going right for us at the moment."

"Are you the happy police? Do you have this conversation with everyone who walks in here?"

James throws his head back and laughs, "No, Miss, I try to read each person and get a feel about them. The first time I met you I felt that you were melancholy."

"Well you were right. Are you an intuitive or something?"

"No, like I said, I just pay attention."

"I guess you do. Well, James, once again you've given me much to think about, not to mention homework!" I shake his hand firmly. "I look forward to our next conversation."

I look around the under lit room and wonder why the cozy booths and tables set with freshly pressed linens aren't full. The food is reasonably priced, for an airport restaurant, and certainly higher quality than most airport bar food. It can't be because of the staff; I can't think of anyone who is more charming and personable than James. Feeling empathy for James, I leave him a tip that is three times my normal amount.

"It was a pleasure, as always, Miss Alison."

Once again, I pull out my pad and pen to start a list. How can I merge my list of what interests me into my real life? I could ride horses in Lake Forest, I guess. It's not exactly the same as riding on the beach, but what the heck? I could also draw in Lake Forest, that's easy. I could take a class or just start on my own. That's two things on the list.

My thoughts roam and I find myself dreading going home. I don't want to feel anyone's pity for me. I just want to fast forward through this part of my life and not have people speculating why I lost my baby.

Rick and I have never even had one discussion about the miscarriage. Isn't that odd? I ask myself. I certainly think so. I also have to wonder, if he's this absent during a miscarriage, what would happen if I were to get sick or something. Would I be able to count on him? I'll have to ask Cassie and see what she thinks.

I fall asleep and I'm instantly back in Mexico; riding horses, drawing and staring deeply into Marco's eyes. I awaken on landing and wonder why I'm dreaming of Marcos and Mexico so frequently these days. I haven't seen him in five years. I only knew him for a week. Isn't it funny how deeply he went into my unconscious. What could it mean?

∾

CHAPTER 10

I arrive home near dawn and I am alleviated to find that Rick has already left for the day. Crawling into my comfy bed, loaded with pillows and crisp, clean sheets, I hope that the dreams of Mexico will return, and they do. It's one way for me to feel as though I live there.

It's late afternoon when Cassie awakens me with a call.

"I didn't want to wake you too early. I know how these marathon flights do you in. How was your trip?"

"It was fine; nothing out of the ordinary. Frankly I was relieved to get out of here for a while and forget about my problems."

"You have problems? Nothing other than infertility I hope."

"I don't know, Cass, I'm feeling uneasy about Rick and me these days."

"What do you mean by 'uneasy'?"

"I'm not sure. What do you think about the fact that Rick and I never discussed the miscarriage?"

"I think that's just typical male behavior. Most of them don't want to talk about anything emotional like that. They just want to move on and forget about it."

"Hmmm, the relationship books I've been reading say couples should be having daily discussions. I think this is pretty abnormal."

"What's normal anyway? Listen, I'll let you go. I just wanted to check in on you. Call me when you get re-acclimated. Maybe we can take a yoga class or walk to the square for coffee."

"Sounds good, Cass. Thanks for checking in on me."

I can't get Marcos off my mind. I miss his gentle strength and quiet nature. I miss our walks on the beach and the long discussions about Carl Jung and the collective unconsciousness. I miss his intellectual curiosity and his eagerness to understand the meaning of life. I miss the sound of his voice when he read his favorite poetry to me. I wonder what he's doing now? Does he ever think about me? Most importantly, does he hate me for taking off without a word? Why am I thinking about him so much?

To distract myself, I check into drawing classes in the area. There are several. It's time to make a quick trip to the local craft store, I decide, to purchase drawing supplies so I can start drawing at home. There are certainly plenty of beginner instruction videos to get started with online.

Rick arrives home and I have my new art supplies spread out all over the shiny kitchen counter.

"What's all this?" he asks without saying hello.

"My new hobby. I decided to try my hand at drawing."

"Where did this come from? You're not creative. What on earth are you thinking?"

I feel as if someone is deflating my balloon. Why is Rick being so negative? He really hurt my feelings, but I try not to show it.

"Haven't you ever wanted a hobby?" I ask, trying to sound unaffected.

"Never, hockey and golf are all I need. I wouldn't change a thing."

Wow, Rick really has a closed mind. I wonder why I never noticed that before? Quietly, I put my art supplies away and decide to bring them out only when Rick is not around.

Horseback riding! I forgot about it being on the list. I discreetly do an Internet search while Rick plants himself in front of the TV with a beer. James will be impressed that I've followed through with my list.

Rick is so distant. I wonder if he's always been that way and I just never noticed, or has he withdrawn since I lost the baby. It feels as though we almost have no relationship at all. All he does is work and play golf and with his limited free time he's coaching hockey. There's no conversation and no shared experiences. What do we really have? It seems like we share a house and a dog and not even much of that lately.

I book my first riding lesson at the equestrian center in Libertyville. My only riding experience was in Zihua and it only required a pair of shorts and no shoes. The horses were docile and walked at a snail's pace along the shoreline. There was no skill or experience required.

The equestrian center offers an entirely different experience, one, which requires proper riding gear and knowledge about horses. They start me from the very beginning with lessons in brushing and grooming my horse before outfitting him with the proper tack.

This was way more than I expected to take on; seriously, I just wanted to ride and trail riding would have been fine.

My instructor is a petite brunette in her late teens named Samantha. She takes me directly to a freshly raked stall to meet my horse, Sunshine, a handsome Bay of medium height.

"You have to properly groom your horse before and after each ride," she says, seeming aloof as she hands me an unfamiliar tool. "This is a curry comb," she says as she demonstrates brushing in a circular motion on Sunshine. "Here, now you try."

I get the feeling she is bored with her job. Is all of this really necessary? "When do I get to ride?"

"Soon enough. You must learn the proper care for your horse first. There's a lot of time involved in riding, you can't just jump on the horse and run off."

That's what we did in Mexico. The lesson continues with a soft brush and a pick for Sunshine's hooves. At long last, after a lesson in proper bridal and saddle application, we are in the ring.

"When his left forelegs move, you need to lift yourself slightly from the saddle. Squeeze those legs!"

I had no idea how complicated riding could be and I find it difficult to follow Samantha's instructions, there's just too much to remember at once. At the end of the hour, I'm worn out.

I thank Samantha for her time and tell her that I'll be in touch when I'm ready for the next session. Once home, I crawl into a hot bath and soak for an hour. I decide to shift my focus on hobbies to drawing for the time being.

While Rick puts in long hours at the office, I pass my time with the online drawing classes and Internet searches on parallel universes. James was right, there's a ton of information here. As I watch the videos the idea of other universes becomes more and more plausible and my mind is overloaded with the possibility of infinite Alis. I refocus my efforts into drawing classes and am surprised that I seem to have a knack for caricature and it makes me smile to see what I can create. My first attempt is a sketch of Gracie and I quite successfully capture her essence.

It's time to move on to something a bit more difficult, so I retrieve a photo of Cass and go to work. I have no idea what I'm doing, but I'm enjoying myself and the results of my efforts.

In the morning, Cass and I take her two youngest kids on a walk to get coffee at the Market Square. We find a table in the back patio and after I surprise her with the drawing I did.

"You did this?" Cass exclaimed.

"Yes, be honest. What do you think?"

"It's awesome! It totally looks like me...though a little grotesque," she says while tipping her head sideways to get the full effect of the super sized lips and butt. "When did you learn how to do this?"

"I don't know," I shrug. "I just started."

"You've got some talent. You must keep doing this, Ali, you're really good."

"Do you really think I'm talented?" I ask timidly.

"Yes, of course you are. Just look at this. Will you do my kids? I'll frame them and hang them on the wall."

"Sure, I'd be glad to. Rick says he thinks I'm not creative."

"What does he know? He's a lawyer after all."

I burst out laughing and oh it feels so good to laugh. My list is already working.

∽

CHAPTER 11

My newfound hobby is giving me a much-needed break from my obsession with pregnancy. Christmas is approaching and I volunteer to help Cass with her annual Christmas party; something that everyone who knows her looks forward to every year.

Cassie is a perfectionist and a natural hostess. I can't imagine putting together such a large event in my home, let alone with four little ones running around, but she makes it all look effortless.

"Cassie, how do you do it?" I finally ask her one day while unpacking one of many boxes filled with Christmas decorations.

"Do what?"

"How do you do what you do? You always seem so capable. It's like you do the work of ten women and make it all look so easy!"

"Have a seat, Ali, I want to tell you something about me."

I pull up a stool to the kitchen counter and refill my

water glass from the large pitcher sitting on the counter. "See this is what I mean!"

"What?" Cass scoots her stool closer to the counter.

"You even have little slices of lemon in your water. It's all just picture-book."

"I'm not without fault, I'm just doing what I love so it all comes easy to me. If I had to do what you do, I would never make it. George, the kids, the cooking and decorating, that's what I love most in this world. It's not an effort to me; I'm just being myself. Don't ever think of me as flawless, it's not the case at all."

"But you are always well put together; impeccable makeup and clothes. Where do you buy all of those great workout clothes? And, by the way, I've always wanted to ask you how you stay in such great shape when you rarely work out."

"There's a great place for fitness clothes in the Water Tower on the fourth level. As far as staying in shape goes; sex, lots of sex. I love my husband. Oh and there's the housework too, and chasing after four little girls - that will burn a few calories!"

I feel a slight pang of jealousy as she mentions their active sex life. My sex life with Rick is far from satisfying these days. Almost nonexistent is more like it.

"As far as the makeup goes, I love the stuff and want to look good for my husband. Doing my hair and makeup everyday is not a chore to me, it's fun."

"You really do love George, don't you, Cass?"

"I really do with every fiber of my being."

How I wish I could feel that way about someone. Part of me always wondered if Cass had married George for his money. For Christ sake, their marriage does look so damn idyllic; I just thought that it couldn't really be that way and he is older and not particularly attractive, not to me anyway.

"Ali, just be yourself, and you can be happy too. Stop trying to please everyone else. If I cared about what my mother thought, I would be an executive, living in the city with a six-figure income and no family. In my mother's eyes, I am a failure, but I don't care. Some day I'll tell you the story about my mother. She's miserable and I'm not. Do yourself a favor and stop thinking how your mother feels. Remember that happiness is the best revenge. Now let's get back to work!"

I've never been exactly jealous of Cass, but I admire and envy her and wish I could be more like her. Her words have given me much to think about. I continue to unpack the boxes, while deep in thought about Cass and her seemingly ideal life.

The night of the party arrives and Cass' house is decorated like a five-star hotel. I can't imagine how many thousands of dollars she spent on the decorations alone, not to mention the caterers and live music. She has four different fully decorated trees placed throughout the house. I can't wait to see what she will be wearing to wow her guests.

I do my best to look pretty. I find a red taffeta strapless dress at Neiman's that I think suits my small frame, and I wrap my hair up on the back of my head and fasten it with a decorative clip. My skin is so light that I must be meticulous not to overdo the makeup. It's easy for me to look like a clown if I'm not careful.

I complete my look with a large pair of shiny, crystal earrings and matching choker necklace. Black tights, a pair of low black heels and I'm pleased with my appearance, though I know I will pale in comparison to my good friend, Cass.

"Al, are you ready?" I hear Rick call from downstairs. "We're going to be late!"

"Give me a minute, I just need to find my lipstick."

I rummage through the bathroom drawers looking for my one red lipstick. There's a full box of tampons in the cupboard and I suddenly realize that I'm late…really late. Let's see, when was my last period? I count backwards and discover that I'm over two weeks overdue! Quickly I search for a pregnancy test and find several.

Rick calls to me again, "Al, come on!"

"I'll be right there, I just have to pee!"

I quickly pull down my tights and pee on the stick. It turns positive immediately. Oh my God!

CHAPTER 12

I swiftly pull myself together and take a quick look in the mirror before facing Rick. I feel numb. This pregnancy has taken me by surprise. It's only been six weeks since the miscarriage and Dr. Stevens told me to wait three months. After all of these years of trying, somehow I'm feeling totally unprepared for this pregnancy. We did have sex twice this month, though I thought we were protected by the condoms we used.

"What took you so long?"

"I couldn't find my lipstick."

"You look beautiful. Come on, we're late."

I throw on my thickest faux fur and brace myself for the slush and I shuffle in my pretty shoes across the street to Cass and George's house. The party is in full swing when we arrive. Cass has hired a valet and cars are parked down the street for blocks. Cass and George greet us warmly at the door and she is dressed from head to toe in gold, and strongly resembles a Greek Goddess.

My head reels as I assimilate my surroundings and at the same time digest my news. My brain is on sensory overload as I take in the massive Christmas decorations, people, noise from chatter and music as well as the various aromas coming from the kitchen. I suddenly feel nauseous and take a deep breath to compose myself.

Rick heads directly to the bar and brings me a glass of champagne and I accept it, not wanting to tip him off to the pregnancy. Why is that? I wonder? Why wouldn't I want my own husband to know that I'm pregnant?

"Thanks," I say simply, pretending to sip the champagne. Rick takes his scotch and water and makes the rounds as I search for someone familiar to converse with. I find a couple of acquaintances from the neighborhood and try to follow their conversation. They are having a heated discussion about a local couple who are separating, but I have no idea who they are talking about. Traveling and not having any children keeps me out of the loop with this crowd; something that I am grateful for. I have no interest in who is doing what to whom around here. I chat with the group superficially all the while feeling deeply content that I'm holding a special secret, an exciting one that is just my own.

I make my way through the crowd to the bar to exchange my glass of champagne for a club soda. Cass sneaks up behind me and grabs me by the arm.

"You scared me!"

"What do you think? Is it a good party?"

"Are you kidding? It's the party to end all parties! You've done it once again."

"You're my friend, you have to say that."

"No, I don't, I mean it." I lean in a little closer and whisper in Cass's ear, "I just found out I'm pregnant."

"That's wonderful news!" Cass grabs me and squeezes me tight, the scent of her perfume makes my eyes water.

"Shhh! I'm keeping it a secret, you're the only one I'm telling."

"Even Rick?"

"Yes, I'm not even telling him."

"That's a little odd, but I'm glad for you. Your secret is safe with me! I've got to go mingle with the guests. Enjoy yourself and we'll have a real talk tomorrow." Cass plants a big kiss on my right cheek.

I watch Rick from across the room, but he doesn't notice me. He talks enthusiastically with his hands and laughs raucously at his owns jokes. Poor guy needs to get out more, I conclude. He really seems to be enjoying the interaction.

I continue to watch him and hope he catches my eye to flirt with me; something we always do at parties and it serves well to revive our attraction to one another.

There's no one here that I feel a need to talk to and my husband isn't flirting with me, so I start to feel tired. I approach Rick to see if I can talk him into going home.

"Something you want to tell me?" He takes a sip of his bourbon.

I could feel my face flush. "No, what do you mean?" How could he possibly know?

"You have lipstick on your cheek, have you been kissing someone?"

"Oh that, it's Cass' of course, she's always hugging and kissing."

"That she is!"

"Can I talk you into leaving? I'm ready to go home."

"Do you mind if I stay? I'm really enjoying myself. Please?" He makes a pitiful face.

"Sure, no problem. I'll see you at home later."

I'm surprised that I'm relieved about Rick wanting to stay at the party. I'm certainly not pleased that he didn't flirt with me at all. I walk home feeling safe and secure about my little secret. Once home I quickly get ready for bed and fantasize about the baby. What will it look like? What will it like to do? Play sports? Music? I am filled with anticipation and am unable to get to sleep.

I pull out my book, *Mindful Relationship Habits*, and begin to make a simple list of things I can do to improve my marriage; touch often, pay compliments and converse daily. These are all things I can implement immediately. I complete my list and turn out the light. I fall asleep feeling content that a baby is on the way and my marriage is improving.

CHAPTER 13

I sleep hard in that pregnancy sleep that takes you to a level of deep slumber like no other. The sun shines brightly through the small crack in the window shade and I see that Rick has not come to bed, once again. Are we tired or just lazy?

Gracie is eager to go outside, and I let her out into the backyard through the den door. Rick is snoring loudly on the sofa. I try not to disturb him, assuming that he is sleeping off a hangover.

My cell rings and I grab it before it wakes up Rick.

"Hello," I say quietly.

"Can you come over for coffee?" Cass asks. "I'm buried in dishes and I just want to sit and talk before I tackle any more of this mess."

"I'll be right over."

I throw on a pair of jeans, winter boots and a heavy winter coat before finding Gracie' leash. We sneak out without disturbing Rick.

Cass hands me a warm cup of tea. Her hair has been straightened and makeup applied.

"Where's the coffee? I need coffee." I look around at the neatly stacked piles of clean dishes on the countertops.

"Not while you're with child."

"Oh, yeah," I smile proudly.

I catch a glimpse of George in the den with the girls. He has them occupied with building a fort out of blocks, so that they are out of Cass' hair while she cleans up. He's such a thoughtful husband thinking of ways to make Cass' life easier. I imagine that Rick will do things like that for me when our baby arrives and I imagine that I will be as deeply, fully happy in my marriage as Cass is in hers.

"So talk." She pulls up a stool.

"About what?"

"About the baby, Rick, you, everything. Fill me in! I thought you guys had put the whole baby thing on hold."

"We did. This came as a complete surprise. The doctor had told us to wait three months and it's only been six weeks. I hope that isn't a problem."

"I think that just means that your body has gotten used to the idea of being pregnant and it likes it. I would think that is a good thing! Why aren't you telling Rick though?"

"I don't want anyone to know this time. It was humiliating losing the baby before after having told everyone. I don't want to go through that again…having to face them all if it happens again. I want to wait until I get through the first trimester this time."

"Won't it be hard to keep it a secret? Are you at least going to go to the doctor?"

"Of course, I'll see the doctor, but that's it!"

"I don't understand it, but I will support you in whatever you want to do."

"That's all I ask, thank you. I'm so elated I could hardly get to sleep last night."

"Are you eating and taking care of yourself?" Cass

looks at me with one eyebrow lifted as she shoves a small plate towards me loaded with fruit and assorted goodies from the party.

"You want to know if I am eating? Yes, I'm doing my best, Cass, really I am, but it's not easy changing a pattern that has been in place for most of my life." I think of how I've added six bites to my daily consumption. Is that enough for a baby? I wonder.

"No excuses, Ali, you've waited for this baby a long time and you are going to do everything you can to make sure that both of you are healthy. I'll be watching you."

"I know you will, Cass, and I appreciate that."

She pushes the plate a little closer to me, "Now eat!"

A small slice of apple catches my eye and I keep track of my nibbles as I look around the kitchen at the mass of clean plates, glasses, silverware and serving dishes.

"You continually surprise me, Cass!"

"What do you mean?"

"There were over 200 people here last night and you've already done all the dishes and organized everything and it's not even 10 o'clock yet. How do you handle it? I haven't even managed to wash my face yet. Really, how do you do it?"

"With four kids I have to be organized, it's the only way it will work. If I didn't stay on top of things, this house would fall apart in two days. It's second nature to me I guess." She shrugs.

"When I grow up can I be just like you?"

We both giggle happily.

~

CHAPTER 14

I go about my business over the following weeks, humming quietly, deep in thought about the new life that is about to enter our lives. How can Rick not notice how preoccupied I am? I do my best not to show my anticipation and it seems to be working.

We spend New Year's Eve the way we always do...a quiet evening at Cass and George's house with all of the kids, watching the ball drop at midnight on the television. It is my favorite holiday of the year, just my closest friends and no hoopla.

The New Year is blessed with joyous anticipation; I am bursting at the seams with expectancy. Quietly, I continue to share my deepest thoughts and desires with my best friend, Cassie. She listens patiently though I know she doesn't understand why I am keeping my pregnancy a secret from Rick. She could never imagine keeping secrets like this from George; maybe that's why their marriage is much better than Rick's and mine.

I want nothing more than to decorate the baby's room, but I control that urge, instead throwing my motherly energies into art. The online classes help me tremendously, plus some natural abilities are appearing, surprising me more than anyone. I'm able to distort features on a face without losing the likeness of the subject. I innately know which features to maximize and which to minimize.

With only three weeks left until my twelfth week of pregnancy and the big announcement, I beg my boss, Katherine, to postpone my January trip to China and instead take a domestic trip, one that I can drive to, instead of fly. Reluctantly, she agrees, and I promise to make it up to her in February, knowing full well that I have no intention of keeping that promise.

I sleep twice as much as I normally do, but Rick doesn't seem to notice. He's too busy and focused with his work, and golf, and for once, I'm grateful for that. I've never been a good liar and keeping this secret is a challenge for me.

From time-to-time I think about my friend, James, and wonder how he is doing, and if he ever wonders about me. It's already been over two months now since the last trip and my last visit with him. I know I'll see him again eventually, and I'll have a chance to show him how fulfilled I've truly become and even thank him.

I check in with Dr. Stevens every week until we make it through the first trimester. She checks the baby's heartbeat, which is strong and monitors my weight gain and blood glucose levels. She informs me that the test results show that I do have the MTHFR mutation and that I should be taking a specific prenatal vitamin, one that contains high levels of good quality folate and not folic acid. She writes me a prescription and encourages me to eat as many leafy greens as possible.

"You need to gain more weight. Are you adding more calories to your diet?"

I think of how I'm adding two extra bites to each of my meals and answer, "Yes."

"And your progesterone?"

"Yes, but it makes me sleepy sometimes."

"Just push through it or better yet, take it at bedtime. It will help you sleep better. With MTHFR your body is unable to process estrogens and it throws all of your hormones off, we need to keep your hormones in balance."

She sends me home with a list of do's and don'ts for pregnancy.

As I drive home, I fantasize about decorating the baby's room and what it will be like to have the family I've always wanted with daily walks with the stroller around the golf course, playing in the backyard and weekend getaways with just the three of us.

Carol calls and annoys me once a week with stories of her impeccable son and the twin grandbabies on the way. I want to scream every time I have to listen to this, but I'll show them all in the end. They will see what a wonderful mother I am, and that I'm just as capable as my brother, William, of being an exemplary parent.

I quietly sit on the bed in the gray-blue guest room and try to imagine what it will look like as a nursery; I visualize the room with a bunny theme, with white furniture and lace curtains. The pastel bunny colors will work well for a boy or girl. This room will be full of life and expectancy. I can't wait to watch how my child's life will unfold.

I think this is the most joyous time of my life, carrying private knowledge and realizing that everything in my life is going to be just the way I've always imagined it, finally.

～

CHAPTER 15

As promised, I make plans for my domestic road trip with appointments in Toledo, Cleveland, Buffalo and several other stops along the way. It's a lot of driving, but I can spend the night wherever I need to and Rick will never need to know that I'm not on one of my routine trips to China. I will have plenty of time to rest.

"Are you nuts?" Cassie exclaims as I share with her my plans. "There's no way in hell you should be driving alone, that far, while you're three months pregnant!"

"I'm not three months pregnant yet."

"Geez, Ali, you're only a few days away, why don't you just swallow your pride and tell your husband for God's sake?"

"I know you don't understand this, but please support me. Just go along with me for a few more days, please!"

"Only if you promise to call me every hour on the hour."

"I promise."

"I still don't agree with you."

"I know."

I pack my suitcase and head out of town after Rick

leaves for work. I'll be glad when I don't have to hide the pregnancy from him anymore; if he had been more supportive during the last pregnancy I wouldn't have to hide this one from him.

I am lost in thought as I make the drive. I fantasize about baby names. It will be wonderful to finally have a child of my own that I can do all the things with my baby that Cass does with her kids and I think of all of the attention this child will receive from Cassie's four girls. My baby will be spoiled to death!

The drive wears me out pretty quickly and I have deep desire to sleep late in the afternoon. I check into the first decent hotel I can find. It's a full 12 hours before I awaken at dawn. Back in my sedan, I drive the rest of the way with time to spare for my first morning meeting.

Cass calls me incessantly. "Have you eaten anything today?"

"Of course I have."

"And your prenatals, did you take one this morning?"

"Yes, Mother! Cass, you don't need to concern yourself so much about me, I'm fine."

"I just hate it when you are so far away, I can't keep an eye on you!"

"I think your ten calls a day will suffice, don't you?"

"I still think you should be at home resting, not gallivanting all across the country."

"It's just a quick business trip. I'll be back before you know it."

"That's not going to happen, just humor me, please."

"I'll call you after my meeting tomorrow. I've got to pay attention to my GPS now, goodbye, Cass!"

I spend the day in meetings with clients, going over endless forms. Worn out, I check in to my hotel and sleep hard again, feeling refreshed for more client appointments the following morning. The meetings move quickly, and I'm back on the road earlier than expected, stopping along the way in Toledo to fill up with gas and use the restroom.

My heart stops as I see the familiar bright red stain of blood on my underwear. No, not again! I feel as though I'm going to faint and rush back to the car as quickly as possible before anyone notices the tears streaming down my face. Now what? What do I do now? Naturally, I call Cass. "Can you talk?" I sob.

"What is it? What's wrong?"

"It's happening again." I'm so upset I wonder if I should even be driving.

"Oh Ali, I'm sorry. You need to come home right away."

"I can't, there's no way I can come home now." I pull another tissue from the box in the passenger seat.

"You have to. You need to be home now."

"That's the last thing I need right now. I need time to think. Why is this happening to me? I'm not a bad person. I don't understand this." I can barely speak through my sobs.

"I don't know, I wish I could tell you why."

"I can't talk right now, I just need to be alone for a while. Promise you won't say anything to Rick! I'll call later."

Before Cass has a chance to answer me, I end the call. My mind is racing. Now what? I quickly find a hotel and check in, hoping that I'm not bleeding all over the place.

Once inside my room, I promptly turn on the shower and undress. My underwear and pants are soaked through with fresh blood. I feel dazed as the tears continue to stream down my face.

Thoughtfully, I run cold water in the sink and place the clothing in the water hoping to remove the fresh stains. As

I step into the shower I see a faint trail of blood intertwining with the water below and making a circular pattern before finding its way down the drain. I feel a slight cramping in my abdomen as I stand directly under the spray of hot water.

Now what? There is no point in calling Dr. Stevens. I've been through this before. There's nothing to do but wait it out. This time, things seem to be happening much more quickly. I hear the sound of Cass's familiar ring tone as I continue to stand under the stream of water. If only the water could take this all away.

I compose myself, dry off, and call the front desk and ask them to send up a package of pads. The cramping increases and I turn on the television, hoping that it offers a distraction. It does not.

I can't face my family and friends right now and I don't want to see Dr. Stevens. I send a text to Cass, letting her know that I'm okay and turn the phone off. What am I going to do? I lie on the bed and to my surprise; fall fast asleep. I'm awakened by severe cramps at 4 A.M. I run into the bathroom and see that my pad is soaked through and I realize that the worst is over and the miscarriage is done.

I feel defeated again. I can't even carry a baby. I have a sudden urge for a friendly face and I know exactly where to find one!

I turn my cell phone on and ignore the many texts and voicemails that have come through. Instead, I focus on my maps app and am glad to learn that my crazy plan is totally feasible. After flipping on the lights in the room, I start a pot of coffee, take a quick shower and throw on a pair of jeans and a baby blue sweatshirt. My lifeless hair lies limp, so I style it in a knot of top of my head. No need for makeup, I conclude, as my tears will just wash it away.

The coffee is ready and I add some powdered creamer and sip slowly as I pack my bag. I leave out several fresh pads to keep in my purse and one to use at the last minute before I check out. If this miscarriage is anything like the last one, most of the bleeding should be over now, but there will still be some residual bleeding for the next couple of days.

Once in my car, I send a text to Cass. *I'm fine. Will call you later.*

With a fresh box of tissues on hand, I head towards my destination.

CHAPTER 16

Three hours later, I'm looking at James' face, as he smiles broadly as I walk in. I make my way to an end seat at the bar that's dark and out of the way of other patrons. I must look a sight I think as James approaches me.

"What a lovely surprise, Miss, it's wonderful to see you again."

James' facial expression changes quickly as he advances towards me.

He clears his throat, "Are you all right, Alison? You don't look so good. You're not wearing your usual business clothes, what's going on? Are you on vacation?"

He has a look of deep concern on his face and I begin to cry before I can utter a word. I pull several tissues out of my oversized purse and try my best to compose myself.

I blurt, "I didn't know where else to go," and start to sob.

James squeezes my hand gently, "There, there, Miss. It can't be as bad as all that. He passes a glass of iced tea towards me.

"Thank you, James. You are kind and I'm sorry. I don't know what I'm doing here."

"Sure you do. You need to talk to someone, so you came to see me. I must say I am quite flattered."

"Yes, I guess that's it. I need to talk to someone and I can't talk to anyone who is a part of my everyday life right now. You have always been so kind and thoughtful." I wipe my nose for the hundredth time.

"Take a sip of your tea, then take a deep breath and tell me what happened."

"I'm so embarrassed. I wouldn't want to keep you from your work." I look around and see two customers.

"It won't be busy in here for quite some time, until then, I'm all yours."

I spill my guts to poor James and cry as I do it. He is kind and listens carefully to my each and every word as he continues to fill my glass. When I complete my tale of woe, James's responds.

"Well, Miss, I see it like this. I'm sorry I have a customer. Don't go away, I'll be right back."

While James is gone, I have a chance to think. Did I really want to have a baby with a man who is so emotionally unavailable to me? Rick isn't mean or anything, in fact, I don't think he cares enough to be unkind to me. We just sort of co-exist together in the same house without any real interaction.

My life will never be like Cass'; she and George love each other, that's why their marriage works. My head is full of thoughts when James returns.

"Where were we? Oh, yes, now I remember."

"James, before we continue on, would you please get me one of those delicious Cobb Salads. I'm suddenly starving."

"Yes, of course, I'll be right back."

James reappears moments later, with a salad in hand. He looks around the dimly lit room.

"I apologize, but it's starting to get busy. Will you be all right here by yourself for a while?"

"Of course, don't let me keep you from your work. I'm fine. I'll just sit here and eat my salad."

I can't explain it, but somehow, suddenly I am feeling better, as if a weight has been lifted and I'm not really feeling sad at all. How could that be? I don't understand it, but I'm starting to feel almost excited about my life and the future.

I sit quietly in the corner of the bar while my mind sorts these new thoughts and it all comes to me effortlessly. Suddenly, I know what I must do. I pull out my phone, do a few searches and find what I am looking for. Moments later I'm sitting at the bar looking quite pleased with myself.

I wait patiently for James as he runs around attending to all of his customers and at long last he returns to my end of the bar.

"It looks like you've worked up a sweat!"

"Yes, I'm sorry about that, it got busy in here!"

"I can see that." I've never seen the restaurant so crowded.

"I must say you are looking much better. Is everything okay now?"

"Yes, James it most certainly is. I've made a decision while you were gone."

"You did? And what was that?"

"I will explain later. I've got to go. I'll be late for my flight. It's been a pleasure, James. I can't thank you enough." I plunk a fifty-dollar bill on the bar.

"But, we didn't really get to talk."

"I know, but you gave me everything I need. I can't thank you enough. See you when I get back." I wave back to James as I head quickly out the door.

CHAPTER 17

I move my little black sedan from short-term to long-term parking and pop the trunk open. Shuffling through my suitcase, I remove most of the clothing and keep the toiletries. Fortunately, I always have all of my travel documents in the trunk of my car: my passport and global entry card are tucked away neatly in a monogrammed leather case. I grab the case and throw it inside my sizeable handbag.

My suitcase feels almost empty as I make my way towards the terminal. I can't believe I'm really doing this! I'm throwing caution to the wind and following my heart and for some reason it just feels right.

I send Cass a quick text before entering security. *Will be out of touch for several hours. I'm fine. All is well.*

Once through security I make a stop in the restroom to freshen up before my flight. The bleeding has almost stopped and, amazingly I'm feeling okay about the miscarriage. It is what it is, I tell myself. At the moment I am more focused on what's ahead of me than what is behind me. There's nothing that I can do now about the babies I have lost.

I check myself in the mirror. I look like a ghost! A little sun would certainly do me some good. I splash cold water on my face and retrieve the only cosmetic in my purse, a pale pinkish lipstick. I rub a dab on each cheek and run the stick over my parched lips, then I try to blend the color on my cheeks using my fingers tips in an upward motion.

Exhilaration runs through me as I get in line to board the plane. I can't believe I'm really doing this, but it just feels right. Before the plane has a chance to take off, I'm fast asleep and dreaming of Mexico.

It has been five years since my last trip to Mexico and I had forgotten how vast the Mexico City Airport is. I have two hours to kill before my next flight, so I decide to bite the bullet and make a call to Cass.

"Where are you? What in the world is going on? Your texts have been so cryptic, I've been concerned that you've gone off the deep end or something."

"I'm fine, Cass, there's nothing to fret about," I giggle.

"You're laughing? How can you be laughing? I've been imagining that you're so deep in depression that you can barely function and you're laughing! What in the world has gotten into you, Ali?"

"I told you I'm fine, there's nothing to be concerned about."

"I was with you when you lost the first pregnancy, remember? You were a wreck. How can you be fine now? Where are you?"

"Slow down, I have a different attitude about these miscarriages than I did before. It just isn't meant to be, that's all." I hesitate and take a deep breath before telling Cass where I am. "I'm in Mexico."

"You're in Mexico! What are you doing in Mexico? Please explain before I tell Rick where you are and send him to look for you!"

"You wouldn't do that to me!"

"Try me! This isn't like you, Ali, please tell me what's going on!"

"It's not easy to explain. I just had a whim, so I'm following it."

"That's it?"

"Pretty much, I just was thinking about how at peace I was in Mexico and felt compelled to go. I need something that brings me joy right now, and as far as I can recall, I was happiest in Mexico. Please promise me you won't tell Rick."

"Only if you keep me informed of your whereabouts at all times. I want the name of your hotel and you need to check in with me several times a day, so I know that you're really okay and that you haven't completely gone insane!"

"I promise. I'll call you when I get to my destination, and please don't worry about me. I'm fine, no better than fine, really."

"I hope so, I really do."

"I love you, Cass. Talk to you soon."

I have to giggle to myself again. Cass is such a natural mother hen and I'm fortunate to have her in my life, fortunate to have someone who worries about me.

Four hours later, the plane approaches Zihuantanejo and I can see the large tower near the runway with the words Ixtapa and Zihuantanejo written boldly in large print as we land. I had forgotten how intimidating the armed guards seem as they line the runway.

As we disembark I am overcome by a strong gust of hot air and momentarily feel as though I can't breathe as the moist air fills my lungs. I can't wait to get out of my baggy jeans, sweater and boots. It is a good excuse to do a little shopping and I adore the embroidered Mexican clothing.

I make my way through the long customs line and ask my cab driver to take me to Villa Del Sol Hotel. My heart starts to beat rapidly as I patiently wait for the driver to get to the hotel.

A staff member at the massive front door greets me warmly and the reception area is just as I remember it; open and inviting. I am given a room assignment and asked if I would like a tour of the property. I politely decline the offer and ask if the gift shop is still open. My excitement accelerates as I realize that I could run into Marcos at any moment. I wonder if he still reads the famous philosophers in English. I must find something special to wear when I see him tonight at his bar.

The gift shop is locked, but there's a sign on the door instructing me to ring the bell for help. I wait for several minutes until a young woman rushes to the door, keys in hand, apologizing profusely.

"I'm sorry, senorita, I hope you did not wait long."

"Not at all."

"Please look around and let me know if you have any questions."

The modest gift shop offers numerous choices for an appropriate garment for dinner. Looking at a beautifully embroidered white dress, I realize how pale I am and how ridiculous I would look in it. Instead, I opt for a couple of brightly colored sundresses, sandals, a bikini, sunscreen and a large, straw hat. These should tide me over until I am able to get to town. I charge the items to my room and thank the woman for opening the shop for me.

The sky is beginning to turn a bright shade of purple and nervousness begins to set in as I realize that I might see Marcos again before the day is over. I take my new wardrobe and quickly find my room.

The hotel looks exactly as I had remembered with the

yellow adobe walls and red tiled roof, so I feel right at home as I hang my few belongings in the meager closet and turn on the water in the large, open shower and wait for it to heat up. I had forgotten how much I love the moist air here, and sound of the pounding waves in the distance.

I love the feel of the warm breeze and dressing in minimal clothing is liberating and so unlike the cumbersome layers of clothing necessary to stay warm at home.

I can't help but wonder how Marcos will react when he sees me. Will he be angry? Excited? What if he's involved with someone? I can feel my pulse race as I contemplate all of the possible scenarios. I feel elated as I dress and try to imagine the look on his face when he sees me.

CHAPTER 18

As I make my way on the bridge over the scenic lagoon, my excitement escalates. My eyes try to focus on the distant Coral bar as I search for Marcos' familiar silhouette. Timidly, I take a seat on one of the empty barstools and order a chilled glass of white wine. I'm unable to concentrate as I continually scan the horizon for Marcos.

Each time I see the familiar white uniform and a head of dark hair, my heart skips a beat, thinking it might be him. I take tiny sips of wine as I sit, watch and wait. With each passing moment, my heart sinks slightly and as I eventually finish my glass of wine I get up the nerve to ask the bartender about Marcos.

"Marcos doesn't work here anymore," he responds flatly.

My heart sinks. This is a response that never entered my mind. I try to appear nonchalant as I probe on, "When did he leave?"

"I think it was last year sometime. I'm not really sure, I'm new here," he speaks with a perfect American accent.

"Do you have any idea where he went?" I ask coyly.

"I heard he went into the family business or something. I can ask around if you really want to know."

I do not want to draw any attention to myself, so I casually drop the conversation as I scan my memory trying to recall what his family's business is. For some reason, I think I remember a conversation about his father having a fishing business.

I can feel all of the muscles in my body begin to relax as I realize that seeing Marcos tonight is not going to happen. It is time to order some food, relax and move on to plan B.

The waiter prepares fresh guacamole for me and as I try to concentrate on his recipe, my mind flashes with images of Marcos and how attentive he was to me, asking questions about me and truly seeming to care about who I was.

Back in my room, I send a quick text to Cass. *I'm at Villa Del Sol in Zihuantanejo. Safe & sound. Will talk to you tomorrow.*

Now, what is my plan B? My mind races as I try my best to recall everything that Marcos had told me about his family.

I surprise myself by sleeping hard, yet again. I dream of Marcos and the scent of the ocean. In the morning, I quickly recall one of my favorite niceties about staying at Villa Del Sol; hot coffee, pastries and a local paper waiting for me inside the cubby next to the front door of my hotel room.

Exhilarated by the sea air, I'm excited to start the day. I can hear the lap of waves as I take my tray to the balcony outside and the birds are chirping loudly. As I pour myself some coffee, the birds approach the pastry basket and attempt to steal my rolls. I cover the basket with a plate and my mind wanders to Marcos and where I might find him. He is close, somewhere, I conclude.

As I take my time, I formulate a plan for the day in my head; it's logical and a good place to start. Pouring a second cup of coffee, I give Cass a call to fill her in.

"Jesus, Ali, I can't take this anymore. Please don't ever run off again and ask me to keep it a secret, it's way too much stress for me."

"Has Rick been looking for me?"

"Well, no."

Of course he hasn't been looking for me, he doesn't even know I'm gone. How odd is it that he and I never talk or text for the entire time that I'm away for work. My books say that couples should be connecting every day.

"He hasn't asked you anything about me, Cass, and he's not going to. You don't need to worry about lying to him, the fact is he doesn't care where I am."

"Why would you say that? Of course, he cares where you are!"

"Really? Think about it, he has never tried to contact me during any of my business trips over the years, out of sight, out of mind!"

"You are really scaring me, I've never heard you talk like this before."

"I'm just thinking clearly. There's nothing to be scared about, I promise."

"When are you coming home?"

"I haven't given that any thought yet."

"You run off to Mexico, after having lost a child, and have given no thought to when you might return? Ali, I think you need help!"

"On the contrary, you keep prodding me to be myself and stop worrying about what others think, well I'm being myself! I'll call you later." I love her, but she sure is smothering me right now!

I take a shower in the ample bathroom and quickly dress in one of my newly acquired sundresses. As I look in the mirror, the overhead skylight accentuates the translucence of my skin. If I don't tan while I'm here, people are going to see me coming from a mile away!

I make my way to the ocean front dining room. The breakfast is just as I remembered it: fresh chunks of seasonal fruit with local yogurt and honey and another basket of fresh pastries; it is just the right amount of food for me; a full fifteen bites. The staff is warm and friendly, fussing over me as if I had been a frequent visitor over the past five years. I repress my urge to ask about Marcos as I enjoy the quiet of the secluded beach cove.

After breakfast, I head to the lobby and make arrangements for a driver for the day. The bellman gives instructions to the driver in Spanish. I tip the bellman as he opens the car door for me.

"Buenos dias senorita," the driver greets me with a smile. "Hoy es un dia precioso."

I understand the first part of what the driver has said, but he's lost me on the second part, so I just smile and nod. "El puerto deportivo," I say looking at my notes.

"Si, el Puerto deport." He nods in confirmation.

The winding road feels familiar as if I had just been here last week, not five years ago. The driver pulls up to the small marina and I instruct him, "Espere por favor."

He nods again, "Si, yo espero." Apparently the bellman had instructed the driver well on my needs for the day.

Where do I begin? I wonder as a walk around the marina hoping to find some sort of clue. Marcos said his father was a fisherman, but I have no idea what his father looks like or the name of his fishing boat.

I stop to ask a man who seems to be in charge, "A que hora vuelven los barcos de pesca?" I use my notes again for translation.

"Media tarde," he responds and I have to look that up in my Spanish translation booklet. The fishing boats will return mid afternoon sometime.

"Gracias, senior."

"De nada," he nods and smiles.

I make a short walk to the shops at the end of the marina. I have several hours to kill before the fishing boats are due to return.

I feel a sense of inner peace as I gaze down the stone streets lined with dozens of tiny shops. This area is familiar to me and I am prepared for a morning filled with bartering with the local merchants.

My first purchase is a large, vibrant striped basket to hold all of my purchases. I quickly maneuver from shop to shop acquiring numerous vibrant embroidered blouses and dresses that I love so much. I even find four matching dresses in various sizes to take home to Cass' girls.

Suddenly I am famished and head away from the shops in search of food. I find a colorful restaurant filled with locals and assume that the food must be authentic to the area. The waiter brings me a basket of homemade tortilla chips and salsa and I begin to taste as I try to comprehend the menu. I look at the tables around me and notice that almost all of them have a large bowl of what looks like soup with several small bowls filled with various condiments. When the waiter returns, I simply point to the next table and he nods, replying, "pozole".

Feeling ravenous, I continue to munch on the chips and salsa. The soup arrives and I am overcome by the scent of fresh cilantro; something that I adore and rarely have an opportunity to come across in Lake Forest.

The soup is delicious and I continue to eat to the point where I am uncomfortable. After paying the check I realize that I forgot to count my bites; something I haven't done in years. I make my way down Calle Ejido and into a nice looking silver jewelry store called Galeria Lupita. This place looks much more upscale than the other stores in the area.

"Hello, senorita. May I help you with something today?"

"Yes, I'm looking for a gift for my friend. She wears lots of silver jewelry, the bigger, the better."

The man motions to his two sons who are standing by and they quickly spring into action, retrieving dozens of items that might fit my needs. After much discussion, I choose a shiny cuff bracelet for Cass and am certain that she will like it.

A pair of large, turquoise and silver dangling earrings catches me eye.

The owner, Roberto, asks, "Would you like to try them on?"

"Oh no, I couldn't. I'm used to wearing small earrings like these. I point to the tiny white pearls studs in my ears.

"Senorita, these would look lovely on you. Just try."

Warily, I try them on and am surprised at how much I like the reflection in the mirror. I will probably never wear them, but decide to buy them anyway.

Roberto sends me on my way with a cold bottle of water and I am grateful.

Feeling satisfied by my lunch and purchases, I decide it's time to head back to the marina and wait for the fishing boats to return. My driver is waiting patiently for me at the same spot where he left me and he helps me with my overstuffed basket full of goodies.

"Puerto pequeno," I say simply and he understands, taking me directly back to the modest marina.

The driver finds a shady spot to park the car and rest while I find a place to sit and wait for the boats to return. I find several white benches with some shade, so I pick one and claim my spot. I make myself as comfortable as possible, pulling out my bottle of water, large straw hat and sunscreen out of my oversized purse. I could have a long wait ahead of me.

I watch patiently as the various boats return to the harbor after a full day of fishing. An old man stops to ask me what I'm doing there and I respond, "esperando." He seems satisfied with my answer and continues to move along.

I scrutinize each boat carefully as they arrive for anything familiar, anything that might trip my memory and I feel more and more anxious knowing that Marcos could disembark from one of these fishing boats at any moment. Having no idea how he will react when he sees me only adds to my level of anxiety.

I reapply my sunscreen. What if he is angry about my abrupt departure? What if he wants nothing to do with me because he's moved on? The longer I wait, the more anxious I become and suddenly feel as though a full-blown panic attack is encroaching. My head is swimming with doubt. I was so sure about seeing him again and now I don't know. What am I doing here? What was I thinking?

My heart is pounding and I can't breathe. It suddenly feels so hot and crowded. Is everyone staring at me? I feel beads of sweat trickling down my back. I don't want anyone to see me like this. I must get out of here quickly and back to the comfort of my air-conditioned room.

In a moment of complete terror, I quickly grab my purse and head straight to the waiting cab. "Villa Del Sol, por favor."

That was close! What if I had actually seen Marcos?

I take a breath and feel liberated as we make our way back over the winding road to my hotel. This may be the last time I ever see this quaint little town.

CHAPTER 19

I quickly pay my driver and leave him with a generous tip, then rush back to my room before the tears that are mounting in my eyes have an opportunity to run down my cheeks. I was so sure about coming here and now I may never see him again. I feel like such a fool! What am I doing here?

I quickly close the blinds and turn the air-conditioning on full blast. I wait for the water in the bathroom sink to turn cold before soaking a washcloth and placing it over my eyes as I lie in the quiet room. All I can think about is how fast my heart is beating, if only it would slow down! I focus on taking deep breaths and after some time I'm feeling calmer and better.

I call the airlines and make arrangements for a morning flight back to Detroit. It is time to stop living in a fantasy world and get back to my real life. Thank goodness Cass is the only one who knows about this trip. I would be embarrassed if anyone else knew.

I decide to call Cass.

"I'm coming home."

"What a relief. What's wrong? I can tell you've been crying."

"I don't know. I felt so sure about coming here, and now I just don't know what I'm doing here. I feel like such an idiot."

"Listen, you've been going through a lot lately, the stress was liable to get to you one way or another. It was probably all of those crazy hormones surging through your body that made you run off to Mexico."

"You know, you're probably right, there's really no other explanation for it. Oh Cass, what have I done?"

"Nothing irreparable. Come home and everything will get back to normal. As long as you are there, you might as well enjoy yourself. Take a swim, walk the beach or have a delicious authentic Mexican meal tonight."

"You're right, you're always right and you always know how to make me feel better.

"What are friends for? Now hurry up and get home. I miss you!"

I pull myself together. I don't want my new bathing suit to go to waste, so I throw it on and covered it with one of my new embroidered dresses.

The pool water feels refreshing after a day in the hot sun. I swim methodically up and down the length of the pool as I think about what brought me here. I honestly don't know who I am anymore. The old me would never have done anything like running off to Mexico. Maybe Cass is right; maybe it was just the hormones.

The poolside bartender motions me over to his bar and asks if I would like a drink.

"Si senor, margarita por favor." I conclude that I can't leave Mexico without at least having one margarita.

There is no more worrying about Marcos' reaction to seeing me, or my running into him. I take my drink and walk to the beach, finding one of the hanging beds, I make myself comfortable as I watch several children at play on the shore and the vendors making their last run of the day down the beach. The breeze picks up slightly and I feel serene. I snap a quick picture of Playa la Ropa and send it to Cass. I can relax now, and enjoy my drink as I watch the sun setting in the cove and look forward to returning to my own life tomorrow.

In the morning I enjoy my last coffee and croissant on my little patio and feel worried. How will I be able to face Rick without his knowing that I've lied to him? I don't want to risk losing my utopian life in Lake Forest. I just want to go home, be a better partner to Rick and have a family. I want us to have the kind of marriage that the Millers have; I know it's possible. I have no intention of telling Rick anything about the second pregnancy or my trip to Zihua. I just hope that he never finds out.

The hotel arranges a driver to take me to the airport and he is waiting for me as I pay my hotel bill. Good thing Rick never checks my credit card bills.

Once settled on the plane, I am unable to stop my thoughts from meandering. What if I can never have a baby? The doctor mentioned that gene thing, but what if that's not the only problem? What would my life look like? What if I run off on a whim over and over and have no control over my actions? Maybe there is something mentally wrong with me. When I get home, I must try harder to do what everyone expects of me.

Eventually, I am able to sleep on the plane and feel agitated as I land in Detroit. There is no way that I'm going to see James this time. I am much too embarrassed and can't face him right now.

I quickly collect my bag at baggage claim, find my car

and head directly to I-94 W. I still have a five-hour drive ahead of me and a lot of thinking to do.

The house is fully lit up as I pull into our driveway on Holland Court. I can feel the knots in my stomach tightening as I think about facing Rick. Why couldn't he be gone when I got home? That would have been much easier.

I take a deep breath and brace myself for anything as I enter through the garage door. Poor Gracie has gone deaf recently and doesn't hear me as I make my way to the kitchen. I can hear the TV blaring and Rick is in his study, working.

"Hi Babe. How was your trip?"

"Same old, same old," I reply, feeling guilty.

"I'll be out in a minute, I just have to finish this up."

"No worries, I'll go upstairs and shower." I'm relived he doesn't look at me. I'll greet him properly after my shower.

Thank goodness I wasn't in Mexico long enough to get a tan. That would have been difficult to explain. I startle Gracie as I lean down to pet her. She is thrilled to see me, but too stiff to get up and greet me.

Feeling exhausted, I quickly undress and throw my clothes in the hamper. The hot water feels good. I wrap myself in my pink robe and return downstairs for a cup of tea. Rick joins me on the sofa and I give him a kiss as we settle in and get comfortable to watch a movie together, just as if nothing out of the ordinary has ever happened.

"You know, I've always wondered about something; do you eat Chinese food when you're over there?"

I giggle, "Not unless I have to. I play it safe most of the time, eating American style food in the hotels."

"Don't you want to eat the native food? I'd think it

would be pretty spectacular, way better then the Chinese food we have here."

"I'm afraid of getting sick in any restaurant outside the hotel. You should come with me sometime, we could try it together."

"That's a long way to go for Chinese!"

CHAPTER 20

I sleep through the night on the new ecru sofa and in the morning find a note from Rick on the coffee table. He was up and out early, as usual.

I check my phone and there are numerous messages from Carol and a text from her as well. *You don't answer your phone. Beth is in labor. The twins are due at any moment. Call me!*

I had to come home to this?

There is a message from Cass as well. *Don't want to wake u. Y don't u come by when ur up and moving so we can have a talk?*

Poor Cass must have a lot of questions. I throw on a pair of leggings and a heavy coat and head across the street to her house. She looks impeccable in designer blue jeans and a fitted royal blue long sleeve tee with her sleek hair ending into a blunt edge just above her shoulders as she answers the door, barefoot, with baby Sophie balanced on her right hip.

"You don't look like you've just been in Mexico."

"I wasn't there long enough."

"Come in and give me a hug!" She wraps her left arm around my waist. "I've been concerned about you!"

"I know. You have enough on your plate without having to worry about me."

"You're my friend, now take off your coat and come in and get warm."

Cass leads me to the massive, brown and red toned sectional sofa, and I know I'm in for a long conversation with her as I see the coffee pot and plate of home made cookies on the coffee table.

Turning to Cass, I ask, "What do you want to know? I'll tell you everything."

She gently places Sophie in her basinet and sits facing me on the sofa. "I've been thinking about you a lot, Ali, while you were away, and I realize that I don't know very much about you. We only met three years ago, when you and Rick moved here. You've told me about your issues with Carol and your brother, but other than that, I really don't know much. I want to understand you, so I was hoping that you could fill me in on your life before we met, but most of all I'm dying to know why in the world you felt compelled to run off to Mexico of all places!"

I giggle and can understand how my behavior would make absolutely no sense to Cass.

"About two years before you and I met, I was invited on a girls' week long trip to Mexico, it was part of a bachelorette celebration for one of my college friends. She picked the place and we all just showed up, there were six of us in all. It was a blast. We sunned, sailed, had spa treatments and danced the night away."

"I had been dating Rick for a few months and had no idea at the time where that was headed, though I did see him as good marriage material. Anyway, on our first night at the hotel in Zihuantanejo, this tall, dark bartender with wavy black hair…"

"Ali, where are you now? You have the goofiest look on your face!"

I could feel my face flush, "I was just recalling how that bartender looked at me that night, as if there were no one else around, no one else in the universe. I swear, he looked right into my soul and I was, well, swept away. I fell for him hard. We met that night on the beach and he kissed me. I've never experienced anything like it or even close to like it. We were together every night after that. And you know it wasn't just the physical connection with him. I was intrigued by how intelligent and well read he was. He went to school, but he was mostly self-taught. On his own he read all of the philosophers in English; Jung and Camus were his favorites. We would walk the beach and have long discussions about the meaning of life. It was quite romantic. He also read poetry. I went to college and never read any philosophy or poetry books."

"Why did you never tell me about him?"

"I guess I thought it didn't matter anymore. It was in the past, and now I have a stable life with Rick. Marcos was just a fantasy, a fling."

"Marcos? What an exotic name! Apparently he was more than just a fling if you went back to Mexico to see him again."

"I'll get to that." I pour us both a second cup of coffee as my mind wanders back to the nights on the beach with Marcos and how I felt as I looked up into his dark eyes with the waves and moonlight dancing on the water behind us. "I fell hard for Marcos and I didn't believe that Rick and I had any sort of commitment to one another yet."

"Why didn't you continue in your relationship with Marcos?" Cass scoots closer to me.

"I just couldn't. I couldn't see how our lives would work

out together. I felt as if I would disappoint everyone if I ended up with someone like Marcos…a bartender at a resort in Mexico. What would my family say? What would people think?"

"Maybe they would say that you are brave for living your life differently than theirs."

I shake my head; "I didn't see it that way at the time. I had to get Marcos out of my mind and get on with my life, the way it is supposed to be. The only problem was that I couldn't face him to tell him, so I just left without a word, no forwarding address, nothing."

"That was mean."

"I know." I lower my eyes to the floor. "It worked for a long time. I didn't let myself think about him and then I started to dream about him more and more often and think about how joyful I was there when I was with him. It was like a nagging feeling that just kept growing and growing until I couldn't ignore it anymore. I guess losing the second baby just set me off and I just had to go see, if it was real or just my imagination."

"I had no idea you were harboring a secret love all this time."

"Neither did I, really. There's another piece to the story that I never told you about, it's the oddest thing."

"There's more?"

"Just before I started dreaming about Marcos, I developed an unlikely friendship with a bartender at the Detroit airport."

"You mean I have competition?" Cass splays her hands in an upward position.

"Ha! Hardly. This bartender, James started asking me all kinds of personal questions about my life and my level of satisfaction with my life. I started to notice that after every time I talked to him, I would dream about Marcos.

He said it was because I was happiest when I was with Marcos, but I don't know. It was all so weird."

"Do you still talk to James? I would love to meet him."

"I see him every time I pass through the airport. For some reason, I totally trust him and tell him everything. He's really a great guy."

"Are there any other secret boyfriends or friends you want to tell me about?" She taps her chin with her forefinger.

"I think that covers it," I giggle.

"Then let's get back to Marcos, did you see him?"

"No, he wasn't at the hotel anymore. I tried to find him and then I just panicked and had to come home. I want to go back to the way things were. I want to try for another baby and a picturesque life here with Rick. I'm going to try twice as hard and be twice as good and hope that I'm never found out."

"I don't know, Ali. I don't know if you can ever forget about a love like that."

"I've made up my mind, I'm going to focus on making the best life I can right here in Lake Forest. I'm going to do everything I can to make my marriage successful."

"I hope that works for you."

"I've been reading some books on marriage and they got me thinking about my relationship with Carol and how she's at the root of everything in my life. I found this one book about healing the mother wound and it really hit home for me."

"In what way?"

"Carol was never there for me emotionally. She was unable to connect with her own daughter. This book talks about that as well as the destructiveness of the narcissistic personality, which she has. It all fits Carol to a tee and explains how that's left me constantly wanting her approval and always being disappointed by never getting it."

"Maybe I should read it too."

I chuckle, "Yes, I think you should. The relationship books talk of how we subconsciously expect our partners to resolve the issues we had with our most challenging caregiver as children, and for me that would definitely be Carol."

"So what are you supposed to do?"

"Can you imagine if somewhere in my brain I'm expecting Rick to resolve my issues with Carol? That's an impossible expectation for anyone! The book says you can't resolve those issues with your spouse, but apparently you can heal them by being aware of your triggers from childhood and talking about them."

"That sounds like a lot of work."

"No kidding. How do you and George make your marriage work so well, do you talk about everything?"

"Not really, we just have lots of sex!"

So much for my books!

CHAPTER 21

I use the white enamel cookware set we received as a wedding present for the first time. I feel a bit overwhelmed with three burners going at once. I'm attempting to brown the chicken without making a huge mess when Rick arrives home. This is my first try at chicken piccata and remnants of flour and butter make a trail along the otherwise clean counter tops.

The unfamiliar aroma catches Rick off guard as he enters through the garage door.

"What is that wonderful smell? Did you bring home Italian take out?"

He kisses me on the cheek as he scrutinizes the pans on the stovetop.

"You did this yourself? Am I missing something? You haven't tried to make a new dish during the entire time we've been married. What has gotten into you?"

"It's the new me, I've decided to try new things and first on the list is cooking. I hope you like it. Why don't you get comfortable and grab a beer?"

"That sounds great, but first I'd like to take a run."

"Don't take Gracie with you this time, she limped for three days after your last run."

"No problem. I'll be back in a half hour," he says as he disappears up the stairs to change out of his suit.

Good, now I have a half-hour to get everything ready. I set the dining room table with our best Limoges china and crisp linens, then I go upstairs to make myself more attractive to my husband. I trade leggings and a t-shirt for his favorite pair of designer jeans, a crisp white blouse and a pair of suede booties from my favorite Forest Bootery.

Carefully, I apply a thin layer of black eyeliner; some mascara and a blush stain to my cheeks and lips. My hair is always the biggest challenge, so I try a new tool to add volume and it seems to work, making my past the shoulder-length hair look about three times as thick as normal.

Lastly, I add a pair of white pearl stud earrings and a splash of my all-time favorite perfume, Chloe, before heading back to the kitchen. I have time to prepare the salad plates before Rick returns home.

"Wow, you look great and so does that table. I don't know what has gotten into you, but I like the new you!"

"Don't you want to shower before dinner?" I ask, noticing the sweat stains on his gray t-shirt.

"No, I'm good. Let's eat, I'm famished." He takes a seat in one of the off-white leather chairs at our small, but exquisite dining room table and waits for me to serve him.

Looking out the French doors, to the newly landscaped backyard, I try to come up with some clever conversation, but I can't think of any. I can't recall the last time Rick and I had a conversation about our life together. The silence at the dinner table is heart breaking.

I feel disappointed as I watch Rick eat the piccata in his sweaty clothes while I went to the trouble to look nice for him. I conclude that he has no inkling about my trip to

Mexico or my second pregnancy. I feel a pang of guilt as we eat our meal in silence.

Before going to bed, I prepare a hot bath for myself and soak as I mull over the state of my marriage. What would happen if Rick and I weren't together any more? I can't even contemplate that or the idea of living in a marriage for the rest of my life having dinners with my husband like the one we had tonight. I don't think anyone should feel as lonely as I do right now in my marriage. I can ruminate over my disappointing dinner or move on to a better plan.

The next day I reluctantly pay a visit to my brother in nearby Highland Park. I'm not sure how I feel about this visit. I love my brother, but seeing his pristine grounds and his small Tudor mansion bring out my feelings of envy. The maid answers the door and, to my dismay, I find Carol sitting in their living room when I arrive; she's perched perfectly in the plaid wing chair in the corner of the living room.

"Alison, dear, what a surprise. This is the last place I would ever expect to run into you."

There it was, the zinger, right off the bat. She isn't wasting any time today. I can feel the knots in my stomach tighten as I approach her.

"Mom, how lovely to see you," I fib.

I kiss her courteously on the cheek and try to step away quickly before her overpowering perfume has an opportunity to permeate my sensitive nostrils.

"What are you doing here, dear?" She arranges the stack of gold bracelets on her left wrist. The sound of those bracelets clanging together is permanently imbedded in my brain from childhood.

"I came to see the babies. I have gifts for them," I say as I awkwardly lift the two wrapped packages up in the air.

"Did William tell you his good news?"

Oh God, now what? Aren't twin newborns enough good news to last for a lifetime?

"No, Mom, what good news?" I brace myself.

"Your brother has been made partner in his law firm."

I can feel my heart sink. Just one more thing to make him look more perfect in our mother's eyes.

"That's wonderful," I can feel the room spinning.

"Congratulations, William." I look over and observe my tall bother, with his well-combed auburn hair and Brooks Brothers clothes. How did it happen that he turned out to be such an ideal child and I ended up as such a seeming failure?

With no escape in sight, I spend a painful hour visiting with my sister-in-law, Beth, and the newborns. I have to admit, they are precious, but they make me long for my own child more than ever.

Feeling utterly rejected, I return home and grab a beer out of the fridge. I find a classic movie to watch as I pull up my fertility chart on my laptop. It looks like my cycle is back on track. I hope so; I really want a baby so that everything in my life can be the way I want it. Maybe Dr. Stevens' vitamins will work.

I add an additional five bites to my daily intake of food and resume tracking my monthly cycle by taking my temperature every morning before getting out of bed. I even go so far as to continue visiting William and the twins as often as possible.

～

CHAPTER 22

Saturday morning I sneak downstairs without waking Rick. I quietly make a pot of coffee and check my emails to confirm my reservations for tonight. Rick is going to be so surprised.

I prepared two spinach and mushroom omelets and place them in the oven on low before sneaking back upstairs and taking a shower, trying not to wake Rick. I hear him stirring as I towel off.

"What smells so good?"

"I made us some breakfast."

"More cooking? Are you turning into Rachael Ray?"

"That's not in the realm of possibilities."

"What's going on then?"

"I'm just trying to give my husband a nice weekend."

I shut the bathroom door, before turning on the blow dryer. Twenty minutes later, I'm fully dressed in jeans, boots and a gray cashmere turtleneck sweater. Rick is drinking coffee at the kitchen counter in his boxers and t-shirt.

"Why are you so dressed up?"

"You and I are going to have a little adventure today."

"You know I like to relax on the weekends."

"It will be relaxing, I promise. Take your time, eat your breakfast, take a shower and put on a pair of nice jeans."

"Are you going to tell me where we're going?"

"No."

"I don't know about this, Al."

"Trust me."

Rick follows my instructions and returns downstairs in a pair of jeans, navy crew neck sweater and his favorite worn-out loafers.

"You look great. Let's go."

"You're still not going to tell me where we're going?"

"Nope," I say with a smile.

Rick sits quietly in the passenger seat of my sedan with his dark glasses over his eyes and I can't tell if he's gone back to sleep. I'm feeling quite pleased with myself for pulling off this little getaway as was suggested in my relationship book.

An hour later I turn down East Walton Place and pull up under the familiar flags. The uniformed bellmen are waiting as I pop open the trunk.

"What are we doing here?"

"We're having a little mini vacation."

"The Drake?"

"Yes, we like the Drake."

"But, I wanted to watch the golf tournament and I don't have any clothes."

I feel my heart sink, but trying to stay positive, I respond, "You can watch the game from Coq d'Or. You love watching sports in there. I packed you a bag. You have everything you need."

"Oh, okay."

Rick and his stupid golf obsession, can't he humor me and forget about it for one day?

We check into our room that overlooks Lake Michigan. "Maybe we can take a walk later," I suggest.

"What's that noise?"

The bellman responds, "That's the heating system. If the noise bothers you, just hit it a few times and if that doesn't work, call the front desk. The workmen are here all the time trying to fix it."

Rick gives me a look of disapproval.

"So, it's an old hotel, it's part of the romance."

"I don't see what's romantic about a broken down heating system."

"Humor me."

"How long are we here?"

"Twenty-four hours. Think you can stand it?"

"Let me buy you lunch downstairs in the Coq d'Or."

"Thanks!" I think Rick is on board.

We enter the dark wood paneled room and adjust our eyes to the lack of light.

"The bar or a table?"

"A table," I respond noticing the TV screens with the golf tournament playing.

"Let's take this one." Rick picks a table with a perfect view of the screen.

"Please don't fixate on the TV, you can do that at home."

"Sorry, force of habit."

"I've booked his and hers spa treatments for this afternoon."

"Why don't you take both appointments? I'd rather stay here."

"Come on, Rick."

"I don't like to have strangers touching me, Babe. You go and relax. I'll buy you a nice dinner tonight and here, go buy yourself something nice." He hands me his credit card.

This is not what I had in mind, but I'm staying positive. At least we can have a quiet dinner tonight.

We order a lovely lunch and I wish Cass and George were here so I would have someone to talk to while Rick is glued to the screen. Maybe we've run out of things to talk about after three years together.

Feeling discouraged, but not hopeless, I excuse myself and head to the spa. I'm greeted by a curvy blonde named Kathy and she informs me that she will be my esthetician for the afternoon. As Kathy massages my face, she asks, "Are you in Chicago on vacation?"

"Sort of. I live in Lake Forest and I brought my husband here for a surprise romantic getaway. He's back at the hotel drinking beer and watching golf; that's how well my plan is going."

"Men and their sports, sometimes you can't separate the two."

"You sound like you've had some experience. Are you married?"

"Not at the moment, but I've been married three times."

"You're brave."

"Or stupid. I'm a hopeless romantic."

"Are you still hopeful?"

"I'll never give up, but I'm taking a break."

"I can't imagine going through a divorce, that's why I'm doing everything I can think of to improve the marriage I have."

"I think we expect too much of our partners these days, we want them to be romantic and best friend at the same time. I've been listening to this relationship expert on YouTube, Esther Perez. She talks about how we want to be close to someone and have our freedom at the same time and that no one can possibly fill the expectations we place on our partners."

"So I shouldn't be upset about my husband wanting to watch TV and drink instead of coming here with me today?"

"Maybe not. Maybe you should let him do his own thing today and you two can compromise and get together tonight or something like that."

"Has Esther been married a bunch of times too?"

"I looked that up and she's still married to her first husband."

"Impressive."

I think about what Kathy has shared with me and make a mental note to watch some of the videos, and I decide to give Rick a hall pass on today. My afternoon is relaxing and I feel fully rubbed, scrubbed and polished by the time I leave. I walk over to the Water Tower and find the sportswear store that Cass recommended to me. I spend more than I had planned on, and don't feel guilty about it thinking that Rick owes it to me for not participating in my plans today.

I stop at Nordstrom to stock up on cosmetics before walking back down Michigan Avenue to the Drake. I'm not surprised to find that Rick hasn't been back to the room in my absence.

I made eight o'clock reservations at Bavette's, so I have plenty of time to shower off the oils from the spa and dress before dinner. The shower doesn't drain, so I call the front desk to complain. Feeling playful, I dress in a revealing, form fitting little black dress, something that is totally out of character for me.

It's seven-thirty and there's still no sign of Rick, but I'm sure he hasn't gone far. I find him sitting at the end of the bar in a heated debate with several men. The conversation stops when I stand next to him.

One of the men blurts, "Is she with you?"

Rick turns around, "Hi, Babe. Wow, look at you!"

He's slurring his words.

"We have dinner reservations. You need to shower."

"I don't feel like getting all dressed up, can't we eat right here? You want me to relax."

"You're not doing anything I had planned for this weekend." I really don't want to go to a nice restaurant while he's so obviously inebriated.

"Maybe you shouldn't have surprised me."

He has a point. "Okay, we can stay, but I'm not eating at the bar."

"We'll get a table, no problem."

"I feel like a fool in this dress."

"It's dark in here no one will notice."

Just what I want is for no one to notice me after I've gone to all this trouble.

I order a drink and listen to Rick and he talks in circles, asking me the same questions over and over. What would my self-help books say about this? They'd probably tell me to run!

I politely make it through dinner and excuse myself as soon as it's over. I want to call Cass and tell her what a disaster my little trip has been, but I'm too embarrassed. Rick stays and continues to drink with his new friends at the bar. I hear him roll into our room at one and I pretend to be asleep.

I lay awake and try to decide whether I'm more hurt or angry. How the hell am I ever going to improve this marriage?

I wake up early and make no effort to be quiet. Rick must have a wicked hangover, I surmise, from the volume of his snoring. I dress in my warmest layers and head out for a long walk up Michigan Avenue. My mind is replaying yesterday's events and I'm so angry at Rick I want to scream. I stop along the way for a cup of coffee and a light breakfast of scrambled egg whites. I pull out my copy of *Mindful Relationship Habits* and try to calm my mind.

Communication is key and Rick and I haven't been doing much of that. Maybe I can talk him in to a couples' workshop where we could work on our communication skills. I order a second cup of coffee and finish reading the entire book. I make notes, and focus mostly on chapter 5, "Practice Acceptance of Your Partner". I need to be reminded of that right now while I'm so frustrated by Rick's behavior. Feeling like I have some tools to work with, I'm ready to face Rick without expressing my anger.

"We have to check out soon," I say flatly while opening the blinds.

"Close them, please."

"Sorry, we have to check out."

"I feel like shit."

"I can imagine."

"Don't be mad at me, Babe. I'm sorry."

"I'm not mad, but we have to go. I brought you some coffee. Go hop in the shower."

"I don't feel up to that. I'll just throw on some clothes and shower when we get home."

Disgusting, but okay. "Alright, let's roll."

My bag is waiting at the door and I wait for Rick to throw his things in his bag.

"At least brush your teeth and splash some water on your face."

"I'll meet you down at the car."

So much for the best-laid plans.

Ali's Portal

CHAPTER 23

Cass calls first thing Monday morning. "How about a walk around the golf course and coffee on the square?"

"Sure."

"Can you come by here, so we can each take a stroller instead of me pushing the double?"

"No problem, I'll see you shortly."

I have no idea that Cass wants to continue our conversation from the other day and she doesn't waste any time.

"You know, Ali, you never talk about your father."

Even though I'm freezing, I'm enjoying our quiet neighborhood as we pass a few moms with strollers along the way plus a handful of power walkers. I've learned to cover my cheeks with Vaseline before these walks to protect them from the bitter cold.

"There's not much to say, poor Daddy is dominated by my overbearing mother. His life must be hell, everything he does is criticized by Carol, so he keeps quiet and stays in the background."

"By the way, why do you call your mother 'Carol'? I've always wondered about that."

"Because she doesn't feel like a mother to me. She's never been nurturing or encouraging like I imagine a mother should be. She's just Carol."

"Do you have a relationship with your dad?"

I shrug, "Sure."

"It doesn't sound like it's very important to you. When was the last time you saw him?"

"I see him once a month or so. We have a pretty good relationship. Daddy was always supportive of me, telling me how proud he was of me whether I deserved his praise or not. I can't recall Carol ever telling me she was proud of me."

"I just find it really strange that you never mention him. When my father moved out, I was devastated, he means the world to me."

"There's just not much to say, period."

"I can take a hint, change of subject. I've been thinking about what you told me about your inability to say the letter "s" as a kid and it really bothers me."

"Why?"

"Because if one of my girls had that issue, it wouldn't concern me and I certainly wouldn't make them feel bad for it."

"You know that Carol is a piece of work."

"Yeah, I guess. How did that make you feel as a kid?"

"It certainly didn't help my self esteem. Basically, it just made me really shy and quiet. I was afraid that I would be made fun of for my speech impediment, so I just stayed silent."

"That's kind of sad. How's the baby making going?"

"Slowly, Rick and I aren't on the same schedule. He's been

working ridiculously long hours and then there are my trips to China. The good news is that I'm on those vitamins now and we've been pregnant twice. The third time will be a charm!"

"Whenever it happens, your little one will have lots of built in babysitters with my brood."

"That will be wonderful, Cass. I really look forward to that."

We walk the rest of the way back to Cass' house in silence. I have a gnawing feeling in the pit of my stomach as I think about the disastrous night that Rick and I spent in Chicago.

February arrives and I have to make good on my promise to go to China, though I am still too ashamed to stop and see James. What must he think of me? A crazy woman who barley knows him hunts him down and pours out all of her problems. Poor guy will probably be relieved if he never sees me again!

I do miss the tea, the salads and the talks. Maybe I will feel better about seeing James after some time has passed, but for now I just can't face him and any questions that he may have for me.

My trip is routine and uneventful, except for an afternoon side trip to the pearl market so I can buy gifts for Cass and the girls. I've become quite experienced at bartering after many dozens of visits to China.

I take the escalator to the fourth floor of the pearl market; a floor known only to commercial buyers and a select group of savvy tourists. It's lunchtime for the merchants and I make my way through the dozens of booths, resisting the foul odor of hot tofu and leeks as it infuses my nostrils. I finally find my favorite vendor at her same booth in the south corner.

I find matching delicate necklaces for the girls and one with large baroque pearls for Cass. I offer the assertive saleswoman 1,000 RMB, knowing she will act insulted and come back with double the amount I offer. I play the game with her and we settle on 1,500 RMB, which is what I wanted all along. I learned long ago that if you don't play the bartering game correctly, the Chinese merchants won't deal with you.

I return to Lake Forest after being gone a week, and as usual, the rain is coming down hard. I pull into my brightly lit driveway at 10 P.M. on a Tuesday night and Rick is nowhere to be found. He couldn't have gone far, I conclude, with the house lit up brightly.

I find Gracie on her bed in the kitchen and try to shake her awake, but she doesn't move. Her breathing is labored and I feel an intense rush of adrenaline followed by an extreme increase in my heart rate.

She's alive, but barely, what do I do? I immediately call Rick and he doesn't pick up, so I leave him a message. I feel calm and terrified at the same time. Where is he? I need him now! I call the vet and she offers to meet me at her office.

I try to pick Gracie up, but to no avail, so I drag her bed to the garage and feel as though my heart will beat right out of my chest. I'm sweating profusely by the time I get her bed next to the car. Now what?

The lights are off at the Miller's, so I don't want to bother them. I walk to the patio and can see that one of my neighbors still has their lights on; I quickly give them a call.

"It's Ali, down the street. I'm sorry to bother you at this hour, but I have an emergency. It's my dog, something's wrong and I can't lift her into the car. Could you come over and help me? It will only take a second. Oh, thank you so much!"

I hold back the tears for as long as I can. Fortunately,

my neighbor, Jim, arrives in his robe and helps me get Gracie into the back seat. As I drive to the vet's, I'm so full of adrenaline that I forget about my jet lag.

Victoria, the thirty-something vet is waiting for me on the curb, in her sweats with umbrella in hand and she helps me to carry Gracie inside, still on her bed. We are soaked through by the time we get inside.

After an excruciating five-minute wait for her assessment, she gives me the bad news.

"I'm sorry, Ali, she's old and her body is giving up. We're going to have to let her go."

No, not my Gracie! I've had her since college. I press my index fingers firmly against the inner corner of my eyes to prevent the tears from flowing.

"Do we have to put her down?"

"I'm afraid so," she looks at me sympathetically. Poor Victoria has to deal with this every day.

I am unready for this but know it's the right thing to do for Gracie.

"Okay, let's do it," I say, fighting back the tears.

"I'll give you two a minute alone while I get everything ready."

The tears flow freely until I am sobbing, completely unable to control my emotions. My sweet Gracie, what will I do without her?

Victoria returns and I quiet my sobs and hold my loving dog for the last time. She soon stops breathing and it's all over before I've have time to think about it. I thank Victoria and step back into my sedan. I cry as hard as I can the entire way home while trying my best to focus on the road through the pouring rain. Rick's car is in the garage when I return.

Dressed in a familiar business suit, he looks up from his computer when I walk in.

"Where were you?" I ask.

He sees my tear-stained face and soaking wet clothes and hair. "Uh, I was out. What happened?"

"Gracie. I came home and she was in distress, so I took her to the vet and we had to put her to sleep," I continue to sob uncontrollably. "Did you notice anything wrong with her while I was gone?"

"Nothing, she just slept most of the time, as usual. Ali, I'm sorry. I know how much you love her." He hugs me and I continue to cry. All of this loss, I don't know how much more I can take.

~

CHAPTER 24

I f only this feeling would pass. How long will it take? I feel dazed and make my way through each day feeling as though I am half in and half out of my body.

Rick tries to comfort me, but is too preoccupied with his work to offer much solace, so as usual I count on Cass to be there for me.

"I'm sorry I'm not more help to you, Ali. With four kids, we just don't have time for pets and I never had any growing up. I know losing Gracie must be a horrible loss to you."

"It probably seems silly to you, but she was a member of the family. She was always there for me, no matter what."

"Have you thought about getting another dog?"

"I couldn't right now, it just wouldn't feel right. Plus, with my travel schedule, it wouldn't be fair to a puppy to be left alone so much. Rick's hours are even more ridiculous than mine these days."

"Speaking of Rick, how are things going between you two?"

"Fine, why do you ask?"

My mind flashes to my recent catastrophic attempts to improve my marriage.

"Not too long ago you were having concerns about Rick and your marriage."

"That was probably just hormones. Everything is fine; status quo, but I'm so weepy these days, Cass, I feel like I can barely leave the house. It has nothing to do with Rick; it's just all of this loss lately in my life. Maybe it's supposed to be making me strong or something, I don't know, but whatever it is, I wish it would just stop. I could sure use some good times in my life right about now."

"No one's life is ever content all of the time, but I'm sure things will start getting better for you."

"You certainly seem to have a good life. Since I've known you, I can't think of anything in your life that has been sad or tragic."

"I've had my share of sadness. I'll have to tell you the story about my mother."

"Why don't we get our families together soon for a barbeque? My house or yours?"

"I think it's time we had a dinner at my house for a change. We can make use of that back yard that we've worked so hard on...if it's warm enough."

I put the finishing touches on the back yard, adding cornflowers, Virginia bluebells and geraniums to the garden. Everyone is going to love spending time here I think as I admire the various vivid blooms. I buy some turquoise and aqua accent pillows for the new patio furniture as well. Feeling confident with the results of my efforts, I finally invite the Miller clan over and keep my fingers crossed.

Rick helps me prepare several side salads and marinates chicken to break in our new built-in gas barbeque. The little girls are thrilled with the swing set and the evening is a success. Rick helps me with the cleanup and I decide to take the opportunity to probe his thoughts.

"What do you think about us trying again for a baby?" I watch for his reaction out of the corner of my eye.

"If that's what you want."

"I'm asking you what you want. What do you think about having a baby? We haven't talked about this for a long time. I really want to know how you feel." I stop what I'm doing and lean up against the kitchen counter to face him.

"I've always wanted children, but if it's not meant to happen for us, I don't want you to keep putting yourself through agony." He's still focused on drying the dishes.

"What if I can't have a baby, how would you feel about adopting?"

"And raise someone else's kid? No thanks. I want to have a kid of my own or none at all."

I can feel a slight tightening in my chest.

"I never knew you felt that way about adoption." I watch Rick and wonder what's going on in his head.

"There's no way I would ever raise someone else's child."

I am quite shocked by his view on adoption, but relieved that he's willing to keep trying for one of our own. We finish the cleanup process together and for the first time in a while, sleep in the same bed together.

I lie awake and think about our marriage. Things aren't exactly the way I would like them between Rick and me, but what marriage is perfect? We all make sacrifices and I'm sure that our marriage is better than most and that we will be all right in the long run. I'll continue to read my books and be more mindful in my relationship with Rick; certainly that will keep things moving in a positive direction and I'll look into a couples' retreat for us.

A week goes by and it is time, yet again, for another trip to China, and I decide that this time I do have the nerve to pay a visit to James on the way back. He is surprised to see me.

"Miss Alison, where have you been? I thought I would never see you again. Have a seat and tell me everything."

"I don't think you want to know everything. I must apologize, James, for my last visit here, I've been quite embarrassed."

"Embarrassed, why?" He looks confused.

"About my behavior. You must think I'm a total nut, coming in here and crying to you about my problems, and then just vanishing without any explanation."

"I was just concerned about you, that's all. I certainly don't think you are crazy. Where did you go in such a hurry?"

"Mexico." I can feel my face flush.

"Mexico? I never would have guessed that. What compelled you to go to Mexico? A craving for a margarita?"

I smile.

"It's rather a long story."

James looks around at the empty bar. "I've got time, probably a couple of hours before it starts to get busy in here."

"Okay, but first I need some of your tea and a Cobb salad, please."

"Of course, how remiss of me not to have offered. I'll be right back." He passes me a glass of tea before disappearing into the kitchen.

I take a sip and wonder how I could have ever gone this long without James' tea.

When he returns, I ask, "What kind of tea is this? Can I buy some and make it at home? I've noticed that it instantly takes my headaches away, even those times when I don't realize I have one until it's gone."

"I'm sorry, but it's an old family recipe and I must keep the recipe a secret, but I hope that since you like it so much, that you will come in to see me more often."

"I would love that, James." I take a deep breath and start my story to James, beginning with the second miscarriage and finishing with the passing of my sweet Gracie. "Are you sure you don't think I'm crazy now?"

"Of course not, but I am curious. What about this Marcos? Do you still love him? Are you going to see him again?"

"Of course not. I was full of hormones that just made me act impulsively. I love my husband and have a good marriage in Chicago."

"Are you content now, or were you only truly fulfilled on your vacation in Mexico with Marcos? What was it about Marcos that intrigued you?"

"Oh, here we go again!" I giggle. "It's the man responsible for making sure everyone is happy."

James leans in and speaks deliberately, "Not everyone, Alison, just you. I'm only asking you. Be honest with yourself. Are you content with your life in Chicago?"

I suddenly feel as though I've been slapped across the face and my mind whirls trying to find an answer to James' question. I cannot come up with any words to convince him or myself that I'm truly satisfied with my life in Lake Forest.

"Why do you do this to me?" I blurt.

"Why do I do what to you?"

"You make me think about things until I'm so confused that I can't find an answer. How do you do that?"

"I'm just getting you to question the things in your life that you take for granted as true. We must constantly reevaluate our lives, to check in with ourselves and see if we are living our lives for ourselves or whether we are living our lives for others, to please them."

"You sound like some sort of ancient philosopher or self-help guru. How do you think of this stuff? I never think about such things."

"Then maybe it's time you did."

"You never answered my question."

"Which one?"

"About Marcos, what intrigued you about him?"

"He was conundrum to me. He had no formal education, but he was one of the smartest people I've ever talked to and he loved to talk about life for hours. He had the ability to listen as well."

"Not many people do both well, do they?"

"No they don't."

"Can you envision yourself living an alternate life with Marcos?"

"Of course not, that's just a silly idea."

I think about what James is saying my mind flashes images of Marcos and me together on the beach in Mexico. I honestly don't know how I feel about anything. I pick at my salad and count my bites while James attends to some customers who just walked in. As he returns, I hand him two 20's.

"You've done it to me again. You've given me a lot to think about and I don't know whether to thank you or slug you," I say with a smile.

"Thank you for coming to see me, Miss Alison, it is always a pleasure." He nods his head like a true gentleman.

～

CHAPTER 25

I am annoyed as I try to make myself comfortable in my stiff airplane seat and I can't stop thinking about my conversation with James. Why is he so insistent about my peace of mind and why am I so uncomfortable about it? Of course I'm satisfied with my life and why does James keep insisting otherwise? And why did he have to plant the idea of a life with Marcos?

Feeling agitated, I pull out my book, *the Five Languages of Love*, and continue to read. I take the test to see what my love language is. I quickly find that there's not just one language for each person, but rather a list of hierarchy from most important to least. My most important is quality time and second is words of affirmation. No wonder I'm frustrated with Rick, he's not giving me his time or his words these days. I'll have him take the test so we will better be able to understand one another's needs and hopefully fulfill them better. While reading, I eventually fall asleep and, once again, dream of Marcos. The dream is so real that I feel disturbed as I awaken, not knowing whether it was just a dream.

I listen to NPR on the drive home, hoping it will keep

me awake. It is almost dawn, as I pull into the driveway on Holland Court and all the lights are on. My heart sinks as I realize that this is my first time returning home without Gracie to welcome me back. The house feels bare.

I check for any messages on the machine, and I see there are several as I hear Rick enter through the garage door. He's wearing a pair of gray sweatpants and a navy blue Northwestern t-shirt.

"Hi Babe, I didn't expect to see you this soon."

That is an odd comment, I think. I look around the room and suddenly I can feel all of the little hairs on my arms standing up straight.

"Wait a minute," I say without thinking first, "you haven't been here all week, have you?" It was if I had been hit over the head; the lights, the messages, and nothing was out of place in the living room or kitchen. It is all just as I had left it seven days earlier. Something is not right.

"Come on, Al, don't make me say it?"

"Say what?"

"You know I don't stay here when you're out of town."

"I do?"

"Of course you do, you must."

"What are you talking about?"

"You know I stay in town with my girlfriend."

I feel a wave of nausea flood through me. "Your girlfriend?"

"Al, come on. You know there is someone else. For Christ sake you and I only have sex once a month at most. What did you expect?"

"I expect you to keep your wedding vows to me! Who is she? Someone I know?"

"It doesn't matter who she is. You must have known. How could you not?"

"Well, I guess I'm pretty stupid, because I had no idea."

"She's young and came after me. What was I supposed to do? I didn't pursue her. She's just been a distraction for me while you're away. It's just sex, Ali, that's all. I'm married to you and I intend to stay married to you. I assume you have someone that see when you're traveling."

"Well, you assume wrong!"

"Calm down. We can talk about this."

"I'm very calm and there's nothing to talk about. I'd like you to get your things and get out."

What a fool I've been by working to improve this marriage; a goal that I alone aspired to apparently.

"You're overreacting."

"I don't think I am, Rick. I think I'm acting appropriately to this situation, now I want you to leave." I am shocked by how serene I feel. "I'm going to bed now, I don't want you to be here when I wake up."

Rick stands there, speechless as I wheel my roller past him and towards the staircase.

I unpack my suitcase, throwing my dirty clothes in the hamper. I take the *Five Languages of Love* book and place it in a plastic bag along with the other relationship books. I also retrieve the numerous baby books from the shelf and add them to the bag. Someone will get use out of these books, but it's no longer going to be me.

Feeling unemotional, I wash my face; brush my teeth and slip on my pink pajamas. Soon I am fast asleep and dreaming again of Marcos.

I awaken in the evening feeling clear-headed, but wonder why I'm dreaming of Marcos all the time. I would have expected to dream about Rick and the end of my marriage. I am surprised that I don't have a desire to pick up the phone and call Cass. Instead, I find myself making a reservation to Zihuatenejo for later that evening.

CHAPTER 26

This time I'm going to find him I tell myself as I drive to O'Hare. With my suitcase packed full of recent purchases from Zihua, I confidently check in for my flight and wait patiently to board the plane.

A text from Cass comes in as I settle into my seat. *R u home yet? I don't want to wake you. Text me when you wake up.*

Shoot, how should I handle this? I really don't feel like telling her about Rick right now.

Had a delay, will be home in a few days.

I hope this will work for the next few days until I'm ready to talk to her.

My mind wanders to Rick and I wonder if I even know who he is, or did I fool myself into seeing what I wanted to see? I had always assumed that we had similar values; that he was a man of integrity and a man who honored his commitments. Was I so distracted by my desire for a family of my own that I couldn't see what was happening with my own husband? If I had known who Rick truly was, I never would have married him.

I sleep soundly and dream of Mexico and Marcos' eyes. A feeling of exhilaration overcomes me as I deplane in Zihua and, once again, feel a familiar rush of hot, moist air. I'm going to see him this time, I tell myself and feel butterflies in my stomach as I think of Marcos.

I see the name "Davis" hand written on a card as I depart from the airport. Villa Del Sol has come through and sent a car for me. My jubilation escalates as we slowly make our way towards the hotel.

The staff greets me warmly and I am quickly escorted to my favorite room near the lagoon. I feel right at home, as I dress for dinner in my orange sundress. I wear my new dangle earrings and feel feminine and colorful. Looking at myself in the mirror, I am reminded at how desperately I am in need of a tan to warm my pale skin.

Plopping myself on one of the many bar stools at Marcos' old bar, I order a glass of Sauvignon Blanc and bowl of fresh guacamole and chips for dinner. This time I am able to pay attention as the waiter adds fresh tomato, onion and lime to the newly chopped avocado.

Oddly, I feel no sorrow regarding Rick and what has transpired between us, instead I feel an enormous sense of relief as if I had just been set free from a prison that I didn't know I was in. Rick gave me a huge gift, the gift of truth and I am grateful for the opportunity to be living a life that is based in genuineness with no more hidden lies. The signs about our estranged marriage had been there all along, though I had refused to see them. I was an unknowing, but willing participant in the façade we were precipitating as a "perfect couple." There is no sadness or anger; just enthusiastic anticipation for what is coming next in my life.

The guacamole and wine satiate me and I am content to be sitting on a comfortable bar stool, watching the last of the boats head back towards the marina as the sky glows a bright orange as it drops into the horizon.

I go to bed early and awaken at dawn, excited for the day ahead and for the coffee and pastries awaiting me in my cubby next to the front door of my hotel room. I slowly sip the coffee and try my best to decipher the local newspaper, but quickly I realize that my Spanish is not nearly keen enough to understand even the simplest of articles. I tear off several pieces of bread and throw them on the ground and watch as the birds fight over them.

With a game plan firmly in mind, I dress for the day and feel blissful as I inhale the salt air and head towards the beach for my favorite breakfast of seasonal fruits, yogurt and honey. The staff waits on me attentively, refilling my coffee and pastry basket, and making small talk about the day. I feel on top of the world.

After breakfast, I return to my room and load my colorful basket with bottles of water, sunscreen, sunglasses and the same large, straw hat.

A local cab driver drops me at the marina where I plant myself on the same bench as before. Several fisherman walk by, giving me strange looks, but I ignore them and instead try to imagine the look on Marcos' face when he sees me. It's hot and I feel as though I will melt under the scorching midday sun, but I am determined to wait out the day until each and every fishing boat has returned from a day at sea. I don't take my eyes off of the dock even though my body is calling me to sleep.

As each hour passes, I reapply sunscreen and determinedly refocus my mind on my one and only task… to find Marcos. At three o'clock I see a small, white fishing boat dock with several people on board. I see two small children disembark, each with a line of small fish attached, behind them is a tall, strikingly handsome man and I suddenly recognize him. Next to him is a stunning young Hispanic woman, with glowing brown skin, mid-back length straight hair and a cotton dress with tiny flowers that flows sensually as she walks in the breeze. They appear happy and he looks even better than I remembered, weathered from the sun and sea. My heart stops and I feel a sense of panic. He has a wife and children, this possibility has never occurred to me!

Quickly I gather my belongings and head to the street before he sees me. What a fool I am! Of course is married and has children, why did that thought never enter my mind? I feel like a childish schoolgirl who has created a fantasy world. I wish I could rewind time and erase the past two days of my life.

I find a cab and return to Villa Del Sol feeling that my last dreams in life have just vanished. What now? It is time for me to grow up!

Once in my room, I make reservations to return home in the morning and order room service so that I can hide. I just can't face anyone right now. I have no marriage, no dog and no hope of a family. How did my life unravel so quickly?

CHAPTER 27

S adly, I drink my last cup of coffee on my spacious patio before heading to the airport. I conclude, once again, that I am nothing but an impulsive fool, running off to Zihua not once, but twice.

With my small suitcase in hand, I make my way to the lobby and settle my bill with the front desk clerk. A driver waits for me and offers to take my bag to the car. As I pass it over to him, I notice an attractive man in a freshly pressed shirt and pants sitting on a bench near the main entrance of the hotel, his head is tilted down slightly, but his eyes are focused on mine. It's Marcos! He quickly stands but does not move.

I have nowhere to run. I can't feel my legs, but they are moving towards him and I hear myself asking, "What are you doing here?"

"I'm the one who should be asking you that, Alison. What are you doing here, and why are you leaving without seeing me…again?"

"You know that I was here before?"

"Of course I do."

"But, how?"

"This is a small town and people talk. You don't exactly look like a local."

I could feel my face flush.

"So, Alison, answer my question. Why are you here, and why didn't you contact me in all of this time?" His penetrating eyes seem to pierce right through me.

"I couldn't. I just couldn't." I nervously fumble with my straw hat.

"But why?"

"What difference does it make? You're a married man with children. I don't want to interfere in your life."

"What are you talking about? I'm not married. What about you? Did you marry?"

I feel a wave of guilt as I try to come up with a response to this question.

"It's not that simple."

"Why did you leave me without a word? You broke my heart."

A feeling of remorse overwhelms me.

"It's all so complicated. I don't know where to start and I have a plane to catch."

"Please, take the next flight. I will let you go after you tell me what happened, I'm begging you."

"All right, just give me a few minutes."

I talk to the front desk clerk and ask her to hold my bag for a while. I call the airlines and change my reservations to the next flight out.

I return to Marcos. "I'm all yours for the next hour. Let's talk." This was my dream come true, so why do I feel like I am about to pass out?

"Come, let's go to the café next door."

I follow him through the unassuming walkway in silence to a plastic table on the beach with blue tablecloths and a red umbrella next door to the hotel.

A waiter quickly appears to take our order.

"Dos café con crema," Marcos says firmly.

"You remember."

"I remember everything."

My heart is in my throat.

"I need to know why you left without a word."

In all of the times I had imagined my reunion with Marcos, I had not imagined this line of questioning.

"I just thought that our lives wouldn't mesh and that we would disappoint everyone in our families if we stayed together. I couldn't face you to tell you, so I did the cowardly thing and just left. I don't expect you to forgive me."

"Did you marry? Have children?"

His gaze is intense and I feel like crying.

"I did marry. I married someone that I thought would make everyone pleased, but it didn't work out. We didn't have any kids. What about you?"

"No marriage or kids. You were the love of my life, Alison. There is no other woman for me."

"What about the woman that I saw you with today at the marina?"

"That is my sister and those are her kids."

"Oh, I just assumed..."

"What else do you want to know about me? I will tell you anything, but first I want to know why you are here."

"I just wanted to see you." I nervously play with my coffee cup.

He gently takes my hand in his and looks directly into my eyes.

"Alison, why are you here?"

"I uh, I just felt like I had to." I still focus on the cup.

"Alison, look up at me, why did you feel like you had to? Tell me from your heart, why are you here?"

I look up at him and swallow hard, "Because I'm still in love with you and I can't stop thinking about you." I quickly search his face for a reaction. His facial muscles begin to relax.

"Now we are getting somewhere."

"You're not angry with me?"

"I was hurt and confused when you left. I went on with my life, but you never left my heart, not for an instant."

"Do you still love me?" I can't believe I have the nerve to ask this.

"Of course I do."

"I'm glad," I squeeze his hand as I search his eyes for a connection. "What do we do now? My plane is leaving soon."

"Are you going to run away again and disappear?"

"Of course not."

"Then we will be fine and figure this all out." He leans across the table and kisses me gingerly on the lips. His familiar scent infuses my nostrils and I feel a wave of euphoria. Oh how I have missed his kisses!

I compose myself and reach for my purse. I pull out a business card and write my home address on the back.

"Here, now you have all of my contact information; phone number email address and physical address. We won't lose touch again."

I hand him one of my cards and a pen. "Please, any information that you can give me. You can include your blood type too," I say with a giant smile.

"I love that you like to play," he leans in and kisses me again. How did I ever walk away from this man?

"I hate to bring this up now, but I must leave to catch my plane."

"I understand."

"Do you? I don't want to leave, but I most go home and take care of some things."

"It's okay, as long as I know that you are back in my life. There is no rush."

"What are we going to do? When will I see you again?"

"I don't know," he says calmly, stroking my hair.

"But," he interrupts me with another kiss. "Do I really have to leave now?"

"It's up to you."

"You're not making this easy for me."

"I don't intend to."

I grab my purse and do my best to compose myself. "Walk me back to the hotel?"

We walk quietly, hand in hand, down the narrow alley. I'm in utter shock, here I am with the man I love, the man I've been dreaming of all of these months, and here we are!

Marcos stops abruptly and leans down to kiss me properly, a deep sensual kiss. My stomach does flip-flops as I am suddenly taken back to our first kiss five years ago. It was a kiss like no other I have ever experienced. Marcos brings an intensity to kissing like I have never known; as if he is giving the kiss his full attention and nothing else exists at that moment.

When the kiss is over, we continue in silence down the alley and my heartbeat begins to speed up knowing that I will be leaving Marcos in a matter of moments.

A car and driver is waiting for me at the entrance to the hotel. The bellman retrieves my suitcase as soon as he sees me. I look to Marcos for some sort of reassurance that we are okay and that we will see each other again soon.

He opens the car door for me, and I throw my arms around his neck and grab onto him for dear life. He hugs me back hard. I slip into the back seat of the small vehicle and Marcos bends down for one last kiss. I can feel the tears building up in my eyes. Without a word, the driver pulls away from the hotel and I watch as Marcos becomes smaller and smaller in the distance. I also know I will see him again, no matter how.

CHAPTER 28

At the airport I check my phone and see a text from Marcos. *I miss u already.*

I respond straightaway. *I miss you too and am not going to let you out of my life this time.*

I have a lot to think about on the plane ride home. I wish I could tell James about the recent changes in my life. How in the world are Marcos and I going to make this work? At the moment, I don't really care, I'm just delirious and I want to relish every moment.

When I return home, the house feels cold and empty. Rick has taken most of his things and without Gracie; there is no warmth at all. I drop my roller in the kitchen and quickly get ready for bed, sending a quick text to Marcos before falling asleep.

I luv u & am so happy 2 b back in your life. He responds straightaway, *I luv u 2, Alison, more than u could ever know.* I think about how quickly things have fallen into place for us after a long five-year separation. It feels almost magical to be together again and for us to both have the love that we've been yearning for all this time. I fall fast asleep.

I'm wide-awake at dawn and start a pot of coffee and a

load of laundry. At eight-thirty I throw on a pair of boots and a winter coat and head across the street to Cass'.

I ring the doorbell and am not surprised to find Cass in new workout gear.

"Ali! When did you get back?" She gives me a giant hug.

"You always smell so good. I got back last night."

"Aren't you exhausted? You normally sleep for at least 14 hours after one of your trips."

"I'm actually feeling pretty rested. Do you have any coffee made?"

"Of course, come in and sit down." She places little Sophie in her ruffled basinet and fills two mugs with coffee.

"I have quite a bit to tell you," I start, watching her face for any inkling of what I'm about to say.

"Did something happen at work?" She passes me a mug.

"You'd better sit down, this could take a while."

I have her attention as she watches me with a look of concern.

"Rick and I split up." I brace myself for her reaction.

"I'm sorry," she says unemotionally.

"You don't seem very surprised!"

"Well, truly I'm not."

"You're not? I thought you would be shocked." I throw my hands in the air.

"I've been feeling anxious about you two for quite some time," she says quietly.

"What do you mean 'anxious'?"

"There are a lot of things, like the fact that you two never looked at each other or talked to one another when you were with us, and honestly, Ali, your face never lit up when you talked about him. It's like you guys were married, but not particularly happy about it."

"Why didn't you ever say anything?"

"It was really none of my business."

"Of course, it is, you're my best friend."

"There's more."

"More?" I can't imagine what else.

"George and I have both noticed that Rick wasn't around much when you were on your trips."

"What do you mean?"

"Sometimes the house looked unoccupied, and we did see one of the neighborhood kids taking care of Gracie several times. Plus, you told me that you've been reading marital advice books, so I figured things weren't going well between you."

"You know, I was reading those damned books since I assumed that our relationship issues were mostly my fault because of Carol. I thought that since I didn't have a bond with my own mother that I couldn't possibly be a good partner. I convinced myself that if I improved my relationship skills the marriage would automatically improve. Stupid me, it takes two to make a marriage work. I wish you had told me about your suspicions."

"Again, Ali, it wasn't my business. I didn't want to create trouble where there wasn't any. I wanted you guys to figure things out on your own."

"You're suspicions are correct. Rick is having an affair."

"Ouch. You must be devastated."

"Oddly enough, I'm not. I feel more relieved than anything. Maybe I knew on some level that he'd been having and affair, but there were plenty of times recently when I questioned our marriage. I knew in my heart that things weren't right between us, but I didn't want to face it."

"You certainly seem calm about everything. Maybe it

hasn't hit you yet."

"I don't think so. I think I'm fine about it." I feel myself smiling.

"What's that about?"

"What?"

"That smile? You look like you have a secret!"

I can feel my face turning bright red and I start to giggle.

"Ali, don't keep me waiting!"

"I didn't spend a few extra days in China, I spent them in Mexico." I can feel my face turning red again.

"Ali! You went to see Marcos, didn't you?"

I nod my head up and down. "I did. Can you believe that I didn't waste one minute hunting down Marcos after I find out that my husband is having an affair?"

"Your face lights up when you talk about Marcos and you smile. He's the love of your life, Ali, it's obvious."

"Really? I had no idea I was being that obvious. This is all so unbelievable."

"It's such a romantic story. So what happened in Mexico? Did you find him?"

"Actually he found me. When I saw him it was as if no time had passed, all of the same feelings were still there, and fortunately they were still there for Marcos as well."

"What happens next? Is he coming here?"

"I have no idea where we go from here or how we make this all work. If you have any thoughts, please let me know."

"I wouldn't think about it too much, Ali, things have a way of working out. Just let things unfold. They already are…for the better."

We both laugh.

CHAPTER 29

Rick is being amicable about the divorce and we decide to put the house on the market right away. With the improvements we've made in the dining room, kitchen, living room and back yard, we stand to make a nice little profit.

More than anything, I dread breaking the news to Carol. I decide to get it over with as quickly as possible and ask her to meet me at the coffee shop at the square. She loves any excuse to come to Lake Forest from Evanston; it's where she has always wanted to live and the reason why I moved here.

She arrives in a multi-colored Dior blouse, bright orange pants and wearing every piece of gold jewelry that she owns. Carol always dresses beautifully, but I wish I could figure out exactly who it is that she's trying so hard to impress.

"This is a nice surprise, Dear. You never invite me for coffee."

She hands me a small white box with a bright pink bow.

"You don't have to bring me a gift every time you see me."

"I can spoil my only daughter if I want to. Open it."

I reluctantly tug at the expensive ribbon and find a large, gold charm bracelet inside and my heart sinks. My own mother doesn't notice that I only wear silver jewelry. Gold looks great on her warm skin tone, but makes my pale skin look like I'm sick and this piece is much too bulky for my tiny frame.

I take a deep breath, "Thank you, Mom. I asked you here because there's something that I want to talk to you about."

"Good news, I hope. A baby on the way perhaps."

I can feel my stomach tighten.

"No Mom, that's not it. Let's order, then I'll tell you all about it."

"Alison, you look tired. You have dark circles."

"I'm getting enough sleep, Mom. You don't need to worry about me. I asked you here today because I wanted to talk to you about Rick."

"Rick? Is he all right? You know I'm very fond of him."

"I know, Mom." She's not making this easy for me. I take another breath and continue, "Rick and I have split up and we're getting a divorce."

"I would have done that if I could have figured out a way to support myself," she says under her breath.

"What was that?" Did I really just hear that?

"Nothing, sorry dear. What happened? I thought you two were happy, trying to start a family and everything."

"I found out he's having an affair."

"That bastard!"

"Mom!" I never expected to hear that coming from her mouth.

"It's not all his fault, really. Things just weren't that great between us. I'm to blame as well."

"Don't be so hard on yourself, dear. You're better off without him." Is this my mother speaking? I fully expected her to take Rick's side. She thinks he hangs the moon. It almost sounds as though she's being supportive of me.

"You let me know if there's anything I can do to help you, dear, we women have to stick together!"

Now she wants to help me? This is not the mother I know at all!

"Thanks, but for now I have things under control. I'll let you know if that changes in the future. It's nice of you to offer." I'm stunned.

She reaches across the table and pats my hand. I can't remember the last time she touched me.

I finish with Carol and decide to stop by Cass' to fill her on the bizarre conversation. She laughs at the ridiculousness of it and is as surprised as I am by Carol's reaction to my news.

"Speaking of moms, Ali, I really want to tell you the story about mine, but it's kind of long. I've wanted to tell you forever. Are you free tomorrow afternoon? I could get a babysitter and we could have a nice quiet lunch at the Pub, just the two of us.

"That sounds great, just let me know what time." My curiosity is piqued, but I'm guessing that she and her mom had some sort of rift years ago and haven't spoken.

It's a rare occasion that I get to spend time with Cass without the distraction of children. She swings by and we make the short walk to the Deerpath Inn. There's a crisp chill in the air and we are both prepared in our winter clothing.

The Pub is empty and we take one of the dark booths for privacy.

"We definitely need wine for this story, red or white?"

"When I talk about my mother, I need the hard stuff, like straight whiskey."

We take off our heavy winter coats and scarves and place them next to us on the hardwood bench seat and leave on our sweaters for the meantime, and still have more layers underneath to remove should we get warm as the afternoon progresses.

"Bring us a bottle of Barolo and two glasses," Cass instructs the waiter.

"I hope we'll be able to walk home."

"I'll carry you if necessary."

Cass starts her story as soon as the wine arrives, "My mom and dad had a terrible marriage. Dad was constantly cheating on her and he even brought home a few STDs to share with her over the years. I don't know why she tried to stick it out with him, but she did. I love my dad, but he was a rotten husband. Eventually Mom got up the nerve to leave him and had a very difficult time financially. She got a job as a secretary and had to go from living the good life in a huge house to barely paying the bills and living in a tiny apartment."

I sip my wine and listen intently.

"She was under a lot of stress and started putting on a ton of weight. Mom had always grown up with everything; money and good looks and now her whole world was upside down. Her self-esteem was rock bottom when she hooked up with a new man. He seemed okay and made her feel better about herself for a time and then things just continued to spiral downwards for her. She was diagnosed with breast cancer and had to have a radical mastectomy."

"Your poor mom."

"I think her anger was mounting after all of those years

with Dad and then it just got worse and worse for her, and then she finally bottomed out."

"What do you mean?" I take another sip of wine, engrossed in Cass' story.

"I mean that she walked in on her best friend and her boyfriend together and lost it. It was the last straw for her. I don't know the details, because she's never admitted any of this to me, but she was convicted of killing the boyfriend and sticking him in the trunk of his car and leaving it at the airport."

Cass studied my face thoughtfully for my reaction.

"She murdered him?" It took a moment to sink in.

"Yes, she's serving 30 years at the federal prison in Aliceville, Alabama. She can get out in 22 for good behavior. She's a model prisoner, everyone looks up to her."

"I have no idea what to say. It must be terrible for you."

"My mother still tries to control my life even from behind bars. Just because her life was ruined by a bad marriage and having kids she thinks my life will be too. That's why she pushes so hard for me to be a career woman with no kids. This is my life, not hers, but she never seems to understand that. Every time I go to visit her, she's gives me grief about the way I live my life."

"She sounds a little like my mother."

"I've thought of that when you talk about her. You've been seeing my life as problem free all of this time, and I just want you to know the truth. Everyone has something that they have to deal with in life, it's just that some are more obvious to the outside world than others."

"Geez, Cass, I'm speechless. Can I ask you a question?"

"Of course you can."

"What does it feel like to know that your own mother is capable of murder?"

"It's complicated. In my mind, I go back and forth about her guilt. She's never admitted to the murder, but she's never really denied it either. No matter what, she's still my mother and I owe her a certain amount of respect."

"I don't think you owe her anything, Cass. When you kill someone, don't you lose all of your rights as a human being?"

"I don't see it that way. I try not to think about her innocence or guilt and just deal with her as my mother, the way I always have."

"That must be very difficult."

"Yes, she's a very demanding woman, even in prison she constantly calls and wants to know every detail of what I'm doing and then tells me how I should be doing it differently."

I'm in shock and have so many questions for Cass and she openly answers them all, one by one. My head is reeling and I see Cass in a whole new light. Actually, I admire her even more now, knowing that she has created such a beautiful life for herself in spite of her mother's choices.

We chat the afternoon away, she's still my best friend and nothing will ever change that.

~

CHAPTER 30

All day I look forward to my new evening routine of locking up the house, taking a shower, putting on my favorite PJs, making a cup of peppermint tea and crawling in bed by 10, in time for Marcos to call. Some nights we talk for hours, learning as much as we can about one another.

"I've been approved for a two-week vacation next month just like we hoped for."

"I can't wait, Alison. I want you here with me all the time."

"I want that too. I don't know how all of this is going to work, but I know it will somehow."

"If we want it to, it will.

"Do you want to come visit me next? See where and how I live? Meet my friends? I know it's harder to get away for you than for it is for me with all of your family obligations."

"Of course, I want to see where you live, but I want you here more. This is where you belong, Alison. This place agrees with you. You even said so yourself."

"Are you planning on helping your dad with his business indefinitely?"

"Actually, I've started my own little business, but it hasn't taken off yet."

"That's exciting. What is it?"

"Last year we took a small group of Japanese tourists out fishing for the day and one of them offered to teach me his business; the traditional practice of gyotaku."

"Gyotaku? What is that? I've never heard of it."

"Neither had I. It was originally designed for fishermen to document their catches. They would take rice paper and ink with them while fishing, so they could record their catch before turning it loose back to the sea. The art was basic then and has evolved into a true art form. He has been very successful, supplying various hotels from around the world with his art."

"That sounds fascinating. I'd love to see it."

"You will when you're here. I've made a little studio where I can work in the evenings. I can't wait to show you."

"I can't wait to see. Tell me about your family. I'm worried that they won't accept me. I'm a Gringa after all and I'm not Catholic."

"It may be an adjustment for them, but they will come around once they get to know you."

"What about your sister? You two are so close. Do you think she will have trouble accepting me?"

"She will love you most of all. Theresa has a big heart. Her husband ran off months ago, so we're all helping to raise the children. She's living with my parents until she can get back on her feet. I spend as much time with the kids as I can."

"That's one of the things I love most about you, your compassion."

"You know that's one of the reasons that I fell in love with you five years ago."

"What is?"

"Your compassion and kindness. The friends you were with were all very nice, but you stood out to me because of your warmth and kindheartedness."

"I had no idea."

"I could see it right away."

"You know why I fell in love with you?"

"Tell me."

"It was the way you thought and talked about life. The long discussions we had about the philosophers you read. You were so inspired by Jung; it was contagious. Do you recall telling me about Jung's theory on synchronicity?"

"Yes, I'm surprised you remember that."

"It made quite an impression on me and I've thought about that quite a bit lately, how life's synchronicities can change everything, like how we met. I just happened to go on vacation to the hotel where you worked and how the discussions I had with the bartender in Chicago got me thinking of you again. It's like life is just one big chain event of synchronicities."

"I think you should become a philosopher."

"That would be hilarious. I want to know more about your family, it sounds like you are close-knit."

"We are. What about you? Do you have a close family? Are they going to object to our relationship?"

"That possibility kept me away from you five years ago and it's not going to happen again. I'm not close with my family and I really don't care if they approve of us or not. I have a very difficult relationship with my mother. She's been distant to me my entire life and I've decided to stop trying to please her since it's brought me nothing but disappointment."

"I like that attitude. Why do you think your mother is like that? Was her mother cold too?"

"That's a good question. My grandparents died when I was young and I don't remember much."

"There's a reason why your mother is the way she is and it probably has nothing to do with you."

"I've never looked at it that why, but it makes sense."

He's right; maybe I shouldn't take Carol's behavior so personally.

"Sometimes circumstances have a lot more to do with what's going on with them than anything you did."

"Wise words. She's such a peculiar person. She brings me a gift every time she sees me, like she's trying to buy my affection."

"Maybe it's the only way she knows how to show you she loves you."

"You could be right, she certainly never tells me she loves me."

"She's never told you?"

"Never."

"Try to forgive her. She's doing the best that she can. We all are. I have lots of plans for your visit."

"Like holding me and kissing me?"

"Exactly."

"I can't wait."

"Neither can I. I love you."

"I love you too. Good night."

I have several weeks to prepare the house for showing before I leave again for Zihua. I'm surprised that I'm not sad about the end of my marriage or moving out of the house. I had so many dreams and aspirations tied to this place and now it just feels like the right time to move on. The only thing I'm truly sad about is moving away from Cass and her family.

I think about the possibility of moving to Zihua and what would that be like. There are many unknowns at this point, but I'm not going to blow it again with Marcos. Work is a big question. Would I be able to do what I do from Mexico? If so, will I still be commuting to China? I hope not, that trip has become quite tiresome for me.

I make an appointment to talk to my boss, Katherine, after my vacation. I have no idea what she'll say and I have to be prepared for the possibility of being let go. I need to have a back-up plan for sure.

I spend as much time as I can with Cass. Our occasional morning ritual of a walk around the golf course with baby carriages and coffee afterward at the square is now a daily event. Poor Cass has to listen to me carry on for hours about my uncertainty about the future.

"What do you think I should do, Cass? I have no idea where I'm going after the house sells. What if it sells right away? I'll be homeless."

"Don't be ridiculous, you can always move in with us."

"There's a good way to end a perfectly good friendship."

"All right then, you can move in with your parents."

"Bite your tongue!"

"Honestly, I don't know what you're worried about. You earn a good living, you can rent an apartment until you figure things out."

"Apartments aren't exactly plentiful around here; this place isn't geared for singles and I'm not ready to move away yet."

"I'll tell you what. You know that old brown house with the green trim across the road on Deerpath?"

"The one that's set back off the road?"

"That's the one. George and I closed on it a few months back. We're renovating it, but the carriage house in the back has been converted into a guesthouse and is empty. It's all yours until we get ready to sell it."

"When did you two get into real estate?"

"Just recently. I thought it would be fun to try my hand at flipping houses."

"Naturally, in all that free time you have, just lying around the house and eating bonbons!"

I get a laugh out of her. "Yes, that's me."

"Well, if that works out, I would insist on paying rent."

"If you really want to, but I wouldn't pay much if I were you, there will be a ton of noise from the workmen to put up with."

"Any way that it works out, it's very nice to have that option. Thank you, Cass."

"What are the plans with Marcos? When do I get to meet him? What do you think drew you back to him all of the sudden, I've wondered about that. You and Rick were going along in your marriage, trying to have a baby, and then out of the blue you start dreaming and thinking of Marcos after five years. What do you suppose brought that on?"

"I've wondered about that myself. I wondered if it was just because subconsciously I knew I was unhappy with Rick, but I don't think that's the reason. It is odd and I can't explain it. I'll be spending my two-week vacation down there and check things out, see how things go between us and if I can envision myself living there. The thought of leaving this area is somewhat terrifying to me, I've only lived in two places my whole life, Evanston and here. I'm hoping that Marcos will come here to visit after that. I want him to meet you, George and the girls and see where I live, but I can't imagine that it would make sense at all for him to live here. I don't know, we'll see. There are many decisions to make, like my job, for instance."

"Slow down, Ali, if you try and figure it all out at once, you will be overwhelmed. Just deal with one thing at a time. Anyway, things never work out the way we plan them as you have already figured out by now."

I nod, "Ain't that the truth!"

CHAPTER 31

I hand the keys over to the real estate agent on my way to the airport.

"I think everything is in working order. Please call me if you need me. Will you do me a favor and make sure that the back yard gets watered every day?"

"Sure, don't give it another thought, go and have a great vacation and I'll take care of things on this end."

It feels different to know that Marcos will be waiting for me at the airport when I arrive and this time I won't be playing spy, looking for clues on where to find him. This is what I wanted and it's happening now.

The customs line seems to take longer than usual and my impatience grows. I know that the love of my life is waiting for me on the other side of these doors and I don't want to wait any longer!

I finally make it through the last set of doors and there he is, looking better than ever; his curly hair has grown long and rests neatly on the top of his collar. He's leaner than normal, giving him a taller appearance than his six-foot frame and showing off his hard earned muscles. His normally piercing eyes appear soft as he grins widely. My stomach does a few flutters as I fling my arms around his neck and take in his now familiar scent; from a distance it's sweet and almost floral, then close up it's more of a clean, sandalwood fragrance. He squeezes me hard with both arms, lifting me up several inches off the ground.

"You are beautiful, mi Amor."

I feel feminine in my chiffon floral dress.

"I'm happy to be here with you!"

"Are you hungry? I thought we could start with some lunch."

"I'm famished."

"Is this your only bag?"

"That's it." I can't count the number of times my bag has been to China and back.

Marcos grabs my bag and wheels towards a small, white, weathered looking truck parked curbside.

"I apologize ahead of time. I tried to borrow a nicer car with air conditioning, but this was all I could come up with. It's my dad's work truck, but I promise that it doesn't smell like fish."

"I don't care about that. I came here to see you, not your car."

"This trip will be a real test for us you know. You will get to see how I live and what my life is really like without the illusion of Villa Del Sol to protect us."

"That's what I want, to know the real you, all about you."

"I hope you still feel that way by the end of your stay."

I reassure him, "I won't still be in love with you by the end of my trip, I will be even more in love with you." I place my hand on his knee and look straight into his eyes. The power of his stare almost intimidates me until he unclenches his jaw and I can see the corners of his mouth begin to relax into a smile.

"I'm taking you to one of my favorite little spots for lunch. It's nothing fancy, but I eat there often after a day of fishing. It's on the beach, right next to the marina."

"It sounds perfect." I fan myself with my straw hat trying to produce some movement in the still air.

Marcos parks the truck near the marina and locks my suitcase in the cab. He takes my hand as we walk towards the beach. This all feels surreal to me, to be here finally with Marcos. I'm finding it difficult to breathe in the heat of the day and I feel a trickle of sweat flowing down the middle of my back. I notice that Marcos isn't sweating at all.

"Aren't you roasting? You have on long pants, I've got on a flimsy sundress and feel like I'm going to die."

"You'll get used to it, you'll see," he chuckles.

We arrive at the modest restaurant and Marcos pulls out a plastic chair for me. I gladly take a seat protected by the expansive canopy. I look around and see two old men down the beach on a bench in a heated discussion about something. There are several dogs wandering around and I feel sorry for them; they look emaciated and thirsty as if no one has ever bothered to clip their long, matted hair to ease their discomfort in the hot midday sun. A young waiter arrives promptly.

"Dos cervezas por favor."

"Thank you, I'm so thirsty!"

Marcos takes my hand. "So, Alison, you are finally here. I used to imagine this day over and over in my mind while waiting for the fish to bite on the boat with my father. I even pictured us having lunch here together." He intertwines is fingers with mine. "How do you feel about this love of ours that has endured five years of separation?"

I deliberately inhale his aroma and feel a rush of euphoria.

"I feel that we are meant to be together and I was just too ignorant to know it then. I'm grateful to have a second chance with you."

"Now that you are here, I want to court you properly, just as you should be treated."

"No objections," I smile broadly. "What did you have in mind?"

"After lunch, we will get you settled in your condo and then I'd like to take you out on my boat, a romantic sunset cruise."

The waiter returns with the beers and Marcos suggests the fresh fish of the day for lunch.

"That sounds wonderful, please go ahead and order for me."

"You're going to have to practice your Spanish at some point you know."

"I know, but it's much easier when you do it for me." I giggle.

The waiter, who I conclude can't be more than about 14, brings two large, plain green salads. The dressing is simple and delicious. I feel right at home as I watch the fishermen coming and going from the now familiar marina.

"I'm sorry, but I do have a little bad news for you."

My heart beats a little faster. Bad news, I don't want to hear this.

"I will have to work some with my father while you're here. He's getting old and can't fish by himself anymore."

"You had me worried for a minute. That's not a problem at all. I never expected you to spend every minute with me."

"I was hoping that I could." He winks.

The main course arrives and it's not much to look at, just one, flat piece of fish drenched in garlic butter and a mound of yellow rice. The flavor is spectacular. I don't know how they could make something that looks so ordinary taste so exceptional.

"This food is amazing. I'll bet you know all of the best places to eat in town." I suddenly realize that I forgot to count my bites, what if I went over?

"I don't know about that, I mostly cook at home. What about you, are you a good cook?"

"I'm embarrassed to admit this, but I can't cook to save my life."

"Then I will teach you. I hope you like Mexican style food, my mother is an excellent cook and she taught me everything that she knows."

Naturally, his mother is an excellent cook!

"Speaking of my mother, when would you like to meet her? My whole family wants to meet you. I've told them all about you."

I feel a sense of foreboding. "Can we just take things slowly? I want to meet them, but first I want to spend some time with you and get acclimated." The truth is I'm terrified that his mother won't like me; after all, my own mother doesn't even like me.

"Whatever you are comfortable with, you just let me know. I won't push you."

"I think we need to get going to the condo, the agent instructed me to pick up the key by three and it's two now."

"Do you have the address?"

"Yes, here it is." I show him a print out from my computer. I chose this one since it's right above Villa Del Sol, I'll be able to find my way around.

"Ah yes, I know exactly where it is. Nice place and an easy walk to the beach."

Marcos maneuvers the truck confidently through the darting cars and pedestrians along the way. Zihua is familiar to me now and feels a little bit like home.

An old man is napping at the front desk when we arrive. Marcos speaks to him in Spanish and is given the key to number 311. Marcos carries my bag up the small stairwell to the third floor and unlocks the door for me.

The condo is one large room with a compact kitchen, open living room-dining room area and a small bed that rests against the farthest wall from the front door. The bathroom is large and private with an adjacent closet and dressing area. The furniture is bright and looks hand painted in yellow, turquoise and orange. The doors in the living area open completely, exposing a panoramic view of the curved beach of la Ropa. The Playa appears to be full of activity, but not overly crowded. It's not Villa Del Sol, but beautiful nonetheless.

"You should be happy here."

"We should be happy here. I hope you will be spending lots of time here with me."

"That is my plan, Alison, that is most definitely my plan." He bends down, puts his arms around me and kisses me passionately for several moments. I can feel my knees buckle slightly and my head feels light. "Now, you get settled. I will be back at six to pick you up and take you to the marina for our sunset cruise."

"That sounds wonderful." I feel a pang in the pit of my stomach as I watch him walk out the door.

I look around my tiny condo; it's smaller than I had expected, but it's clean and colorful and has everything I need. Marcos and I should be very happy here for the next couple of weeks.

I hang my few belongings, take a nice long shower, wrap myself in my new, short, red silk kimono and decide to send a quick text to Cass.

Just checked into my condo. Heading out for a sunset cruise later.
She responds instantly. *How are things going with Marcos? Excellent!*

CHAPTER 32

The boat is docked and ready for us when we arrive at the marina. Marcos has stocked a cooler with snacks and beverages. He takes me to a small cove where we can watch the tortuga engage in their mating ritual.

Marcos explains, "If a male is interested, he will make a clawing motion towards her face and she may or may not respond by doing the same. If all goes well, he mounts her and locks himself into position as she swims, but then the poor male must endure the attack of predators while he is otherwise preoccupied."

"Are you an expert on turtles?"

"I see them here year after year. It's fascinating to watch the females lay their eggs and then watch the babies hatch and try to make it out to sea before any predators get to them. It's almost a miracle that any of them make it at all."

"Look, I see a big one right over there!"

"You will see many more around here. What would you like to drink? I brought you a bottle of Sauvignon

Blanc; I remember that you liked that. There is also beer if you prefer."

"You've thought of everything. I would love a glass of wine, thank you."

I watch him carefully as he opens the wine. I'm enjoying seeing him in his environment and not as an employee of the hotel. He seems so capable, I wonder what else he knows how to do besides fish, cook and make art? I notice a small dimple in the center of his left cheek, funny I wonder why I never saw that before?

He hands me the wine in a plastic cup and opens a beer for himself.

"Tell me about your marriage, Alison."

I gulp, "What do you want to know?"

"When did you get divorced?"

I hesitate, "I'm not divorced."

"You're still married?"

"My husband and I are in the divorce process. It won't be long now."

"I see separated couples get back together all the time."

"That's not going to happen here. My marriage is over and I'm here with you now, completely 100% with you."

"Why didn't it work out? You must have loved him."

"I did, or at least I thought I did. I think I mostly married him to make everyone else happy, especially my mother. What I couldn't see at the time was that I honestly don't think he really loved me either. I found out he was having an affair and I can't say as I blame him. We were both unhappy and too complacent to admit it or do anything about it."

Marcos listens fixedly as he fiddles with the corkscrew.

"The oddest thing started happening, I started having these in depth conversations with an airport bartender in

Detroit about life and doing the things in life that give it meaning and whenever I would have one of these conversations, I would start dreaming about you. It happened more and more frequently until I just couldn't get you off my mind. It made me think I made a big mistake by letting you go. I'm willing to do whatever it takes to make it up to you."

"You can start by kissing me now."

"My pleasure," I smile and kiss him fervently and explore the delicacy of his mouth.

The boat rocks slowly and I notice that the sun is beginning to drop in the sky.

"Come on," he interrupts, "I want to teach you how to fish."

"Now?" It doesn't sound very romantic to me.

"Yes, now this is the best time of day to catch Dorado. We can have it for dinner."

Marcos scrambles and swiftly attaches something to a hook on the end of a fishing line. "Sit here, let me show you."

Reluctantly, I take a seat on the stern of the boat as instructed. He shows me how to cast the line, which I doubt I could replicate if my life depended on it, and hands me the pole. "Now just wait."

He sits near me on the railing and sips his beer. "If you feel the slightest little tug on the line, I'll show you what to do."

"Don't we need to get back before it gets dark?"

"We're fine, we have plenty of time."

Too bad, I'm not enjoying this in the least.

"Oh, I feel something!"

"Now, start to reel him in."

"How? Help me!"

Marcos puts his hands over mine as I have a death grip on the pole.

"See, nice and smooth, just like this. Look you've caught one big enough for dinner, good job!"

I suddenly feel a sense of pride as Marcos pulls the Dorado into the boat.

"My very first fish! I can't believe it."

Marcos hands me my cup of wine, "Here, you've earned this."

He starts the engine and we head quietly back to the marina just as the sun is setting.

I watch helplessly as Marcos capably ties the lines to the dock and helps me to the pier. He grabs the large cooler and carries it to the truck.

"Tonight you not only caught your first fish, but now you are going to learn how to cook it."

"I think that's expecting more out of me than I can deliver."

"Nonsense, it's easy, I will show you. We just need a few ingredients. There's a little store along the way to your condo, we can stop there and get whatever we need. I will take you to the Mercado another time, beside I'm not sure that you're up to that yet."

"What does that mean?"

"You'll see." He laughs mischievously.

The condo feels homey as we enter with our bag of produce and fresh fish. Marcos promptly opens all of the doors and windows leading to the ocean view. The sky is a deep shade of orange as the sun makes its last appearance for the day. I turn on the overhead kitchen lights and unpack the groceries into the compact refrigerator.

"Would you care for some wine?"

We forgot to get any, I'm sorry.

"No, we didn't." Marcos pulls out the open bottle from his backpack. It's ice cold from sitting in the cooler all evening.

"Aren't you the clever one? Is there anything that you don't think of?"

"There's one more thing." Marcos digs into his backpack again and pulls out a large book. "This is for you. Now you have your own copy so we can have many more long discussions."

"Jung! I'm so excited to read this!"

Marcos presses me up against the kitchen counter, takes my head in his hands and kisses me so hard that I can barely breathe!

"Wow! That was amazing."

"We are amazing together. Chemistry like ours doesn't happen every day."

"You can say that again."

"I will remind you of that every chance I get." He kisses me again. "Now, for your cooking lesson. We need a pan." He rummages through the limited cupboards. "This one will do. Will you chop some garlic?"

I watch as Marcos skillfully cleans the fish in under a minute. If I did that it would probably take an hour and I would end up cutting myself in the process!

He retrieves another pan, chops a bunch of vegetables and herbs together and throws them in with some butter while he waits for the butter to heat up in the first pan. I take mental notes of everything he's doing.

"Should we eat on the terrace?"

"Oh yes, I'm standing here doing nothing, I'll set the table." I find a drawer with a few decorative placemats and set them on the bright yellow table along with the utensils.

"Come, Alison, I want you to see this part." I watch and learn. "The trick is to get the butter hot, but not hot enough to burn, add the garlic for just a moment or two and then quickly cook the fish on each side. If the pan is too hot or you cook it for too long, it will be tough. See how easy it is?"

"Only because you make it look easy."

"You can do it too. Now, let's eat while it's hot."

He places the plates on the table.

"Wait, I want to take a picture of my first fish and send it to my best friend, she'll never believe it!" I quickly text the photo to Cass and she replies immediately.

That's nice, but I want to see a picture of the two of you.

I giggle. "Come here, just one second, before we eat. I want to take our picture with the last bit of light in the background."

Marcos and I sit on the adobe wall, with our backs to the Pacific while I take a selfie, the very first picture of the two of us together. I'm hesitant to see how we look together and shocked at what a striking couple we make; a contrast of light and dark, large and small, but we look like we are blissful and in love. I send it to Cass. She writes back one word: *Beautiful!*

≈

CHAPTER 33

The sun wakes me up and I hear the distant lap of the waves and the birds chirping loudly just outside my window. I'm waking up in Zihua! I jump out of bed eager to greet the day as I inhale the humid, salt air. I smile, recalling the events of last night and the kiss that Marcos left me with on his way out the door. I have until noon on my own, what shall I do with myself?

There's no cubby next to my front door with coffee and croissants waiting for me, so I guess I'll have to make my own coffee this morning. Throwing on my kimono, I rummage through the tiny kitchen and find a French press. As the coffee seeps, I make a call to Cass.

"How goes it? Are you in heaven?"

"How did you guess?"

"Tell me everything, I want to hear it all. I'm living vicariously through you now, you know, so make it as juicy as possible."

I laugh. "It's all just been fabulous, so far. We had a lovely lunch on the beach and then a sunset cruise on his boat, and he taught me how to fish. You saw the picture."

"I like the picture of you two. He is a very good looking man."

"Yes, he is."

"Did he spend the night?"

"No, we decided to wait for that."

"But, why? You guys are hot for each other, why wait?"

"He says he wants to court me properly."

"Good looking and a gentleman. Sounds like you've hit the jackpot."

"There's still a lot to work out. Our lives are so different. I still have to meet his family and I'm very nervous about that."

"What's to be nervous about?"

"What if they don't like me? They are a very close family, that could end things for us right there."

"You underestimate yourself and him. He adores you and isn't going anywhere. You need to just relax and have fun. This is the good part, getting to know one another. Tell me what you're up to today."

"I haven't thought about it yet. Marcos is fishing with his dad until noon, so I guess I'll take a walk on the beach."

"Keep me posted, I want to hear all about everything."

"Will do."

I sip my coffee on the deck and watch the boats in the bay, wondering if one of them belongs to Marcos and his father. The coffee is terrible, especially since I don't have any cream, and I'm beginning to feel hungry. I throw on a pair of shorts, camisole and flip-flops and head towards the beach.

The restaurant with the plastic tables where I had coffee with Marcos is open and I take a seat. "Café con crema por favor." When the waiter returns, I order a pastry and wish that Marcos was with me.

As I sip my coffee, I contemplate why my normal life long obsession with counting bites seems to disappear when I'm in Mexico. Maybe it's because I'm relaxed or because I'm just in a different environment, but more than likely it's because Carol isn't around to set me off. I don't even think about calories at all when I'm here, in fact, I utterly just don't care.

I finish my coffee and head out for a walk along the beach. I find pesos, not shells as I walk along the sand. I am approached by several locals who try and lure me to their tents for a facial or message. I realize that they only want 200 pesos or 10 US dollars for an hour, so I decide to give it a try.

A large woman named Marta instructs me to sit on her table and hands me a towel after she washes the sand off my feet with water. She points to my top and gestures her hand in an upward motion. I pull off my camisole and lay face down on the padded massage table.

Marta asks me if I want a medium or hard message, and I ask for hard, wanting to remove the kinks in my back from my many years of travel. Marta's hands are strong and experienced. I can feel my stress level diminish.

At the end of the hour, I feel like an entirely different person and hand Marta 300 pesos and promise her that I will be back again tomorrow. I have just found the best possible way to kill and hour in Playa la Ropa.

I head back up the hill to the condo with just enough time to shower and get ready for my day with Marcos. I'm sitting on the sunny deck when he arrives.

"Let me apologize for the way I look," he starts," I didn't have time to shower."

"Don't apologize, I like the rugged look!" I lean up on my toes to try and reach his lips for a kiss.

"I'm serious, Alison, I stink like fish. You don't want to kiss me right now."

"All right, I thought you were just messing around with me."

"I'd like to mess around with you, but I can't when I smell like this. I don't even want to come inside. I've planned our afternoon. If you just bring your purse or whatever you might need, we can go."

"Okay." I feel that he's being short with me, but I sense that he's embarrassed, not angry. I quietly take my purse and follow him out the door.

"I want to show you my studio today and how I do my art. I have a shower there, so I thought we could go there first. There are several little restaurants nearby where we can have lunch, then come back to the studio. Does that sound good to you, or is there something else you would rather do?"

"It all sounds good to me, thank you for planning our day. I know you have enough to do as it is without having to worry about entertaining me." I study his face to get a read of his mood.

"I don't think of it as entertaining you, Alison. I think of it as showing you my life."

"I like that better."

He seems pleased by my response.

"Don't expect much from the studio, it's just a room with running water, about as basic as it comes."

"I just want to see your paintings."

Marcos parallel parks the truck in a small opening halfway up on a curb. I have no concept of where we are. I follow him two blocks north and he unlocks a padlock with one of many keys on his keychain. The building reminds me of a storage shed, where you push the metal, rolling door upwards to open it.

The interior is simple, just four cement walls and a high ceiling with a wood door on the back wall and two large windows facing the street.

"That's the bathroom. I told you it wasn't much."

I sense a tone in his voice that I haven't heard before.

I'm focused on the rows of fish images hanging from several clotheslines across the room.

"What? Oh the studio is fine. How in the world did you do these?" How did he get a flat image from a rounded carcass? Did he crush the bones first?

"Alison? Alison!"

"I'm sorry! These are fascinating and so beautiful!"

I'm impressed with Marcos' ability to take on a completely foreign art form and make it look like a natural ability. I'm anxious to hear all about his process.

"You keep looking, I'm going to take a quick shower."

"Okay."

Two-minutes later Marcos returns in a white, short sleeved shirt and khaki shorts, with his wavy, black hair combed deliberately back and off of his forehead.

"Feel better?"

"Much. I'm famished, let's get something to eat."

I follow Marcos down the narrow, cracked sidewalk to a walk-up window with just three tables on the curb.

He orders a variety of tacos for us and we take a seat in the hot sun. He pulls a nearby umbrella over our heads and I feel a sudden decrease in temperature.

"Aclamaciones!" he says, lifting his bottle of cerveza in the air.

I decide it's best to keep quiet about his mood and not broach the subject at the moment.

"How was your morning? What did you do?"

I don't think telling him all about my relaxing message is a good idea at this point.

"I got some breakfast, walked the beach, and called my friend, Cassie. How was your morning?"

"Don't ask. Dad has dementia, but still thinks he can run things. It's getting to the point where he shouldn't be out on the boat anymore."

"I'm sorry to hear that. Maybe he should retire."

"That's what we keep telling him, but he's stubborn. You don't need to hear about that now. Let's eat up, so I can give you an art lesson."

We eat our tacos quietly and quickly.

Back in the studio, Marcos hands me a pair of painter's overalls.

"You're going to need these."

"Do I have to? They look hot."

"Trust me, you will thank me later."

I slip the overalls on over my shorts as I watch Marcos lay out numerous paint-stained tarps on the floor. "We're just going to practice with color today. I want you to get used to the textures and hues before we actually get into the process with the fish. Do you have any art background?"

"I just started drawing recently. I'm pretty intrigued by art and would love to learn much more about it. Did you study art in school?"

"The man from Japan taught me everything. We spent several days on color alone." Marcos slips on a pair of overalls and turns on several floor fans scattered around the room. "We're going to start with watercolors. What color would you like to create?"

"Pink is my favorite color."

"Think about what shade of pink you like best, is it dark, more on the purple side or is it more of a rosy pink, like a peach?"

I watch as Marcos collects the necessary supplies and

lays them on top of the tarps.

"What do you think goes into making pink?"

"Red for sure, and maybe white?"

"Good, then let's make some different pinks. You need to get down here and get your hands dirty."

Getting dirty is not my favorite thing; I guess that's one of the reasons I started with drawing. I'm moved that Marcos wants to teach me, so I'm doing my best to be an obliging student.

Marcos is fully focused on the paints and hands me a brush. "Now, take some of the red and make a splotch on the paper, then clean your brush well before adding the white. Watch what happens if you add a touch of yellow."

We spend the entire afternoon making various shades of pink and I have learned more than I thought there ever was to know about the color. I begin to feel restless and take a brush full of pink paint and splatter it all over Marcos' face and neck. Without hesitation, he retaliates and before I know it we are both covered in paint and making out intensely on the wet tarps.

He stops abruptly and sits up, "We can easily get carried away here."

"How long did you say you want to wait?"

I finally get a laugh out of him. "Just a little while longer," he kisses me briefly. "Let's get cleaned up and get in a sunset cruise before the day is over."

Feeling frustrated, I reluctantly agree and head to the tiny bathroom to scrub my face and hands as Marcos tidies up the studio. Far from paint free, we head to the marina and Marcos takes me to the same tranquil cove to watch the turtles.

We sit quietly and sip a cerveza. I get up the nerve to ask him a question.

"Did something happen today? You didn't seem like

yourself earlier, like something was bothering you." I have no idea what can of worms I might be opening.

"There is something bothering me."

"Does it have anything to do with me?"

"It has everything to do with you."

I can feel my heart racing. "Did I do something?"

"No, nothing like that. It's money. I'm poor, Alison. I can't provide for you the way that I want to. I can't even afford to take you out for a nice dinner. You are used to a life of privilege. I can't possibly expect you to be happy here with me when I have no money."

"I had plenty of money when I was married and I was miserable. You and I have something much more valuable, besides I make a good living, enough for both of us."

"I can't let you support me. That makes me less than a man. This worries me, Alison."

"Don't let it. You and I have many decisions to make. Let's just see how things go. I don't know why you don't think you're a good provider, look we have all of the fish we can possibly eat!" I point to the cooler loaded from the day's catch.

"I don't want my concerns to ruin your visit, but it does weigh heavy on my mind."

I'm relieved that Marcos' mood was not related to something I have done and I am also encouraged at how open he is with me about his thoughts and feelings. His mood is improved after our talk, though he does seem very tired.

I've been so carried away with our romance that I haven't given too much thought to the practicality of our relationship. Naturally I don't want to live in poverty, but Marcos is such a capable man, I'm sure that he can find a way to provide ample income from means other than fishing.

Back at the condo, we prepare a simple meal of Grouper and rice. After dinner we settle in together on one of the lounge chairs on the patio. Marcos reads poetry to me from his favorite book of romantic poets, Pablo Neruda's *If You Forget Me*.

"'I want you to know
one thing.
You know how this is
if I look
at the crystal moon, at the red branch
of the slow autumn at my window
if I touch
near the fire
the impalpable ash
or the wrinkled body of a log,
everything carries me to you,
as if everything exists,
aromas, light, metals,
were little boats
that sail
toward those isles of yours that wait for
me.

WELL, now,
If little you stop loving me
I shall stop loving you little by little.

IF suddenly
You forget me
do not forget me,
for I shall already have forgotten you.
If you think it long and mad,

The wind of banners
That passes through my life,
and you decide
to leave me at the shore
of the heart where I have roots,
remember
that on that day,
at that hour,
I shall lift my arms
and my roots will set off
to seek another land.

BUT
    if each day,
    each hour,
    you feel that you are destined for me
    ah my love, ah my own,
    in me all that fire is repeated,
    in me nothing is extinguished or forgotten,
    my love feeds on your love, beloved,
    and as long as you live it will be in your arms
    without leaving mine.'"

"Ouch, why did you choose that poem?"

"I think it's terribly romantic."

"But it's so harsh. He sounds very unforgiving. Are you trying to tell me something?"

"I didn't write it, silly."

I recall the time he read to me from this book five years ago and how I knew at the moment I was in love with him. He continues to read to me until we both fall asleep on the lounge chair and don't awaken until morning.

～

CHAPTER 34

I'm up watching the sunrise from the deck when Marcos stirs.

"Mierda! I've got to go!" He kisses me on the cheek as he runs his hands in a backward motion though his thick hair, trying to flatten the curls. "I'm sorry. I will probably be gone all day. Will you be okay?"

"Of course, I'll be okay. Go do what you need to do. I'll see you later."

"I'll pick you up for our sunset cruise."

"See you then. Have a good day."

I guess I feel a little disappointed, but I'm sure that I can find plenty to do to keep myself busy, starting with breakfast on the beach and a wonderful massage with Marta!

I throw on the yellow bikini that I bought at Villa Del Sol gift shop and cover it with a sheer turquoise colored cover-up. My hair seems to have taken on new life in the humidity, giving it a wave and some body. I scrunch it several times with a little product and dap a touch of pink gloss to my lips. All sunglasses look huge on my narrow head, but my favorite black ones, especially, give me a sort of Jackie O look.

The walk from my condo to the café on the beach takes less than ten minutes and I'm in dire need of coffee by the time I arrive. The waiter remembers me and asks if I want a café con crema and pasteles.

"Si, senor, gracias."

I'm happy that things are going well with Marcos and that he was able to tell me what had been bothering him. In my mind, worrying about money is a waste of time. If you need it, you just go make it, end of story. But, I realize for Marcos, here in Mexico, things are not that simple. He has many talents and I'm sure there must be a way for him to make more money.

I sip my coffee and fantasize about what my evening with Marcos will be like. I want to surprise him somehow, but I'm not sure exactly how yet. For the moment I am satisfied to know that after I'm done with my breakfast, I have a relaxing hour-long message waiting for me on the beach. I could get used to this!

Marta sees me walking up the beach and summons me to her tent.

"Hola, Marta. Buenos dias." I must practice my Spanish more aggressively.

Marta's English is broken, but she tries and we somehow manage to communicate. I stick my face into the padded headrest and focus on the sounds around me. Besides the waves and the birds, I can hear several woman speaking quickly in Spanish and children laughing gleefully as they play on the shore. I want to remember these sounds and how peaceful I feel at this moment.

The hour passes much too quickly and Marta asks me what I have planned for the day.

"No tengo idea," I respond honestly. "I would like to

learn cooking," I say, gesturing as if I have utensils in my hands.

"Ah, si, cocina!"

"Si!"

"You want to learn today?"

"Si," I shrug.

"You wait," she instructs me while she makes a call from her cell. I can hear her going back and forth with a woman on the other end. "Two o'clock okay?"

"Yes, but…"

"Si, si." I hear her say before she hangs up the phone. She writes something on the back of one of her business cards. "My sister-in-law, she teaches the cooking in her home. Here is address. You be there at two. She charge 400 pesos, she buy everything."

Twenty dollars for an authentic cooking lesson and she buys the food, I'm in! Marcos will be impressed.

"Gracias, Marta. Te veho manana." I hand her a 500-peso bill.

How exciting, I get to learn how to cook authentic Mexican food!

I take a cab to an unfamiliar part of town and am greeted by a younger, rounder version of Marta.

"Adelenta."

I can tell at once that we are going to have a communication problem. Isabella leads me directly to her modest kitchen. All of the food has been premeasured and chopped.

"Tamales, si?"

"Si."

Isabella shows me a large pot simmering on the stove with meat in it then points to the sink which is full of cornhusks soaking in water. I have no idea what she's doing and since her instructions are lost on me, I resign myself to just watch and video record her as she makes the tamales. She removes the meat from the pan and places in a bowl, then strains the juice through a strainer. I continue to film as she adds pork lard to a bowl of masa and kneads it as she pours pork broth and a chili puree that she's made from scratch. This all seems like a lot of work to me for a simple tamale!

Isabella meticulously spreads the masa mixture onto the husks and capably places them into a large steam pot. She indicates that we have one hour until the tamales are completed. I help her with the clean up process and at the end of the lesson, she hands me a bag with numerous tamales wrapped inside. I return to my condo and refrigerate the tamales for our dinner tonight. Even though I didn't actually make them, I feel that I could possibly make them on my own sometime by just watching the video.

I'm freshly showered and dressed in my favorite orange sundress and dramatic new earrings when Marcos arrives.

"I have a surprise," he says.

"I can see that," I reply, looking at the two little faces staring up at me from behind him.

"My niece and nephew, my sister had to go to work unexpectedly. I hope you don't mind. She'll pick them up later."

"Of course I don't mind, come in!"

"This is Luciana, she's five, and Matias here is three."

"They're adorable."

Luciana stares up at me with her big, round eyes. She looks like a little doll, wearing a pink floral dress and matching pink sandals. Matias, on the other hand, looks like he is all boy, smeared in mud on various spots of his face and body.

"They don't understand a word of English."

"Then you will have to translate for me. Tell them that I'm very happy to meet them."

"We are still on for our sunset sail, they love the boat and they have been on it almost every day of their lives."

"Then let's go."

"Again, I apologize."

"Don't be silly. This will be fun." Marcos has no idea how much I adore children.

Once in the cove, the children take out their miniature fishing poles and maneuver them like little pros. I can't understand any of their conversation with Marcos, but I am enjoying watching the children in their element.

Luciana places her rod in the holder and crawls into my lap. She stares at my hair and strokes it with fascination while saying something in Spanish.

Marcos laughs out loud.

"What is she saying?"

"She wants to know how you painted your hair yellow."

"Ha ha, that's funny. Can you explain to her that it's not painted, that I was born this way?"

"Are you sure you want me to tell her that?"

"Yes, it's my natural color! Now, tell her."

Luciana picks up her fishing pole and returns to my lap and waits patiently for a fish to bite. She is such a sweet little girl and so trusting to come and sit with me.

Marcos helps Matias with his pole until he catches a Mackerel just in time for us to make it back to the marina by dark. The children are excited by the catch and chatter away with one another.

Back at the condo, I surprise Marcos with the tamales and heat them up for our dinner.

"You made this by yourself?"

"Not exactly, but it's a start."

"What compelled you to take a cooking class today?"

"I don't know, it just sounded like a good idea."

"I'm impressed by your initiative and I can't wait to try it."

The children help me set the table and they eat quietly. At their young age, they already have developed impressive manners.

"You did great!" Marcos compliments me on the meal and delivers a kiss to my cheek.

After the table is cleared, I have an idea of how to keep the children occupied and retrieve my sketchpad and a pencil. I draw a caricature of each of them and they giggle madly.

"Ask Luciana to tell me what she thinks is the most distinctive thing about her brother."

"She says his round nose."

"Okay, good. I start to draw where they can see what I'm doing as I exaggerate a round nose on the paper." Luciana squeals with delight. I hand her the paper and pencil.

"Now, tell her to give it a try."

Grudgingly Luciana tries to replicate the nose image and looks at me for approval.

"Muy bien!" I nod.

I hear a knock at the door and Marcos answers it before I have a chance to get up from the table. It's Theresa and I'm suddenly faced with meeting the family, ready or not! The children run to her, sketches in hand, filling her in on their latest adventure.

The Aiza family must have some strong genetics: Theresa is as beautiful as Marcos is handsome. She could easily pass for an actress or model, though I doubt she is aware of her natural beauty. Her simple, white cotton dress hugs her curvaceous figure subtly and she exudes a quiet sensuality, not unlike her brother. I would describe them both as sultry. Her hair is cut exactly like Luciana's; longish with short, straight bangs.

I feel almost intimidated by her beauty as she extents her hand cheerfully to me as Marcos introduces us.

"Thank you for watching the children. I am sorry we had to interfere with your romantic evening." Her English is perfect.

"Don't be silly, they were an absolute pleasure, not in the way at all."

"I think you are being polite, but thank you."

I like her instantaneously.

The children each hug me goodbye and I remind myself to work on my Spanish so that I will be better able to communicate with them next time and not have to rely on Marcos for translation.

"Now, it's back to just us," Marcos puts his arms around me.

"Thank you again, for being so nice to the children. My family is going through a hard time right now and it's been an extra strain on all of us. Bad timing that it's happening while you're here."

"It's called life and it happens. The kids are great and so is your sister."

"I knew you would like her. Next you'll be ready to meet my parents."

"I'm not sure about that."

"It will be easy, you'll see. They spend every Sunday afternoon at the beach, I thought that might be a good time for you to meet them."

"Sunday?" I could feel my blood pressure increasing.

"Sunday."

~

CHAPTER 35

The dreaded Sunday arrives and I am a bundle of nerves. Everything rides on how well this day goes, I tell myself. We have arranged to meet Marcos' family at Marisqueria Mary's (the place where I have been getting coffee and pastry) after they return from church and spend the afternoon on the beach with them.

How in the world is his mother going to accept me, a skinny, white, protestant, soon-to-be-divorced, blonde from Illinois? She will probably detest me the moment she sets eyes on me. Funny but when I imagined being with Marcos again in Mexico; it never entered my mind that his family would be part of the picture.

"Is my bikini too revealing? Maybe I should run out and buy something a little more conservative for today, like a one piece."

"Have you seen the way the women dress on the beach? They let it all hang out. It doesn't matter what size or shape you are, you show it off proudly around here. Stop concerning yourself about what my mother will think, just relax and be yourself today and they will love you."

I've never seen Mary's on Sunday afternoon and I am shocked at the number of local families inhabiting the beachside tables. Everyone looks relaxed and like they are having a good time. I search the sea of faces, looking for Theresa, Luciana and Matias. Naturally, Marcos spots them before I do and I can feel my pulse quicken as we walk towards Marcos' family. Theresa quickly jumps up to greet me and offers me a warm double cheek kiss welcome. I can see the children playing at the water's edge.

Marcos' parents look nothing like him; his mother is short and quite rotund and his father is small in stature with a thin, oval face. He does not look well. Marcos' uncle resembles a younger, stronger version of his brother.

I extend my hand to Marcos' mother first as I attempt to read the expression on her face. "Encantada de concocerte, Senora Aiza." I have been practicing "nice to meet you" in Spanish for the past two days.

She nods, shakes my hand and simply says, "Alicia."

Marcos interrupts and introduces me to his Uncle Jorge and father, Arturo. They both nod and smile.

Theresa grabs my shoulders from behind, "Come, sit next to me and relax. Would you like a beer?"

"Yes, thank you, Theresa." I feel like I need about three to calm my nerves.

"I want to know all about you. Tell me about your life in Illinois. I've always wanted to go to the states, maybe one of these days."

I look across the table and Marcos is occupied in a conversation with his father and uncle and it looks like some sort of debate is taking place. Alicia is watching the children intently.

"Don't worry about Mama, she doesn't understand a word of English. You can chat with her later and either

Marcos or I will translate. We're going to be here all afternoon, there'll be plenty of time."

I straightaway like Theresa the same way that I took an immediate liking to Cass, in fact there's something about Theresa that reminds me of Cass, maybe it's the dark hair and skin and voluptuous figure. It certainly can't be the makeup; Theresa doesn't wear any.

I give her my life in a nutshell, leaving out, of course the part about my current divorce and possibility of losing my job and she shares with me all about her life and how devastating it was when her husband walked out on her. She is open and frank with me and I feel as though I've known her my whole life.

"I've never seen my brother this crazy about anyone. I'm glad you came back into his life. He was a wreck without you. He is the best guy in the world and he'll treat you like a queen, I promise."

"He already does."

Alicia speaks up, "Conquian." She gestures towards me.

"What does that mean?" I look at Theresa.

"She wants to know if you play a card game called conquian, I thinks it's a little like your gin rummy. We usually play cards every Sunday."

"No, I'm sorry I don't."

Alicia speaks ups again, "Poker?"

"Si."

"Bueno, poker!" Alicia pulls a deck of cards out of her straw bag.

"Oh, no, Mama's talked you into a game of poker? Watch out, she's a shark," Marcos remarks.

"Yes, but so am I."

"This, I've got to see."

Alicia deals to everyone at the table after she orders

another round of food and cervezas from the waiter. Alicia and I are neck and neck for most of the afternoon, but in the end, I win thanks my numerous experiences in college late night in the dorms.

"You are the first person to beat Mama in years," Marcos explains. Everyone seems delighted that she has finally lost, I only hope she is not mad at me. I probably should have lost intentionally to make a good impression.

Alicia reaches out her hand to shake mine, "Usted debe ser una mujer muy inteligente para poder vencerme."

Everyone at the table bursts into laughter and I look at Marcos questioningly.

"She says you must be a very smart woman to be able to beat her. I think you've just won her respect. Come on, let's go for a swim."

"Wait, I have an idea."

I grab two of the plastic beer cups and two plastic spoons from the table.

"Sigueme!" I say to the kids as I motion for them to follow me to the water's edge.

They eagerly run behind me with Marcos in tow. I drop to my knees on the shore and speedily start to fill the cup with wet sand.

"Just a second," I say as they watch me curiously.

I return to the table and grab two plastic ice buckets and dump out the water, then I place them on the sand about ten feet from the shore.

"Explain to them that we're going to take teams, and whoever fills their bucket with sand first wins."

It's the girls against the boys and the children are delighted, filling their cups with overflowing spoonfuls of sand. Marcos encourages them and so do the adults from their table, cheering them along.

The girls win and Matias demands a rematch, so we

make it the best two out of three. If they had their way, the children would play into the night, but instead we take a swim close to shore.

After playing in the water, we aid the children in their sand castle making and Marcos builds a giant moat around their creation, much to their delight. The sun begins to set and I am sad to be ending such a lovely day with Marcos' family. I can't believe that I was actually nervous about meeting them!

Marcos and I head back to the condo.

"What would you like to do tonight? I feel like we've been eating and drinking all afternoon, so I don't really want anything else. What about you?"

"I think it's time we made love, Alison."

"Oh you do, do you? And do I have any say in the matter?" I smile.

"Of course. I just think we've waited long enough and you're leaving tomorrow. I need to be with you before you leave, I just do. I have to be close to you."

"You don't have to convince me, I was ready when I got here!"

"Come let's take a shower and wash away the sand from today."

I suddenly feel nervous about being with him. I wasn't nervous about being with him five years ago, so why now?

Marcos starts the shower and I follow him in. Soon my worries dissipate as we lather one another with liquid soap and Marcos tickles me numerous times along my waist. I giggle as I recall how much I had enjoyed showering with him in the past. I admire his body as we dry off, especially his muscular arms, which he has worked hard to earn.

Marcos extends his hands to me, "Come, I want to show you how much I have missed you, even if it takes all night." He leads me to the tiny bed and pulls back the sheets. "Tonight will have to tide us over until we can be together again."

We make love with the same intensity with which he kisses.

After little sleep, I'm up at dawn, showered, packed and ready for Marcos to take me to the airport. I can't believe I'm going back home.

I'm taking one last look at the view of la Ropa from my patio when Marcos grabs me from behind.

"Good morning," he gently pushes the hair away from my ear and slowly sways his body from side to side.

"Good morning," I smile.

"Are you okay?"

"Better than okay, but I hate to leave you."

"How are you feeling about us after last night?"

"I feel closer to you than I thought possible."

"Maybe I should kidnap you and lock you away somewhere. We could make love endlessly and no one would ever know what happened to you."

"As enticing as that sounds, I do need to go deal with reality unfortunately."

"I have to confess a part of me worries that you will vanish from me again."

"We're way past that; I hope you know that by now."

Marcos turns me around and kisses me like it's the last time we will ever see one another. He leaves me speechless.

∼

CHAPTER 36

It feels almost eerie to come home to a house that has been visited by numerous strangers in my absence. The realtor says she has several interested parties, but so far no solid offers. I immediately check on the back yard and am pleased to see that the plants have flourished in my absence and that the hydrangeas are actually changing front blue to pink thanks to my addition of lime to the soil.

I've missed Cass terribly and pay her a visit as soon as I return. Without warning her, I ring her doorbell and am surprised to find the Miller household in a state of disarray; even Cass looks a bit disheveled, with her hair tussled and some of her makeup has worn off.

"Oh, Ali, come here let me give you a hug!" She pulls me in with one arm while she holds Sophie in the other. "You've caught us at a terrible time, just look at this mess! We had a birthday party here today and everyone just left."

"Whose birthday is it?"

I look at the mass of toys and crumbled wrapping paper in the living room.

"Nicole's, she's four, can you believe it?"

"I have a gift for her, for all of the girls actually."

"That's sweet of you to think of them. Do you want to come in? You'd be doing so at your own risk."

"That's okay, I just wanted to let you know that I'm home. I have a lot of work to catch up on."

"Listen, George will be home around five and he can watch the girls then. Why don't I come over with a nice bottle of wine and we can enjoy that back yard of yours that you worked so hard on. I'll be ready for a break by then."

"Perfect, see you then."

I feel a little lost in my house. The past two weeks in Mexico are like some sort of dream and now that dream has ended suddenly. Is that my real life or is this?

Reluctantly, I open the piles of work emails that have been waiting for me. These forms are all tedious and boring, I'd much rather be catching fish with Marcos and the children!

Cass arrives a little after five with a very expensive bottle of champagne.

"Is this a special occasion? I don't want you to waste this on me."

Nonsense, this is the perfect time to drink great champagne, for no particular reason at all!

"Come on in, I just put the cushions out on the patio furniture. I want us to enjoy this setting while we still can. Does it feel odd in here to you? It feels weird to me with no more Gracie or Rick. It's like I don't know where I belong anymore."

Cass skillfully opens the bottle of champagne.

"It looks like you've done that a few times before."

"I do like my champagne! Tell me about your trip. I want to know everything about Marcos."

"I don't think there's anything left that I haven't already told you."

"It all sounds heavenly, even with the kids around and everything, right? And you like his family?"

"Yes, it certainly wasn't the romantic trip that I had envisioned, just the two of us walking hand and hand into the sunset, but it was all very positive. I was able to learn a lot about Marcos, who he is and how he lives his life."

"Can you see yourself living there?"

"I'm not sure about that yet, at least I have time. I can keep visiting and get a better feel for it until the house sells."

"It all seems terribly romantic to me, but then again anything would to me these days, running after four little kids all day long."

"You wouldn't have it any other way."

"You've got that right. Listen, Ali, there's something that I need to tell you and I'm not sure how you're going to take it." She refills my champagne flute.

"Uh, oh." My pulse quickens.

"It's about Rick."

"What about him?"

Cass looks up before speaking, "He's engaged."

"Engaged? How can he be engaged when we're not even divorced yet? I thought he didn't love the girlfriend; that she was just a convenience in his life."

"I don't know anything about that, but that's not the worst part."

"Oh shit, what else?" I brace myself.

She hesitates before continuing, "They're getting married because she's pregnant."

I feel a sharp pain in my chest. "What? Cass, that's just unbelievable!"

"I know, honey, I'm sorry. I wanted you to hear it from me and not someone else."

"Why is that I try and try to have a baby without success, and they have one just by accident? It's a cruel turn of events."

"Maybe you just weren't meant to have a baby with Rick and this woman is. Maybe you will end up having babies with Marcos. Think about how complicated your life would have been if you had a baby with Rick, then split up and wanted to move to Mexico. You could never leave the country with joint custody. Things have a way of working out."

"That's true, I never thought of it that way. It would have been a huge mess."

"Maybe not having a baby with Rick was a blessing in disguise."

"I guess so, but it still hurts."

"I have something else to tell you."

"There's more? I'm not sure I want to hear any more."

"This is going to surprise you I think, it sure surprised me."

"I can't imagine what you're going to tell me next, please just get it over with!"

"A few days after you left for Mexico, I was out in the driveway watching the kids on their tricycles and I saw someone ringing your doorbell, so I called out to him. It was your brother, William."

"I guess with everything that's been going on in my life, I forgot to tell him about my trip to Mexico."

"He seemed rather upset and nervous and he asked if he could talk to me. We brought the girls inside and got them busy with coloring so we could talk uninterrupted. He started sobbing, Ali, right off the bat, I didn't know what to do."

"What happened? Is he all right?"

"Yes, he's fine, just emotionally drained. It turns out he's getting a divorce too."

"The perfect couple is getting a divorce? I wonder what Carol thinks of that?"

"He's not so much upset about the divorce as he is about the reason why they are divorcing."

"Don't leave me hanging, what is it?"

"He's gay."

"What? He can't be. I would have known."

"He cried and cried, Ali. Poor guy has been terrified to tell people and he thought telling me would be easier than telling you."

"I'll call him right away and let him know that he has my full support. Does Carol know?"

"Yes."

"That explains why I haven't heard from her in weeks. I wonder how she's taking it."

"I can only imagine."

"Did William say anything about his plans? Is he moving away?"

"Not really, just that he's found someone and wants to be with him."

"Carol must be having a stroke. Is that it, or do you have more shocking news for me?"

"I think that about covers it for now."

"Geez this will teach me not to go away on vacation again!" We both giggle. "Maybe I'm better off on a beach in Mexico!"

CHAPTER 37

I call William and invite him over for dinner, something that I haven't done in ages. I've missed my brother over these past years. We got along growing up and I always looked up to him. I blame our estrangement on Carol more than anything else. The fact that she always compared me to him makes me want to stay away from him and it's certainly not his fault.

He looks distraught as I answer the door.

"Thank you for having me over, I wasn't sure if you would want to see me."

I reach up and give him a big hug. "Of course I want to see you, nothing would ever change that. Come on in."

I hand him a glass of his favorite scotch and soda. "Where are you living now?"

"I got a small apartment in the city, it's pretty nice."

"And how is Beth taking everything?"

"She's being great, actually. She knew all along what I was probably better than I did. I've been in denial for so long, my whole life."

"She's not fighting you on the divorce or custody?"

"Not a bit. She just wants me to be happy and to get on with her own life."

"That must be quite a relief. What about Mom, how is she taking the news?"

"That's a good question. I thought she'd be furious, but I've barely heard a peep out of her. She literally said nothing when I told her and I haven't heard from her since. Does that mean she's cut me out of her life? I have no idea. Naturally, Dad is being supportive, but Mom? I was hoping you could tell me something."

"Sorry, she hasn't been communicating with me either and honestly, it's been a welcome change. I have news of my own that I'm not too anxious to share with her."

"Are you gay too?" It was the first smile I'd seen from him all night.

"No," I chuckle, "but I am in love and he lives in Mexico."

"Mexico, wow, Ali, when did this happen?"

"It's a long story and you don't need to hear it all now. Let's sit down and enjoy our meal. You're my guinea pig tonight. I took a cooking class in Mexico and I'm practicing the recipe tonight on you."

"I'm impressed, sis, you must really love this guy if he's inspiring you to learn how to make his native food."

"I do love him. I have no idea how Mom is going to take my news either."

"I wouldn't worry too much about that. I think I've paved the way for you on that one!"

"That's my big brother, making my life easier for me!"

"Any time, Ali, any time."

Our evening is pleasant and relaxed and I feel closer to my brother than I have in years. I only hope I can continue to keep things this way between us.

In the morning, Cass and I get back to our routine of

walking and coffee on the square. I treasure my neighborhood; the expansive homes with their immaculately manicured lawns always remind me of the *Stepford Wives*. It all looks so idyllic, right down to the adorable brick train station looks like it's from a 1950's movie set.

"I'm not sure what's going to happen with my job. I don't want to travel to China anymore, so I'm not sure if they will keep me on. What if I move to Mexico, then I would probably be out of a job entirely? Then what am I going to do?"

"You could always go back to school and become a lawyer!"

"That's not funny!"

"Sorry, I couldn't help it."

"I'm really nervous about my meeting tomorrow with Katherine. I have to prepare myself for the possibility of being let go."

"You'll be fine, Ali. Even if they fire you, you'll find something else."

"It would all be much easier if I at least knew where I will be living."

"One thing at time."

I make a rare trip into the city for my meeting with Katherine and try to keep my mind calm while listening to NPR as I fight the traffic.

"What can I do for you today?" Katherine greets me with an air of coolness that I take as professionalism and not a personal grudge. She looks polished, as always, in a gray designer suit and simple, yet elegant jewelry. I conclude that she must spend at least an hour every morning straightening her dark blonde, super long hair to perfection.

"I want to talk to you about China. I was hoping that I could step back from the overseas travel."

"When you say 'step back', what does that mean?" Katherine looks imposing from behind her masculine black desk.

"It means that I would prefer not to go at all anymore. I was hoping that I could take over things on this end and stay in the country."

"But with your experience, you're one of our top people in China. We need you over there," her tone softens.

"I know; it's just that the travel is getting to me, the same place over and over again. I need a change. I know how to deal with the clients on this end."

"I have no doubt that you are capable. I'll have to think about it. In the meantime, I can offer you another one of those domestic assignments to Toledo, etc., like last time. That's all I can promise for right now."

Katherine stands and shakes my hand. I leave feeling somewhat disappointed and quite unsure about the future of my career.

Marcos and I talk every night and I sometimes feel as though I'm right there with him when he talks about his day and his family. I have more airline miles than I will ever know what do to with and I convince him that he should use them to visit me in Lake Forest. I know that money is a concern for him, so I take that issue out of the equation, telling him that I never eat out and spend my time taking walks and enjoying my back patio.

He is also concerned about leaving his family while his father's dementia is escalating and his sister is still going through the transition of her divorce. That issue is taken off the table as well when his family decides to move in with his uncle, so he reluctantly agrees to visit me.

"I've never been outside of Mexico, what if I don't fit in? What if your friends don't like me?"

"I felt the same way about meeting your family and see how well that all turned out?"

"That was different."

"You're being silly. Cass will love you and I don't care what my family thinks." I don't mention to him that I haven't told my parents about him yet.

I'm surprised to learn that Marcos is this insecure, but delighted that he talks to me so candidly about everything.

Marcos' trip to visit is planned for the following month and I pass my days with a routine of daily walks with Cass, showing the house as often as possible and a domestic trip for work. I think about visiting James on my road trip and decide to wait until I'm more settled in my life. If I went to visit him now, I would not have any answers for his incessant questions. I wonder if he is moving forward yet with his own restaurant.

As Marcos' visit approaches, I receive a call from him in the middle of the night. I can barely understand him through his hysteria.

"Marcos, what is it? What's wrong?" My heart is pounding, waiting for the worst.

"It's Theresa."

"What about her?"

"She's dead," he sobs uncontrollably.

"Oh my God! What happened?"

"She was killed in a car accident tonight."

"Was she alone? Are the kids okay?"

"Yes, she was alone. Luciana and Matias don't know yet, they're asleep and we don't want to wake them. Those poor children, first their father disappears and now their mother is gone," he continues to sob.

"I'm sorry, Marcos. You two were close and I know how much you love her."

"I do love her and now in an instant that's all changed, everything has changed. Nothing will ever be the same."

"I'm sorry," I don't know what else to say to comfort him.

"There's no way I will be able to come visit you now. I have to make plans with the family."

"Don't be silly, I don't expect you to come under these circumstances."

"Is there any way that you can come here? I need you now, Alison, I really do. Is that possible?" I'm not sure that anyone has ever told me that they needed me before.

"I'll be there as soon as I can. I love you."

"Thank you, I don't know what I would do without you right now."

I lie awake for hours thinking about poor Marcos and his family and realizing how quickly those we love can be taken from us. My heart sinks as I think about Theresa's children and how they are about to have the worst day of their lives.

Inspired by my brother and his coming out to Carol, I decide to invite her for coffee so I can share my news about Marcos. I have no idea what to expect as I meet her at the square.

She arrives without a gift in hand. "Hello Alison, dear, the last time you invited me here for coffee you dropped the bomb on me about your marriage. I can hardly wait to see what news you have in store for me today!"

"That's a rather cynical attitude, Mom. Maybe I have good news to share with you today."

"I certainly hope so, this family could use some good news for a change."

"Is everything all right, Mom? Is Daddy okay?"

"Yes, of course. Don't dally, Dear, tell me what's on your mind."

I'm surprised by how relaxed I'm feeling. Normally I would be tense as heck delivering news like this to Carol. I guess I really don't care how she reacts anymore.

"I've fallen in love."

"This is awfully sudden. Were you having an affair too?"

"No, but I met him before I was married. We've just recently reconnected. It's sort of a long story."

"Is that it? Is that all of your news or is there more?"

"I guess that's it."

"All right, I'll be going then." Carol stands up and straightens her designer belt.

That's it? No reaction? I don't even get to tell her about Marcos and Mexico?

"Okay, Mom. Don't you want to have a conversation? Don't you want to know anything about him or about our plans?"

"No, Dear, I really don't. It's your life and there's nothing for me to say. Goodbye, Alison." Carol grabs her Birkin bag and leaves an almost full cup of coffee on the table.

This is the strangest encounter with Carol yet. I naturally head straight to Cass' house to fill her in on Carol's odd behavior.

"Maybe she's having an affair," Cass speculates.

"More likely that she's dipping into the scotch with her morning coffee."

"I know; she's planning on coming out of the closet too!"

We both roar with laughter.

~

CHAPTER 38

I arrive in Zihua two days after Theresa's death. I have no idea how to prepare myself for what I'm walking into, as I've never lost anyone close to me. My heart breaks the moment I see Marcos' grief-stricken face at the airport.

His embrace feels like a vice as he weeps silently. Eventually, he loosens his grip and composes himself.

"I'm grateful you are here."

This is the first time I've seen him with an unshaven face, and the circles under his eyes are deep.

"I'm afraid this trip isn't going to be much fun for you."

"I'm not here to have fun. Have you had any sleep? You look like you've been up for days."

"I've had a few hours here and there. We've been having Valerio at my uncle's house...it's a prayer vigil for the first few days after someone dies. We've had lots of guests and I need to get back there right away. I will take you to your condo later. I hope that's okay with you."

"I'm here for you, whatever you need from me, that's why I'm here. How are the children holding up?"

"I'm not sure they understand that their mother is gone for good. We've tried to get their father to come see them, but he wants nothing to do with them." Marcos begins to sob again, so I reach my arm behind him and gently rub his back. "My mom can't take care of them, she has her hands full with my dad. We are trying to figure out what's best for the children."

We arrive at Marcos' uncle's house and it's fully decorated with candles and brightly colored flowers. Theresa's body lies on a table in the back of the living room and it's covered with a white sheet. There are a dozen or so family members milling about, drinking beer and talking. This seems shocking to me that people are socializing while there's a fresh corpse in the room, but I understand that this is a tradition that is familiar to Marcos and not to me.

Marcos introduces me to each family member and I feel completely out of place, as if I shouldn't be there at all, until Alicia greets me warmly and offers me a cold cerveza and I accept.

Matias and Luciana run in from the kitchen and each grab one of my legs and squeeze tightly.

"Alison, Alison!" they squeal in unison as they jump up and down. They certainly don't seem to have any concept of the permanence of their mother's absence.

They invite me to watch them play "avion" in the street, which I quickly learn means hopscotch. Matias is at a definite disadvantage with shorter legs than his sister, not to mention a lack of developed coordination skills. I gladly watch them while Marcos fulfills his obligations with his family inside.

After an hour or so Marcos comes to find me.

"I'll take you home now, but I have to come back later. It's the last night of Valerio and I need to be here."

"It's okay, I understand. I was very lucky to get the same condo again, it just happened to be empty this week."

"Yes, it's a nice place."

"When do I get to see your place by the way?"

"Never, we've talked about this before. My place is tiny and I just don't want you to see it."

"Okay, but I wish you would get over that male pride of yours!" I see a faint hint of a smile on his face for the first time since I arrived.

The key is waiting for us in the lobby and Marcos carries my bag up the familiar flights of adobe stairs. Once inside, he embraces me.

"I need to make love to you."

"Now?"

"I mean it. I need to be with you right now, to connect with you. I can't go back there until we've made love."

I'm more than happy to comply with his request and his lovemaking is intense and fiery, even more so than usual. I feel almost intimidated by his fierce emotion.

"We are alive, and we must remember to celebrate that every day." He kisses me passionately and pulls me so close that I can barely breathe as my face presses snugly against his perspiration soaked chest.

"I must leave now. I have no idea when I will be free tomorrow, but I'll call you in the morning and hopefully will know by then. He quickly dresses and is out the door.

I take a long shower and think about Marcos' family and what they are going through. I can't imagine how I would feel if William were to die suddenly.

I dress in a sheer cotton shift and walk to down the hill to the local upscale market which is geared for the tourists. I find a few snacks and a bottle of white wine and head back up the hill to the condo. Wondering what my condo would sell for, I pull out my laptop and begin a search of real estate in the area.

Much to my surprise there is a vast supply of available condos and the prices are better than I would have expected. Some come fully furnished and even have a car thrown in with the deal. It makes sense, people move here and acquire furniture and cars, but when it's time to leave, they don't want the hassle of taking all of that with them. For fun, I send emails to a few realtors and ask to see the properties.

I pour some wine and sit on my deck to enjoy the view. I give a call to Cass.

"How's it going?"

"Okay I guess. It's hard to tell. Marcos is very emotional and the kids don't seem to understand what's going on which is just as well, though Marcos says they've been having terrible nightmares. We went to his uncle's house today and I was really nervous about seeing his family and just being around them when they've just lost a family member. It was all fine though, they're all so nice to me, especially Matias and Luciana."

"They probably sense what a soft spot you have for children."

"That wouldn't surprise me. I've decided to look at some real estate while I'm down here. If Marcos is tied up with family obligations, I may end up with a lot of free time and I may as well make the most of it."

"You really think you're going to move there?"

"I don't know, but I had better start looking seriously into that possibility."

"Things must be going well between the two of you?"

"They are. We are still getting to know one another, but I love him more now than I did the last time I was here. He is so open about his feelings, it catches me by surprise sometimes, but I love that about him. I never have to wonder what he's thinking or if he's being up front with me."

"He sounds like a true Latin lover."

I giggle. "I guess you could say that. What about you, anything new on the home front?"

"Just stuff with the girls and you know how determined I am not to bore you or anyone else with endless stories about my adorable children."

"You know that wouldn't bore me, I love your girls."

"Trust me, even you would find the stories boring. Call me tomorrow and let me know how things are going."

"Will do."

Inspired by Marcos, I retrieve the book he gave me, *the Archetypes of the Collective Unconscious*. I decide it's high time I read this classic, if Marcos can do it so can I. I refill my wine glass before settling in comfortably on the brightly painted patio chaise lounge.

This book looks intense and complicated! Maybe if I take it slowly I can digest it bit by bit. I thumb through the pages and find a chapter entitled, "Psychological Aspects of the Mother Archetype". This book now has my full attention. I start to read the chapter and feel overwhelmed until I doze off.

I'm startled out of a sound sleep by the familiar ring of my cell phone and see that it's Marcos.

"It's daylight, what time is it?" I ask, trying to get my bearings.

"Of course it's daylight, it's 7:30. You're usually up by dawn. Are you okay?"

"Yes, I must have fallen asleep while reading last night. How are you doing? Did you get some sleep?"

"Yes, a little. I need to go to the Mercado for my mother and I thought I could swing by and get you, so we could load you up with supplies for the week. I'll take you back home after and come back, finish up here and then we can spend the evening together. How does that sound?"

"Great. Are you sure I can't help you with anything at your uncle's?"

"Thank you, but no. It means a lot to me that you came yesterday and the rest of this is all boring family stuff. Just knowing that you are here and that I can see you and hold you at any time is helping me get through this. If I pick you up in an hour, will that give you enough time?"

"Yes. I'll wait for you downstairs."

I have just enough time to walk over to Mary's for a coffee and pastry and still get in a shower.

Marcos arrives right on time, as usual, in his father's white truck.

"Good morning, beautiful," he greets me with a kiss.

"Good morning. You do look better today. How are the children holding up?"

"They keep asking when their mother is going to return. They have plenty of people to entertain them for the time being, though, they are upset."

"Tell me about the Mercado, what do they have there?"

Marcos laughs, "It's more like what don't they have there. They have everything, you'll see. Make a list of what you need. You might be overwhelmed and forget once you get there."

"Can't wait to see."

Marcos finds a spot to parallel park on the street. We walk across the street and into what looks like a children's clothing store.

"This isn't what I expected."

"Just follow me." He reaches his hand behind his back and takes my hand as he walks determinedly through the dozens of shops, ranging from toys, to baked goods and much to my dismay, rows of animal carcasses. The pungent odor fills not only my nostrils, but coats my tongue as well, so I can taste the rotting flesh no matter what I do to try and make it go away.

I hold my breath as much as possible and try not to let on how repulsed I am by my surroundings. We stop at a bakery first and load up on breads and rolls, then on to buy fresh produce. I follow Marcos dutifully without uttering a word.

"What else do you need?"

"I'll just get some of whatever you're getting." I try and smile, but I feel as though I'm holding back a desperate need to vomit.

Marcos catches on and laughs, "Would you rather wait in the truck?"

"Yes." I do not hesitate.

He hands me the keys to the truck and I run out of the Mercado as quickly as possible before I throw up in front of everyone. Once inside the truck, I breathe deeply and deliberately, trying to eliminate the disgustingly foul taste in my mouth. I can't erase the image of the blood dripping on to flattened cardboard boxes along the floor.

I run into a nearby drug store and purchase a coke and a pack of gum hoping they will remove the taste from my mouth.

Marcos returns, loaded with bags and packs them into the bed of the truck.

"Are you going to be all right?" He seems amused.

"Yes, I'll be fine. I don't want to talk about it." I feel like a silly tourist who can't handle the realities of every day life in Zihua.

I can hear Marcos chuckling under his breath. I continue to breathe deeply the entire way home. Marcos removes numerous items from several bags and loads them into one for me to keep. He carries it upstairs for me and reminds me that he will be back to spend the evening with me.

Feeling sorry for myself, I head to the beach in search of Marta. She will know how to make me feel better!

When I find her, she is busy with a customer and instructs me to come back in a half-hour. I make good use of the time, walking the beach and still trying to clear the stench from my nostrils. James pops into my mind and I wonder how he is doing and if he has brought his family to Detroit yet. I hope I get to meet his mother one day; I'll bet she's a real kick, having raised a son like James.

I enjoy my hour with Marta more than I have in the past, appreciating the way that she is able to zero in on and remove the kinks in my back and neck. I am inspired to give Marcos a message tonight; he could sure use one after everything he is going through.

Before heading back to the condo, I stop at Mary's for a fish taco and a sparkling water as I contemplate what I might prepare for dinner tonight from the food that Marcos left me.

Once back in the condo, I dig through the groceries and realize that I have no idea what half of them are, let alone how to prepare them. Suddenly, a thought occurs to me and I do an Internet search and am pleasantly surprised to find that Zihua offers numerous choices for pizza delivery!

I take special care in my look; using a lavender salt scrub in the shower and a mud mask on face to tighten my already small pores. Examining myself in the mirror, I find that I look a bit plumper all the way around; my skin is rosier, my hair is thicker with some wave and I even look as though I've put on a few pounds. The absence of my habitual life-long obsession with mentally tracking calories with each and every bite vanishing while I'm here is beginning to show.

Styling my hair and wearing makeup are nearly futile in this humidity, so I opt for a touch of product in my hair and a dab of pink stain on my lips and cheeks.

As I answer the door, I can tell that Marcos has put some effort into his appearance for the evening as well, wearing freshly pressed khaki shorts and a navy shirt. His hair is freshly washed and combed deliberately straight back and the curls are tucked neatly behind his ears. My breath is taken away for a moment as I inhale his fragrance.

We share some Argentinian wine on the patio before the pizza arrives.

"You found pizza delivery! What an industrious woman you are!"

"Since I can't cook, I have to get creative and ordering pizza is one of my specialties."

"I've never had pizza before."

"You're kidding!"

"No, never."

"You are in for a treat then."

Marcos devours the pizza in record time and I am convinced that he is now completely hooked.

"Let's make love."

"Don't you want to wait a while? I would think that you're full after all of that pizza."

"It gave me fuel," he laughs.

Marcos gently pushes my hair off my face and I wonder about my breath after having just eaten garlic-laden pizza. Not seeming to notice, he kisses me languidly as he leads me to the small bed.

"Alison, I want you all the time."

His fervor alarms me, but I willingly comply. He is right about the pizza, it does feed him with extra fuel.

∼

CHAPTER 39

Marcos seems to be fueled again in the morning and takes his time as the sun shines brightly through the open patio doors.

"Would you like some breakfast?"

"I thought you couldn't cook."

"I know how to make an omelet. Café con crema?"

"Si senorita, gracias." He smiles broadly as he continues to recline in the tiny bed.

"What is the plan for today? Do you need to go back to your uncle's?"

"We took care of everything yesterday. Theresa's body is gone and the house is back to normal. Everything is just as it was except for the children. I need to check on the boat today. How would you feel if we took them out fishing?"

"That would be great!"

"Are you sure? My mother could use a break, she can't do it all by herself."

"You need to stop apologizing when it comes to Luciana and Matias. They are a joy to be around and they need all the support they can get right now. Anything that we can do to make them feel better I am willing to do, you just name it. Let's go get them and take them fishing!"

I quickly change into my bikini and shorts and we are out the door. The kids are playing avion again when we arrive at Marcos' uncle's house. They are eager to get in the truck and leave with us.

Like little professionals, the children help prepare the boat for a day of fishing, putting on their own life vests and untying the ropes from the dock. Once inside a quiet cove, they decide to teach me everything they know about fishing and with the language barrier I try my best to follow their instructions while attempting not to break into a laugh. Marcos observes quietly and smiles.

After a couple of hours, we end up with quite a catch and Marcos decides we should have lunch in Las Gatas. He pulls our small boat up to the dock and a man helps us off. Marcos carries a line with several of our recent catch attached.

"Why are you bringing that?"

"You'll see."

The man takes the boat for us, like valet parking, while we walk to the nearby beach and take a seat at one of the many ocean front plastic tables. There are numerous families eating, drinking and playing in the ocean. Marcos excuses himself and returns without the fish.

Marcos orders for us and the children ask if they can play at the water's edge. Marcos and I both watch them carefully as we sip our cervezas.

"This is a pretty nice spot. It looks like it's mostly locals here."

"Usually, but you can take a boat from Playa la Ropa and spend the day here. The food is cheap and the beaches are pristine, as you can see."

The water is clearer and a much more vibrant shade of blue than the murky water in La Ropa.

"And the best part is coming."

I turn behind me and see our waiter carrying several plates of food and one is full of the fish we just caught! What a treat to have someone cook the fish that we just caught less than an hour ago. The children join us for food and quickly return to the water, giving Marcos and me an opportunity to talk, something we haven't done since I got here.

"How are you holding up?"

"I miss her terribly. She was my best friend. I feel a void in my life, but at least I have Matias and Luciana, through them I still have a piece of her."

I reach out and hold his hand.

"What happens now? Has your family discussed what's going to happen with the children?"

"For now, nothing happens, everything stays the same. They will continue to live at my uncle's and I will help as much as I can."

"What about the family business? Your father can't work any more and you don't seem very interested in being a fisherman for the rest of your life."

"You've got that right. If only I had an education, I could do something to earn some real money."

"I've been thinking about your art. Do you have any buyers yet?"

"Just a few here and there."

"I've got an idea. Let's spend some time on the Internet tonight and I'll show you what I'm thinking."

"Alison, if you could help me get out of this life as a fisherman, I would be forever indebted to you."

"You already are," I bend in and kiss him.

Marcos and I join the children in another game of

filling the bucket with sand for the rest of the afternoon and we are all exhausted by the time we return to the marina. The children are fast asleep the moment we enter the truck. Marcos carries them inside to his uncle's and we head back to the condo.

"You should leave some clothes at the condo so you don't have to keep running home every time you want to take a shower."

"Are you inviting me to move in with you?"

"That wouldn't be so bad, would it?" I smile widely.

"That would be heaven." He gently pulls my hair behind my ear and whispers, "Let me show you what it would be like if we lived together."

An hour later, Marcos opens a chilled bottle of wine and offers to prepare an authentic Mexican meal. I offer to get to work on the Internet researching as much as I can find about Marcos' artwork.

This has been an ideal day, I think as I open my laptop. I find a ton of information on gyotaku and formulate some rough price points for the canvases and prints. My first job out of college was in marketing and I think I could help make his business successful on the Internet.

We share a meal of Dorado from our catch with a Verde sauce and polenta. For desert Marcos makes a chocolate mousse with a hint of chili pepper and fresh mint on the side.

"This is fabulous. Forget about me learning how to cook, you can cook for us every night!"

"Does that mean that we are going to be together every night? I hope so, Alison, I hope you decide to move here."

"I must say, things are pointing in that direction at the moment. I can't wait to see some condos this week to get a better idea of what's available here. I need to figure out how I'm going to support myself if I live here."

"You and me both!"

"We may have your problem solved already. Let's take a look." I pull open my laptop.

"I did a search of artwork like yours and there isn't any coming from this area. You could easily have the local market all to yourself. Your work is distinctive; I think you could do very well. How do you feel about selling prints of your work in some of the local stores? You could even start a little charter fishing business and offer canvases of their catches to your customers. They would have a trophy of sorts to take home. Your only problem may be your ability to fill orders quickly enough."

"But, I don't know how to do any of this."

"You get busy making the paintings and I will come to your studio tomorrow to photograph what you have. I can quickly throw together a decent looking website for you. We can even start a social media campaign and you will be able to manage it quite easily. I'll show you how to do everything. You're smart; you'll get it in no time. We need to figure out your price points."

"What if it doesn't work?"

"It will. I will have you up and running with a business of your own by the end of the week. You just need to think of a name for the business."

I think I'm more excited about starting this venture than Marcos is. I've always worked for a large company and now I get to be a part of a small business starting from the ground up!

I can hardly sleep, thinking about the details of getting Marcos set up so that he can do everything when I leave in a few days.

In the morning Marcos and I enjoy our café con crema on the patio while I check my emails.

"Shit!"

"What's wrong?"

"I had a phone appointment with my boss and I missed it. She must be really mad; she wants me to call right away. I hope she doesn't fire me! Shoot, what am I going to do if I lose my job?"

"You can come work for me," he says with a straight face.

"Very funny."

"Just call her and get it over with, then you'll know."

"Oh, no!"

"Now what?"

"My house just sold! I may be out of a job and a place to live all at the same time!"

"Relax, Alison, you're not going to be jobless or homeless. You are a very capable woman." Marcos stands and kisses me on the forehead. "I'm going to make us some breakfast while you call your boss back."

I dread this call, Katherine must be pretty mad and she has every right to be.

"It's Alison Davis for Katherine," I take a deep breath.

"Alison? Where are you? Do you even care about your job any more?"

"I'm sorry, Katherine, I had a personal emergency and I just forgot. There's no excuse."

"You're right about that. First you tell me you don't want to travel to China any more and now this, I don't know what to think. You've been a very dedicated employee until recently. I know you're going through a divorce, but this is inexcusable."

"Katherine, I know, I'm sorry."

"You be here in my office next Tuesday to discuss this and if you don't show up your job here is finished."

"I understand, Katherine. Thank you."

I've worked for Katherine for five years and I barely

know a thing about her. She has always been completely professional with me and I admire her work ethic. I suppose some would describe her as icy, but I see her as competent and I certainly understand why she is upset with me.

"How did it go?" Marcos calls from the kitchen, so I step in to refill our coffee cups.

"I'm still employed, at least for now. I have to be in her office on Tuesday or I'm fired. I'm going to call the realtor now and see what's going on there. Thanks for making breakfast." I lean up on my toes to kiss him before heading back out to the patio. I return after a few minutes to deliver the latest news.

"I've got 30 days to move out."

"That doesn't sound like very much time. How big is your house?"

I don't want Marcos to know that my house is six times the size of his parent's home.

"It's a good size, I just don't have a game plan yet. What am I going to do?"

"Do you want me to go back with you and help you move everything out?"

"Where to? I can't bring it here. I need a place to live."

"I wish I had a home for you to move into."

"I know you do, but you have enough on your plate here without worrying about helping me move. I'll figure it all out somehow. Cass will help me. I'll call her later. Let's enjoy our breakfast."

My mind is buzzing with to do lists; make plans to get home, get a hold of Rick and see what furniture he wants, find a place to move it, find a place to live, keep my job! I wish I hadn't looked at my emails this morning!

After breakfast, Marcos leaves to take the kids and check on the boat while I get ready to meet with a realtor.

Fortunately, she speaks English and has four properties to show me and they are all in the Playa la Ropa area.

I'm surprised by how similar the condos are: all three bedrooms, multi level, adobe, fully furnished, less than 2,000 square feet, access to a pool with a patio and a view of Playa la Ropa. I like them all and try to imagine myself living in them. What would my day-to-day life be like? I certainly wouldn't be spending my time shopping at the Mercado!

I thank the realtor for her time and tell her that I will be in touch. I will show the properties to Marcos on my laptop and see what he thinks; after all I myself also hope he and I will be living under the same roof!

I text Marcos. *Heading back to the condo. Pick me up when you're done so we can take photos or your art, ok?*

I should be there about two.

Now I have a little time to get my life in order. First on the list are plane reservations home for Sunday, that only gives me two more days here, but I don't want to lose my job.

I send a text to Cass. *House sold I have 30 days to move. Help! Call u later.* She will have ideas for me, I have no doubt.

I change out of my dress and into a pair of shorts and camisole. I wrap my wavy hair up into a knot on the top of my head and am downstairs and waiting for Marcos when he arrives. We stop at his favorite little taco place on the way to the studio.

"How do you get them to look so real?"

"I use the whole fish. First, I clean and sterilize the fish, then dry it with a blow dryer, which makes the fish more receptive to the paint. I then create matting for each, cutting out an area the exact size of the fish. The fish is then placed in the hole and the fins, etc. are pinned to the matting. I choose my color or colors, placing the darker color around the outer perimeter, using a dauber, not a brush. When it's covered with paint, I carefully take rice paper and press it in all around. I finish with some watercolor around the eyes to make them stand out. It can make it more complicated with ghost images, but that's the gist of it. The final step is a red stamp called a hanko."

"Wow, I had no idea so much work was involved. How do you manage with a giant fish?"

"Very carefully!"

"How many do you think you have?" I ask, looking around at the lighting in the room.

"Right now, maybe a dozen or so. I sold a few recently."

"Are you happy with the price that you selling them for?"

"I guess so. I don't know how much to charge."

"I'll show you the prices I found when we get back to the condo. Let's start with the most colorful ones first."

I choose several options for lighting and decide to try them all with the same painting and see what works best. Marcos watches me quietly and seems focused as I ask him for help with various shots. We move quickly through the paintings and I take numerous pictures of each one, hoping that at least one of each will turn out well enough to use for Marcos' website. After two hours we are done.

"See that wasn't bad. Let's go back to the condo and make you a website. Have you had a chance to think about a name for your business yet?"

"I don't know, you seem to know much more about this than I do. What do you think?"

I can see that Marcos needs to get his hands involved in this project in order to get enthused about it.

Back in the condo, I quickly load the pictures on to my

laptop and start a template for the website. Marcos watches attentively as I drag and drop the first picture, then play with the image size and color.

"We can go back in later and fill in the description and price. Now you try one."

"I couldn't do that."

"Sure you can, it's easy."

I talk him through the process and he is quite pleased with himself and the result of his efforts.

"Keep going, I'll be right back."

I turn on some soft music and retrieve a couple of cold bottles of water from the fridge.

Marcos is mesmerized as he figures out the best image for each painting and then follows the steps to add it to the template. He completes all the images within an hour.

"See, you're a natural. Soon you won't need me for any of this."

"That's where you're wrong, I will always need you for all of this and for everything."

CHAPTER 40

I t's our last day together before I head back to Lake Forest, so we try to pack as much in as we can. I call the realtor and take Marcos along to see all four condos.

"What do you think?"

"I think they are all magnificent. I could never afford them."

"You're not thinking right. Once your art starts selling you will be able to afford 10 condos. That's how you need to think!"

"I would feel funny living in a place that you are paying for."

"That's ridiculous. You can fish and paint and I can't. Right now I make more money than you do, but that could change at any time, so you need to get over that."

"If it's the only way that I can have you here, then I guess I can suffer through living with you in one of those spacious gorgeous condos." He smiles.

"That's more like it. Which one do you like?"

"I do have a thought…"

"Speak up, what is it?"

"The one with the carport, I was thinking that it would make a nice art studio."

"That's a great idea! Why didn't I think of that?"

"It was just a thought. I know you're not ready to buy yet and that you haven't even decided for sure if you're moving here, but if you do, it's just something to keep in mind."

"I love the idea and you're right about me not knowing what I'm doing yet. I'll have a better idea about things after my meeting on Tuesday."

We spend the rest of the day working on the website and quit in time to take Luciana and Matias on a sunset fishing trip. I'm sad about leaving them and wonder what will happen to them without a mother or father in their lives. They are certainly well loved and don't seem to be lacking for anything. They cling to me when I inform them that I'll be going away for a while. Poor things probably can't comprehend the difference between permanent and temporary absence at their age. I feel guilty about leaving them right now when they need me.

Marcos and I have the last night alone to ourselves and he prepares a special meal with ceviche from our catch and a chilled bottle of my favorite Argentinian wine. After we eat, he hands me another present. It's a tiny package wrapped in pink tissue paper and a red bow. I can tell that he wrapped it himself.

"I made this for you."

It's a delicate silver band and when I look closely, I can see that it's designed with intertwining fish.

"You made this?"

"Yes, it's my first piece of jewelry. You don't have to wear it, but I thought you would think of me when you see it."

"I will always wear it and think of you, thank you,

Marcos. I love it and I hate to say it, but you should think of making these too for your business. It's so unique."

"You sure know how to spoil a romantic moment by turning it into a business conversation."

"Speaking of rings makes me think; you know, we've never talked about marriage or children. Maybe it's time we did that since we could have some obstacles in our way should we decide to get married."

"Like what?"

"Like I'm not Catholic and your family is pretty religious."

"Not an issue. What else?"

I swallow hard knowing what I'm risking by bringing up this topic. "Do you want children? What if I can't have any?"

"Again, not an issue."

"You can't just leave it at that."

"Yes, we should discuss all of these topics, but the bottom line is that nothing is going to keep us apart, so it really doesn't matter, does it?"

"I guess not." Why was I terrified to talk to him about children?

"Yes, I want to marry you. If for some reason we can't get married, then we will live together. Yes, I want babies with you, but if for some reason that doesn't happen, then we'll spend our lives without children or adopt or something. It doesn't matter. You and me, that's all that matters."

"You are something else."

"It's about time you figured that out."

It feels marvelous to have Marcos' arms wrapped snugly around me all night.

In the morning we silently have our coffee and breakfast on the patio before he drives me to the airport.

"Call me tonight?"

"Of course." He looks like a puppy who has just been scolded by his master.

"Get busy with those paintings, that's an order!"

I'm unable to quiet my mind on the plane ride home.

I send a text to Cass the minute I land at O'Hare. *On my way home. Up for a walk in the morning?*

If you're home in time, join us for dinner tonight. Just a casual meal at home with the family.

I would love that. See you soon.

How nice to come home and be able to have a family meal prepared for me with the closest thing I have to family in this town. I realize that this will be the last time I will be coming home to this house; it's sad and exciting all at the same time.

The house feels like a model home without life being lived inside as I enter through the garage. There's a note on the kitchen counter from the realtor and she wants to meet me tomorrow to sign the papers. This is all happening so fast!

I check on the garden first and think of how I will miss coming home to it. I start a load of laundry and shower. It feels foreign to put on real clothes; it's so much easier just to throw on a shift or a bikini and cover up with a pair of thong sandals. I find a nice bottle of Italian wine in the pantry and head across the street to the Miller's. I'm going to miss being so close to them and seeing them so frequently.

The two oldest girls answer the door and they are excited to see me, "It's Auntie Alison, Mom!"

"Tell her to come in."

Cass is busy cooking barefoot in a pair of skin-tight jeans and a form-fitting white silk blouse with white piping. How does she cook a tomato sauce in a white blouse? Baby

Sophie has graduated from the basinet to a playpen and is occupied with sticking numerous plastic toys in her mouth. It must be teething time.

"Sorry, my hands are a mess, come here and give me a hug."

I put my arm around her shoulder and give her a squeeze while she's occupied at the stovetop.

"It smells wonderful in here! You must be using lots of garlic."

"Let me look at you. Mexico agrees with you or maybe it's just Marcos. I've never seen you look this great, Ali, really. You've got a little color, you look relaxed and I'd speculate that you've gained a pound or two."

"Thanks, I feel pretty good. You look great too, as always. Here I brought a bottle of Italian wine."

"What a coincidence, I just happen to be cooking Italian tonight."

"What a surprise." Italian food is all Cassie knows.

"Do you have any plans yet about moving?"

"No, I was hoping that you might be able to help me with that. I'm supposed to meet with the realtor tomorrow to sign the papers, then I'll only have 30 days to be out of the house and I have nowhere to go."

"Don't say that, of course you have somewhere to go. I told you about the carriage house."

"I appreciate that, but what do I do with all of my furniture? I have no idea how much of it Rick is taking, if any. I need to call him tomorrow and find out."

"You could store it all in the garage across the street while they're working on the house, though I can't guarantee that it wouldn't get damaged. They're using part of the garage as a workshop."

"That's very nice of you to offer, but I think I'll just get some movers and stick it all in a storage unit until I figure out the next steps."

"How were the condos that you looked at?" Cass nods her head as she talks.

"I'll know more after I meet with Katherine on Tuesday and see if I still have a job or not. The condos were all livable and quite similar. They were all very colorful with spectacular views of the Pacific, two-story with three bedrooms and two baths. I could easily see living in any of them."

"And Marcos, can you see living with him?"

"I can definitely see living with him. Things are very different there, but his family is great and they make me feel so welcome. Did I tell you that his sister reminded me a lot of you?"

"No, you didn't, how odd. How?

"She was dark, beautiful and very warm."

"Open that wine; we'll be ready to eat soon. You can tell George and me all about your wonderful alter life in Mexico so we can fantasize through you."

Dinner with the Millers is homey and trusting and just what I need.

I meet Cass for our walk and coffee in the morning. I feel sad that this may be one of our last walks together. There are many things I will miss about living here, but I'm happy to trade walks around the golf course for walks on the beach.

"I wanted to tell you about Marcos' art. It's very exciting."

"I'm listening."

"He learned something called gyotaku; it originated in Japan. You basically take a whole fish, daub it with paint and then cover it with rice paper. The end product is quite stunning. Here, take a look.

I show Cass some images on my phone.

"Those really are spectacular. You've got a talented guy there."

"I know."

The realtor and notary show up promptly at nine and I sign what seems like dozens of papers. As soon as we're finished I text Rick and he agrees to come to the house after work and go through the furniture with me.

I find a storage unit that's easily accessible and schedule movers for a week before the closing. That should leave a little cushion just in case things don't go exactly according to plan.

I spend the day catching up on work emails and before I know it, the day is almost over and Rick is at the door. Funny, I haven't seen him since he moved out and I feel no emotion towards him as I open the front door. He feels more like an old friend than a soon-to-be ex-husband.

"Come on in." He looks a little tired, still in his suit from work.

"You look great, Al, have you been on vacation?"

"Sort of." I don't feel like sharing the intimacies of my life with a man who barely gave me the time of day when we were married. It's a little late to get close now, maybe we can be acquaintances, but I have no interest in anything more than that and I also feel no ill will towards him.

"Have you given any thought to what furniture you want?"

"Not really. I'm living in a furnished apartment now, but soon I'll be getting a new house and will have a better idea of what I'll need. What about you, what do you want?"

"I'm kind of in limbo myself. I have an idea that might work for both of us. I've scheduled movers and a storage unit. Why don't we move everything into storage, share the cost until we each figure out what we need. I don't really have any emotional attachment to anything here, do you?"

"Really, you don't, I kind of thought you would want to hang on to some of the memories from our marriage."

"No, not really."

"Okay then, it's a plan. Just let me know what I owe you. By the way, I have our final divorce papers here for you to sign. You should have your lawyer take a look first. Would you be able to get them back to me by the end of the week? I'm kind of in a hurry."

"So I heard."

I think Rick is more uncomfortable about this topic than I am.

"Sure, no problem."

I walk Rick to the front door and am astonished that I feel nothing for this man that I was married to for three years. How does that happen?

Cass and I get in an early walk before I have to head to the city for my meeting with Katherine.

"Are you nervous about your meeting today?"

"Oddly enough, I'm not. There have been so many changes in my life lately that I've just decided to go with the flow and not fight things when they happen. If I get fired today, something else will work out."

"That's a great attitude! Worrying doesn't benefit anyone. I'll be anxious to hear what happens."

"I'll call you on my way home."

I listen to NPR and feel calm as I drive to the city and fortunately miss the morning rush hour traffic. Katherine exudes her same cool demeanor as she greets me.

"Have a seat, Alison. I've been thinking quite a bit about your situation and I have some ideas, but first I want to hear your thoughts about your job as it is and I want you to be completely candid with me."

This is not what I expected. "To be perfectly honest, Katherine, the job has served me well in the past. I didn't realize this at the time, but one of the reasons that it worked well for me was that it took me away from my marriage frequently enough that I could pretend that things were fine between us. I looked forward to being away from my husband and my problems at home. Now that my marriage is over, I don't have a need to run away and I really don't want to travel as much as I was."

"I can understand that. How would you feel about traveling to China a few times a year instead of every six weeks?"

"That sounds doable."

"This is what I am thinking. You are a valuable asset to our firm and I don't want to lose you. I thought we could move you to an advisory position were you could train and supervise new hires. Most of your work would involve emails and phone calls from your trainees. There's a catch though."

So far this is sounding pretty good. "What is that?"

"Technically, you would be getting a pay raise, but your hours would be cut back tremendously. It would end up being a large pay cut for you, but it would also give you the freedom that it sounds like you're looking for."

"Does is matter where I live?"

"As long as you have Internet, cell service and make it to China about four times a year, you can live anywhere you like."

What a relief to hear that.

"It sounds ideal, Katherine. Would you draw up a proposal for me, so I will have an idea of salary, etc., before I commit?"

"Certainly, I hope this works out, Alison. You're one of our best employees and we want to keep you."

"Thank you, I think this is going to be a good solution for me."

While fighting the downtown traffic on my way home, I think about my job and what it means to me. I wouldn't exactly call it my dream job, but I do take a certain sense of pride in my ability to do it well. Would I consider another career? Absolutely, but what I do not know. In the meantime, I think Katherine's offer is a reasonable transition for me. The pay cut scares me a little, but it helps to know that I can always go back to my old job if necessary.

I call Cass on the way home, fill her in on the meeting and invite them over for dinner. I have an idea, but I need to make a couple of phone calls first.

CHAPTER 41

I stop at a Mexican grocery store in Highwood on the way home and load up on masa and cornhusks for dinner. I cut the pork roast into cubes and leave it to simmer on the stove while I make a couple of calls and Internet searches and gather the information that I'm looking for. An email comes in from Katherine with an attachment laying out the details of our agreement, should I accept. The salary is a big cut, as expected, but so are the hours.

Carol has been incommunicado since our coffee date and I'm beginning to get concerned. I call her, but she doesn't pick up, so I try Daddy next.

"Do you have any idea what's going on with Mom? She's not talking to me and last I heard she wasn't talking to William either. It's so unlike her, is everything okay?"

"You know your mother, she never tells me what's going on. Yes, I would say she's acting strange, but she never lets me in on anything. I would just let it go for now and give her time, she's obviously going through something and I'm sure it will pass."

I know Daddy is trying to make me feel better, but I

can't help but feel uneasy about her silence, so I call William to see if he knows anything.

"She still hasn't spoken to me since I came out to her. I know nothing and honestly I prefer her silence to the barrage of her opinions."

"I know what you mean. Listen, while I've got you on the phone, why don't you pick a night and bring your new friend over for dinner. I would love to meet him."

"Really? That would mean a lot, Ali, thank you. I'll get back to you."

I watch Isabella's video again as I try to perfect the tamales one more time. I set the patio table for dinner and am fully prepared for the Miller's when they arrive.

"You're cooking and it's not spaghetti, I'm impressed."

"Don't be until you've tried it."

"Seriously, Ali, you really are embracing this whole Mexico thing. I wish I could be more like you. I'd be too afraid to run off to a foreign country and jump in with both feet."

"Hey, do you mind if I watch golf until dinner is ready?"

Poor George doesn't have Rick to hang out with anymore.

"Please, make yourself at home, George, we'll be outside."

Cass and I make ourselves comfortable where we can keep an eye on the girls who are busily playing on the swing set.

As I look as the backyard, I think of all the dreams I had that were attached to it. How I imagined our children playing here and lots of family barbeques. Now all those dreams have vanished so quickly.

"So there have been a lot of changes in my life today."

"Like what, other than your meeting?"

"Like I feel as though I've signed my life away today. I signed the papers on the house, the divorce papers and the agreement with Katherine, that's a lot of change for 24 hours."

"You already signed the agreement? Is it what you wanted?"

"Not exactly, but I think it will work out pretty well. This is what I have in mind, are you ready?"

She nods, smiling.

"Rick and I agree to put everything in storage and divide it up later as we need it. I called the realtor in Mexico today and explained that my house is in escrow, but that I'm interested in one of the condos."

"You've decided to move there for sure?"

"I'll get to that. Down there you have to pay cash, so she's going to do her best to hold the condo for me until I have the cash in 30 days. I will have enough from the sale of the house to pay cash and have plenty left over as a cushion in case I need it. I will be taking a big pay cut, but the cost of living is so much lower there and I could pick up something part time if necessary. It's all just falling into place, Cass, and I have nothing to lose by trying this, nothing. The only thing I will miss here is you guys and we can still talk every day and visit often I hope."

"I'm not worried about that, I'm just sort of stunned at how quickly this has all come together."

"I haven't even told Marcos yet."

"There are just a couple of loose ends."

"What's that?"

"Do you think George will sell the sedan for me? The other hitch is how much I'm going to miss you."

"Of course George would do that for you and I'm going to miss the heck out of you, too. But we'll talk all the time. Friendships don't die."

I tell Marcos my news on our nightly phone call and he is so surprised he's almost speechless.

"You mean you will actually be living here in a month?"

"Yes, hopefully in the condo with the carport. Wouldn't that be ideal?"

"There must be so much for you to do."

"Not really, I'm just bringing my summer clothes and everything else goes in storage."

I just can't believe it. Have you told your parents yet?"

"My mother is sort of MIA at the moment, I haven't talked to her in quite some time. She's acting very odd and we don't know why."

"Are you worried about her?"

"I was, but Daddy says she's fine."

"Is it easier for you when she's not around criticizing you?"

"Sad to say, but it is."

"Have you ever thought about talking to her about her criticism?"

"I think she would have my head if I did that."

"Maybe she doesn't hear herself and how negative she sounds. What have you got to lose?"

"I'll think about it. I'm going to have plenty of free time to help you with your business. Have you been painting madly?"

"As a matter of fact I have. My goal has been finishing two a day and I've been keeping to it."

"Do you think you could make some that are really big, like big enough to cover an entire wall, like a mural?"

"I guess so, I could use several smaller fish. It would require a lot of work."

"Would it be worth $5,000 US to you?"

"Are you kidding?"

"No, I'm not. I've been researching and I think you could get $5,000 for the murals and $700 and up for the small ones like you've been making. I have lots of contacts and I think people will be very interested."

"Alison, I would be rich!"

"That's what I've been trying to tell you!"

Two nights later, William arrives for dinner with his friend, John, a commodities broker from New York. He's young and energetic and he seems to make William very happy. I break my news to William during dinner.

"Little sister, I didn't know you had this in you, I'm so proud of you, following your heart and just starting a new life. You're fearless, I had no idea that timid little Ali was hiding a tigress inside!"

"Let's not be too dramatic, William, it's only Mexico, it's not like I'm moving around the world."

"It's still a bold move and I can't wait for you to get settled so we can come and visit."

"I hope you mean it."

All of my loose ends continue to tie up quickly and I spend every free moment with Cass, George and the girls. If only I knew what was going on with Carol, but I've never understood her and maybe I never will.

Thirty days fly by and before I know it, Cass is dropping me at O'Hare with the two biggest suitcases I could find. We hug goodbye and I say so long to my life as I know it in Illinois.

～

CHAPTER 42

I am surprised to see the entire Aiza family when I
pass through the doors at the Zihuatenejo airport.

"Wow, I never expected all of you to come!"
Everyone hugs me, including Uncle Jorge.

"I'm sorry, Alison, they insisted. I couldn't stop them."
Marcos looks much more relaxed than the last time I was
here.

"Don't be silly, it's a wonderful surprise."

"Don't worry they're not coming with us to the
condo."

"It would be all right if they did. We'd better hurry
though, the realtor is meeting us there in a half-hour."

"Thank you, everyone for coming, I'll see you soon."
Matias and Luciana wave enthusiastically as they walk
away.

"Hello, by the way," I say as I deliver a kiss to my
driver.

"Hello, nice to see you."

"Is it weird that I won't be leaving any more?"

"Weird, it's fantastic. Let's get married," he grins.

"Now?"

"No, but soon."

"The ink isn't dry on my divorce papers, let's give it a little time – the weekend," I laugh. I roll down the window trying to circulate some air.

"I'm excited that you're here. If I'm too intense for you with my eagerness, just tell me to back off and I will."

"I don't want you to back off, okay?"

"Okay, I just hope I don't drive you crazy."

How could having the man that I adore paying attention to me drive me crazy?

Mrs. Vasques is waiting for us at the condo when we arrive. She has received partial payment and preliminary paperwork from me, so we are here to do a final walk through and finish the signing the contracts.

The condo is fully furnished, including a completely stocked kitchen and an old VW van in the carport.

"Do you have any questions for me?" Mrs. Vasquez asks.

"I don't think so, thank you."

"Call me if you think of anything. Here are your keys."

"Thank you so much."

"I can't believe I'm a home owner in Mexico!"

"Quick, let's christen the house."

"Now?"

"Yes, before my family shows up. I'm kidding about the family, but not the christening. What room shall we start with?"

"I think I'm going to like living here!"

We spend the next couple of days settling in to our new place and fortunately Marcos volunteers to stock up for me at the Mercado.

"Do want me to bring back some fresh steak for dinner?"

"Disgusting, just the thought of that. There will be no

eating of beef or pork while I live here, it's fish or nothing."

"You're going to get awfully tired of fish."

"Never!"

Marcos brings his few belongings and permanently leaves his little apartment. Matias and Luciana spend as much time as they can with us at the new condo and Marcos keeps them busy with lots of chores.

"What do you think if I convert the carport now to a studio. Is it too soon? Am I crowding you?"

"Of course you're not crowding me. You should renovate it right away, so you can get to work making your millions."

"It's going to take a little time to pour a new floor, add walls with windows, add electricity and running water. Plus I think we'll need lots of shelving."

"You know how to do all that?"

"Who do you think has been doing all of the repairs on my parents house for the last 20 years?"

"I'm impressed. Do you really need running water and electricity? Isn't natural light enough?"

"I don't want to be tracking paint into the condo. It will be much better this way. I also thought it would be fun to have a place where Luciana and Matias could paint too. I want to teach them."

"Only on the condition that you teach me as well."

Marcos invites me on a surprise afternoon cruise on his boat and takes me to the same cove where we first saw the Tortuga mating. He stops the boat and drops anchor.

"You're in a romantic mood."

"I have a surprise for you."

Marcos hands me a pair of flippers and a snorkel with a mask. I can feel my heart rate increase.

"We're going to snorkel?"

"Yes. I want you to see what's underneath the surface."

I'm too embarrassed and too proud to mention to him that I have a fear of snorkeling.

"I haven't done this is years, remind me what to do."

The truth is that I tried this once as a kid and had such a terrifying experience that I've blocked out what to do.

"Get the fins wet first."

I'm silent as I copy what Marcos is doing. I can do this, I tell myself. Just don't think about it!

My heart beats faster as I watch Marcos slide into the water. Reluctantly, I slowly climb down the step ladder and gently do a breast stoke towards him. I don't take my eyes off Marcos as I do my best to stay calm. I follow him towards the shore and actually find myself enjoying the warmth of the water and the movement of the small sea life around me. As long as no large creatures appear out of nowhere, I'll be fine.

We make it to shore and find that the rocks are rugged and too dangerous to touch, so we turn around towards the boat and I feel unnerved when I see how far we are from the boat. Without trying to be too obvious, I make a direct line back to the boat, pull myself in and towel off. Marcos takes his time, entering the boat about 15 long minutes behind me.

"You didn't stay in very long."

"I had enough," I respond nonchalantly.

That evening I confess to Marcos how fearful I had been in the water.

"I had no idea. You should have told me. I would have stayed by your side."

"I was too embarrassed to tell you."

"I'm your partner, if you can't tell me who can you tell?"

After a week of settling in, we invite Marcos' family

over to spend Sunday afternoon. Even though I barely knew her, it feels strange not to have Theresa there. I realize that this is the first time in my life that I've felt like part of a family, except of course for being around the Miller's. I love the mayhem.

"I've been thinking," I mention to Marcos after everyone leaves.

"And what is that?"

"I think Matias and Luciana should live with us. Your father is getting worse every day and they're here all the time anyway."

"That's a big step."

"Not really, to me it makes perfect sense."

"Theresa would be very pleased."

"Good, then it's settled, from now on they live here with us."

"I have a surprise for you, the turtles are laying their eggs tonight and I want you to see it."

"I've always wanted to see that."

"Let's go then, my friends at Villa Del Sol just called and they're already down there."

We arrive at high tide in front of the hotel. It's pitch dark, but we use our cellphones as flashlights. There are a dozen or so large females making their way up the beach looking for just the perfect spot to lay their eggs. I get a good look at the face of one and she looks like she's crying. I wonder if the turtles feel pain in labor just as humans do.

The ancient creatures are single mindedly determined to carry out their genetic mission and they work tirelessly flapping their legs methodically back and forth until they have a hole big enough for their eggs.

"How many eggs is she laying?"

"Average is 110."

"Wow!"

As soon as the Tortuga is finished laying her eggs, Marcos retrieves a large bucket and shovel and begins digging up her eggs.

"What are you doing? She just worked so hard to did that hole!"

"We're protecting the eggs."

I look down the beach and see that Marcos' friends are all digging up eggs too.

"Can't someone just watch over them?"

"24 hours a day? It's not practical. There's a sanctuary down the beach that's designated just for the baby turtles. They will stay there until they hatch and then we help them get safely to the water. Without it, most of the babies are eaten by predators before they ever make it to the water."

I don't know about this. Something always seems to go wrong when man interferes with Mother Nature.

The mothers disappear back into the sea as quickly as they arrived and the excitement is all over.

The next day we give the children the news about them living with us full time and they are ecstatic. There isn't a transition period for any of us. We naturally develop into a routine that works for all of us; one that involves afternoon painting sessions in the new studio.

A couple of months into our new life, I hear the doorbell ring for the first time at the condo. Everyone has always knocked, who would be ringing our bell? I open the front door and am astonished to see Cass standing on the other side, holding a potted plant.

"What are you doing here?"

"I came to bring you a house warming gift. You didn't think I was going to let you move away without me checking out your new life did you?"

She's dressed in an adorable white romper.

"You're so tan! Are you by yourself?"

"I have my lover waiting for me back at the hotel. Of course, I'm not alone; I came with George and the girls. We've rented a condo up the hill for the week."

"Come in. You did a good job of keeping this a secret from me."

"I can keep secrets when I have to."

"Where is that man of yours? I'm dying to meet him."

Cass scopes out her surroundings.

"He's around. Let me show you the place first. Follow me."

"It's all so bright and vibrant. Did you paint all of this furniture yourself?"

"It came like this, I didn't have to buy a thing. Do you like it?"

"It's sensational, Ali, really spectacular. Your view of the Pacific is impressive, even better than our view of the golf course."

We find Marcos in the studio with the kids and they're working on a fish painting. They're covered in green paint.

"Marcos, we have a visitor."

He looks up from his kneeling position on the floor.

"Oh, hello," his smile is magnetic.

"This is Cass."

"From Illinois?"

"Yes."

Marcos quickly stands and attempts to straighten his shirt and hair. He extends his hand, and then quickly retracts it once he sees how much paint is on it. "Nice to meet you."

Cass whispers in my ear, "He makes Rick look like dog meat."

"Cass!"

"Nice to meet you Marcos. It's nice to finally put a face with the stories that I've been hearing about you for the past months."

I interrupt before she says anything else embarrassing, "This is Luciana and Matias."

"Hola," they say in unison.

"Look at you all domestic and everything."

"Cass, stop."

"Okay, I'll behave."

"What are your plans while you're here?" Marcos asks.

"To spend as much time with Ali as possible."

"How about a sunset cruise later? We could catch some fish and then come back here and cook it for dinner, sound good?"

"That sounds phenomenal. Who are you, Ali? A fisherwoman, cook, my goodness I can't wait to see what's next."

"Enough of the sarcasm, we'll see you back here about five? Do you have a car? Marcos can give you a ride back now and pick you guys up later."

"We're just up the hill, within walking distance. See you at five."

"Thank you for coming, Cass. I'm pleased you're here."

"That's the whole idea."

I watch her head up the steep hill and am impressed by what a good friend she is and how fortunate I am to have her. I find Marcos and the kids still working on their painting.

"How much longer do you need to finish that? We're meeting them at five and everyone needs a good scrubbing before we leave."

The children look at Marcos questioningly, so he

interprets for me and I can tell by their tone that they're unhappy about the prospect of a bath.

"Cass seems like a nice woman. You had no idea she was coming?"

"None. Do you see why she reminds me of Theresa?"

"A little, yes I do."

At five, we all pile into my beat up old van and Marcos drives us to the marina. It will be a while before I have the confidence to drive around Zihua, if ever. The drivers are crazy around here and I'm not sure I would do well at dodging cars.

Even with the language barrier, Matias and Luciana take control and direct everyone where to sit and what to do. We soon find one of our favorite coves and they take over with fishing lessons.

"They're a riot," Cass whispers to me.

"Aren't they though?"

"You'd never know they just lost their mother. They seem pretty happy."

"I think they are, they have a lot of people who love them."

"Mostly you and Marcos, it looks like you got your family, Ali."

Cass is right and it never even occurred to me what a ready-made family I stepped into; I haven't thought about having a baby of my own for months now.

The children catch enough fish for our meal and we end up making the trip a nightly event while the Millers are in town. Marcos prepares a Veracruz style dish with our catch that is to die for and the Miller girls become fast friends with Matias and Luciana despite the not speaking the same language.

For the rest of the week, we take turns taking care of all six kids. George and Marcos, who have hit it off, watch them so Cass and I can walk La Ropa and have massages, then we return the favor so the men can fish by themselves and go golfing. It turns out that Marcos is quite a golfer thanks to one of the regular guests at Villa Del Sol who insisted on teaching him.

We eat at Mary's as often as possible, so the children can play on the shore. On their last night, the Miller's share some news with us.

"This isn't a one time trip for us. We've been checking into real estate this week and have put an offer in on something. See that big house up there on the hill?" Cass asks.

"You mean that huge one in the middle with all of the windows?"

"That's the one. We're turning it into a vacation rental, so you will be seeing lots of us. We're going to get down here as often as we can. We see why you love it as much as you do. Who knows, we may buy more properties and make them vacation rentals as well."

Cass and I take a long morning walk together on the beach on her last day. I watch the sun glisten on the water as the waves splash against the shore.

"What do you think about this setting? Does it compare to our walks in Lake Forest?"

"There's obviously no comparison. This place is really special. You're so fortunate to be living here. You know how you said you were always envious of me?"

"Sure."

"Now the tables have turned and I'm envious of you. Don't get me wrong, I love my life, but you've got something incredible here, Ali. You were brave enough to change your life and look at you now. You positively glow, it's like you've stepped into your own. Marcos obviously adores you and it's so nice to see your face light up when you talk about him, and the way you two look at each other. I'm just very happy for you, and so proud of you."

"Thanks. I am happy and I'm glad you understand why I changed my life so drastically. It all just fell into place as soon as I stopped trying so hard to make a life work that wasn't working."

CHAPTER 43

Over the following couple of months we settle effortlessly into our new lives. On most days, I enthusiastically greet the day by dawn. We have a breakfast of pastries or eggs on the patio before Marcos drops the kids at preschool. I normally have time for a long walk on La Playa and by the time I return, Marcos is working away in the studio. I spend a few hours marketing on the Internet or packaging his paintings. We have a lovely lunch, of fish, then it's off to post the art and pick up the kids. We spend an hour or two all together in the studio, with Marcos giving us lessons mostly and before dinner we have time for a sunset cruise and fishing. We all prepare the evening meal together, more fish and fresh vegetables. The days are so full that we're all happily exhausted and ready for sleep by the time it arrives so we can be rested when it's time to get up in the morning and do it all over again.

I'm astonished that's there's really nothing that I miss from my old life, especially since Cass will be visiting regularly. I feel a contentment that I've never known before. I don't worry about whom I can please and how or what I can do to fill a void in my life, like having a baby. We are a family; and we don't look like any kind of family that I ever would have imagined for myself.

Marcos and I work diligently at getting his online business up and running and, as predicted, demand is superseding supply. He works tirelessly creating new canvases while I do most of the shipping.

I become involved in the local elementary school by teaching an English class once a week. It doesn't pay anything, but I am inspired by the level of English that both Marcos and Theresa learned from Americans living in the area when they were in school.

Marcos and I are preparing for our wedding as I also prepare for my first trip to China in many months.

One afternoon, while planting bougainvilleas, dahlias and birds of paradise in numerous pots on the balcony, I see an unfamiliar number of my cell.

"Hello?"

"Alison, it's your mother."

My heart races, "Mom, I haven't heard from you in so long, I was wondering if you were all right."

"I'm fine, dear. Your father and I are staying at a place here in your town. I can never remember the name of this place. We're staying at Villa Del Sol."

"You're here in Zihua?" My heart is pounding.

"Yes, that's right. We came to see you."

"Why didn't you tell me?"

"We just decided to make a little vacation out of it. We've never been to Mexico. You don't need to entertain us. The hotel has scheduled several excursions for us, but we would like to see you. They've made us a reservation at a little place called Amuleto. May we stop by for a drink on the way? We just need your address and a driver will bring us."

"Okay, but I don't think we have time to get cleaned up before you get here."

"Don't worry about that. See you soon."

"Who was that?"

"My mother, she's on her way over!"

"She's here? I thought she had gone missing."

"She had. Quick, everyone we need to get cleaned up fast! Baths and showers and your best clothes."

"Alison, it's just your mother, she's not going to care what we're wearing."

"You don't know my mother."

How did Carol find me? As far as I knew, she knows nothing about my move. This could be a huge disaster!

We scramble to get ourselves ready. Marcos helps bathe the kids while I frantically try and pick up the numerous toys and shipping supplies strewn about the condo. Marcos gets the kids settled with colored pencils and paper on the patio while I fill the ice bucket. Do we even have any scotch? I doubt that mom will drink tequila.

The doorbell rings and I try to calm my nerves before answering.

"Mom! Daddy! What a surprise! Please come in."

I watch Carol's face to read her reaction to the condo and I see no expression at all. Daddy speaks first.

"This is just lovely, Alison. I'll bet you never tire of the view."

"How did you find me?"

"I called your friend, Cass. She filled me in on everything."

By everything, I take it that Cass informed her about Marcos and the kids.

I take my parents to the deck and Marcos stands, looking neatly pressed and showered.

"Mom and Daddy, this is my fiancé, Marcos, and his niece and nephew, Luciana and Matias."

Carol still shows no expression as she calmly shakes Marcos' hand and says hello to the children.

"What would you like to drink? I don't think we have any scotch."

"Some wine or a beer will be fine."

My mother drinking a beer?

"A beer is fine with me," Daddy chimes in.

I frantically attempt to assemble a plate of hors d'oeuvres as Marcos chats with them casually on the deck. This all feels like a dream to me.

We chat superficially until the topic of Marcos' art comes up and my parents ask to see it. Marcos proudly takes them to his studio and shows off his latest creations, which includes one of his murals; a four by twelve foot canvas with, what looks like, the skeleton of a giant fish in various shades of black, orange and gold.

Carol tilts her head from side to side as she studies the massive canvas.

"How in the world did you do this? Is this from a real fish?"

How odd that Carol is this interested in Marcos' painting.

"Yes, I caught it myself. It's a tuna."

"But, how did you do this? It's quite stunning."

"It's not as easy as it looks and would be difficult to explain. I have to clean it first, there are many stages."

"How long does it take you to make one of these?"

"From beginning to end, a few days. The smaller ones go quicker, of course."

I can't believe Carol is asking him so many questions; she genuinely seems interested.

"And how do you make them look so real?"

"Because I'm using the whole fish, gills and all."

"I still don't understand how you do it."

"I'd be happy to show you if you like."

"Would you give me a lesson and teach me how to do it?"

I somehow can't imagine Carol scrubbing the slime off a fish then fluffing its scales.

Their conversation is interrupted as a cab arrives to take Carol and Daddy to dinner.

"When will I see you again?" I ask.

"Soon, I hope."

"Enjoy your dinner, you're in for a real treat."

Carol and Daddy politely say goodbye and they're gone as quickly as they arrived.

"They seem very nice. Are you hurt that they didn't invite us, or at least you, to have dinner with them?"

"Not at all. Showing up here was a big deal for my mom; I'm sure that having dinner with us too would have unhinged her!"

I call Cass and pick her brain about what she had told Carol. She doesn't know much. Cass decided to fill my mother in on everything and save me the trouble later, she also promised to keep Carol's upcoming visit to Zihua a secret. "No reason for you to get all stressed out about it."

"Did she react at all, or say anything about William?"

"Not a thing."

"By the way, Carol's weird behavior continues. She's requested an art lesson from Marcos. Who ever would have guessed she be bonding with him over anything!"

Two days later, I receive a call from Carol and she asks me to join her for a drink at Villa Del Sol and I agree. It feels funny to be visiting Villa Del Sol as a local who is now engaged to one of their ex-bartenders! I feel like I fit in with the staff now, though I certainly don't look like them, more than with the vacationers who fill the leather woven chairs around the Coral bar. Carol and I enjoy the view of the Pacific as we place our drink orders.

"I can see you've been doing a little shopping."

"Oh, my clothes? Aren't the colors just wonderful?"

Apparently Mom likes the embroidered clothes as much as I do.

"Mom, I have to say, you've got me stumped. I have no idea what's going on with you."

"What do you mean?"

"I don't hear from you in months and then you show up and don't criticize me once, that's not like you. What's going on? You know I tried to call you."

"Is that how you see me, as critical?"

"Of course I do, you've been criticizing me my entire life."

"You shouldn't speak to me this way."

"But, it's true. Why have you always disliked me so?"

"Dislike you? I adore you."

"You do?"

"Of course I do, that's why I've always been hard on you. I didn't want you to end up like me."

"What do you mean, like you?"

"I loathe myself. I've been miserable my whole adult life and I didn't want you to end up feeling as miserable as I do."

"But, why are you so miserable? You have a pretty good life, Mom."

"I wanted a career and I ended up being pressured into an early marriage with your father. All these years I've blamed him for feeling as stuck as I do. If I had been a successful career woman, like I wanted to be I wouldn't have been stuck in a bad marriage with two kids and no where to go."

I can see tears developing in the corner of my mother's eyes.

"That's why I pushed you so hard, so you wouldn't end up like me."

"But that's what you wanted, it's not what I want and Daddy has never stood in your way of anything. If you had wanted to pursue a career, he would have supported you."

"It's not that simple. When William told me about his sexuality and how he was moving on with his life, I was so envious. He was brave enough to make a move to have a more content life...and then you; you did the same thing. Do you know how extraordinary I think you are for making such brazen changes in your life? You and your brother have done something that I never had the nerve to do. You've found a man who cherishes you and you're wonderful with those children; you don't even speak the same language and you just took them in as if they were your own. Look at you; you've blossomed into a formidable woman. You left that fragile, little Alison back in Illinois. I'm so proud of you." Carol dabs her tears with a tissue.

I've waited my entire life to hear her say that.

"I had no idea you felt this way. I always thought that I was nothing but a big disappointment to you."

"Well, you're not."

"But, still, I have to ask."

"About?"

"The speech classes. Certainly you were embarrassed by me then."

"What on earth are you talking about?"

"Every year when I got tested for speech and failed, I could feel you pull away from me until it seemed that we had no connection at all."

"You think I was embarrassed by your speech class?"

"Yes, admit it, Mom."

"I was never embarrassed, and I can't believe that is what you've been thinking all this time. If I pulled away it was only because I felt that I had failed you somehow. I had no idea how to help you, so I just left it to the professionals."

"But I needed you then."

"I'm afraid I wasn't a good mother. My mother was overbearing and overly involved in my life and I didn't want to be like that."

"Is that why you never came to any of my school events?"

"Yes, I wanted to give you lots of space."

"I didn't want space, Mom, I wanted you and your attention."

"I'm sorry Alison, I wish I had been one of those great moms who their daughters adored, but I didn't know how. It's not an excuse, just a fact."

"I'm sorry you had a difficult relationship with your mom. You've never talked about her. I hope you'll share more about that with me. You know, Mom, it's not too late. What did you want to do with your life?"

"Seriously? I always dreamed of being an interior designer."

"That makes sense, you've always managed to create beautiful houses. You should do it! Daddy will support you, he's not the enemy, Mom, he's a good man. Go back to school."

"But, I'm too old, I've missed my chance."

"There are lots of older people in school now, you'll fit right in. I'm sure you could take classes online if that's more comfortable for you. No excuses, Mom""

"You're right I guess."

"I'm glad we had this talk. I hope you will come back for the wedding."

"I'm glad we talked too, and of course I'll come back for your wedding."

"You can help me design the wedding, it could be your first assignment, what do you say?"

Carol's face lights up. "Of course, I would love that!"

The following week, I'm on my way to China and I'm excited to be seeing James after all this time. He is going to be surprised at how the changes have all been in the direction towards my personal fulfillment and expansion.

I have a special gyotaku print tucked neatly inside a tube mailer for my favorite bartender. I step inside the dimly lit room and scan the area for his familiar tall frame. The place is packed; each seat is taken and there is a line out the door. I steadily focus on the tables and notice clearly that every person is drinking James' tea. Suddenly it occurs to me. It wasn't just the conversations with James about my personal fulfillment that made me think and dream of Marcos. The periods of cognitive clarity and lucid dreaming were a result of his tea. I remember reading something about a tea like that once; in fact I think it was the same color. That scoundrel tricked me into a blissful life with his brew!

I find one open seat at the bar and wait patiently for James to notice me as he busily waits on his customers. Eventually he sees me.

"Miss Alison! How are you? I thought you had gone forever."

"I will always reappear, James. You cut your hair! I have to ask you…"

"Ask me what?"

"It was your tea, wasn't it?"

"You finally figured it out. I knew you would eventually."

"What the hell is in it?"

"Just a little something to open the pineal gland; to help you see the world through a clearer lens."

"I'll be damned."

"The tea is just a vehicle to open you up to what you truly want in life and not get distracted by all of the things we're told that we're supposed to want. You were so dismal the first time I met you; now look at you! You are blissful now, aren't you?"

"Yes." I feel stunned and am trying to comprehend that these last months of change have been a result of a tea!

"Did you notice that it lasted a little longer each time you drank it?"

"Yes, I guess I did."

"And it would wear off suddenly and you would revert back to your old self until you drank it again?"

I recall my sudden changes of heart in Zihua, "Uh-huh."

"Until it finally changed your way of thinking forever?"

"Yes, now I see."

"That's why I wanted you to make those lists while you were still under the influence of the tea and why I wanted to start thinking of other universes so you could open up to the possibilities of what your life could be. I hope you're not angry with me."

"Are you kidding? You changed my life!"

~

ALSO BY SAYLOR STORM

Thanks for reading *Ali's Portal*. If you like **fun trivia** books, check out my love trivia book:

Love Trivia & Other Fun Facts That Will Make You Blush
    https://amzn.to/3Jraplw

ABOUT THE AUTHOR

Born with fertile mind and a passion for the great outdoors, Saylor Storm spends her days exploring the majestic mountains and scenic hills from the Sierras to the Appalachians. When she's not lost in thought on a hike, she can be found in her cozy writing nook, conjuring up tales of strong determined women who navigate the challenges of life with unwavering determination.

Whether it's through her writing or her adventures on the trails, Saylor inspires others to live their best lives, to embrace the beauty of the world around them, and to never stop learning and growing.

facebook.com/SaylorStorm

twitter.com/SaylorStorm

instagram.com/SaylorStorm

Cover design by Lesia - germancreative